What the critics are saying...

ઐ

"...ANOTHER LOVE is one hot, erotic ride." ~ *Bea Sigman, Romance Junkies*

"You won't want to put it down for one second. I know I didn't!!" ~ *Crimsonpen, Romance Junkies*

"...a very moving story." ~ *Sinclair Reid, Romance Reviews Today*

~A Mutal Favor~
Winner of the 2004 Golden Quill Award for best hot, steamy romance from Desert Rose RWA chapter

~Bittersweet Homecoming~
Winner of the 2004 More Than Magic award for best erotic romance from Romance Writers Ink RWA chapter.

Ann Jacobs

ANOTHER LOVE

ELLORA'S CAVE
ROMANTICA PUBLISHING

An Ellora's Cave Romantica Publication

www.ellorascave.com

Another Love

ISBN # 141995329X
ALL RIGHTS RESERVED.
Another Love Copyright© 2003 Ann Jacobs
Cover art by: Syneca

Electronic book Publication: August 2003
Trade paperback Publication: December 2005

Warning:

The following material contains graphic sexual content meant for mature readers. *Another Love* has been rated *E-rotic* by a minimum of three independent reviewers.

Ellora's Cave Publishing offers three levels of Romantica™ reading entertainment: S (S-ensuous), E (E-rotic), and X (X-treme).

S-*ensuous* love scenes are explicit and leave nothing to the imagination.

E-*rotic* love scenes are explicit, leave nothing to the imagination, and are high in volume per the overall word count. In addition, some E-rated titles might contain fantasy material that some readers find objectionable, such as bondage, submission, same sex encounters, forced seductions, etc. E-rated titles are the most graphic titles we carry; it is common, for instance, for an author to use words such as "fucking", "cock", "pussy", etc., within their work of literature.

X-*treme* titles differ from E-rated titles only in plot premise and storyline execution. Unlike E-rated titles, stories designated with the letter X tend to contain controversial subject matter not for the faint of heart.

Also by Ann Jacobs

ഇ

Books In Print

Another Love
Black Gold

ଛଗ

Prologue

ഇ

You're pregnant.

The implication of those two words hadn't registered right away, but as Erin Winters sat by her son's hospital bed two weeks later and watched him sleep, it hit her hard.

She was pregnant again, yet she was not going to keep the baby. And she knew nothing about her baby's father except his name—James Blake Tanner IV—and the fact that he and his infertile wife apparently had money to burn since they hadn't even haggled over paying the fifty thousand dollars she'd asked for to bear his child.

It was just another job. A job that paid so well that she'd been able to come up with the deposit the hospital had demanded before admitting Timmy for the operation he'd had earlier today.

But…it wasn't just another job. A tiny human was growing inside her, developing his or her own unique features and personality. Would he be like Timmy, cheerful and bright in spite of his immobility and the pain that often dulled his eyes and made him look older than his seven years?

Erin would never know, because she'd agreed to relinquish this baby the minute it left her womb. Closing her eyes, she lay back in the recliner and tried to rest.

What if she weren't a single mom? What if this unborn baby had come not from a test tube but as a result of hot, steamy sex? Sex like she hadn't enjoyed for so long she'd almost forgotten what it felt like to take a man's hard cock in her pussy and have his spurting climax trigger her own.

She creamed her panties when she imagined her dream lover—tall, dark, handsome and just a little bit dangerous. Even though she was tall, her head would barely reach his shoulder. She'd have to stand on tiptoe to look over it. He'd be big, possessive, protective…a man she could lean on.

A white-collar man with blue-collar calluses. A horseman who loved the outdoors. Adventuresome but not a daredevil. Never another one of those! He'd start out kissing her silly, then move on to the fun stuff. All sorts of fun stuff. There wouldn't be an ounce of reserve in his gorgeous body when it came to sex.

No use fantasizing. Erin closed her eyes and drifted off to sleep. *Her nipples tingled. His mouth descended, and he sucked one in. Oooh. Just the right suction to set off bursts of sensation that had her whole body aching. She skimmed her fingers over the rippling muscles of his shoulders…his chest…his ridged belly. Lower.*

He raised his hips, as if to give her better access to his big, hard cock. His heavy balls. God, how she wanted to taste the moist pearl that glistened at the blunt tip of his cock, suck that plum-like morsel and swirl her tongue around it.

A playful lover, he gave her nipple a quick bite, then switched his mouth to the other aching bud. He used his hands, too, sliding his callused fingers over her bottom, her back, the incredibly sensitive spots behind her ears. And oh, yes. Now he'd found her clit and was nibbling and tonguing it. God, yessss.

Her pussy clenched, her pulse raced. He wrenched himself free, straddled her, and rammed his cock inside her. He was so big, so powerful, so incredibly male. His breath smelled sweet, yet when he kissed her she tasted herself on his sensual lips. He rammed into her over and over, faster and harder with each thrust until moments later she slumped against him, drained. Aftershocks coursed through her as he flooded her with his hot, spurting essence.

Erin woke, trembling, her skin clammy and her panties soaked. She was pregnant, for real, but the closest she'd come to a lover lately, dream or otherwise, was a sterile syringe and her trusty vibrator.

Chapter One

Five months later

&

Glenna Tanner had just died in surgery at Parkland.

Erin set down the phone. Like a zombie, she sank onto the worn sofa in her living room, sobbing as she hugged her distended abdomen.

She'd worried about this surrogate arrangement from the beginning. But she'd never imagined some deranged maniac would go on a shooting spree in the infant department at Neiman Marcus and take out the mother of this baby. A sob tore itself from Erin's throat. She'd liked Glenna, appreciated how much she'd wanted this child. Now the sweet woman who'd thanked her so profusely for carrying her baby would never get to rock it to sleep in the antique chair she'd told Erin about last week when they'd met for lunch.

"What will become of you?" The baby's only response to her question was a hard, swift kick to Erin's ribs.

Though Erin had never met Glenna's husband, her heart went out to him. This time the man had lost something no amount of his money could replace.

* * * * *

She's gone.

Blake stared at the bleak white closet wall that just this morning had been hidden behind Glenna's bright colored dresses. Why had he told Mary to get rid of them today?

Why the hell did he care? It wasn't as though seeing her clothes would have cheered him. The memory of watching them lower Glenna's coffin into the icy ground lay heavy on his mind, so heavy he doubted he'd ever smile again.

Like a robot, he shrugged out of the jacket of his dark gray suit and hung it up. Sliding the mourning band off the sleeve, he felt tears well up in his eyes. His fingers tightened around the scrap of black material as he walked back into the bedroom he'd shared with Glenna for nearly fourteen years.

Three days ago, they'd laughed and made love in this room, and he'd teased her gently about the baby they'd bring home in less than four months. Then she'd gone shopping for a layette and gotten in the way of a stray bullet.

Why in hell had he ever agreed to her insane demand that they find a surrogate mother to bear the child she'd been unable to carry? If he hadn't given in, he'd still have had Glenna. She wouldn't have been in harm's way when that crazy bastard had peppered the infant department at Neiman's with gunfire.

How the hell was he going to survive? "Oh, God." Suddenly it struck him that the baby Glenna had wanted so damn much was still alive, still safe inside the body of the surrogate mother her gynecologist, his good friend Greg Halpern, had found.

Blake stripped off his dark tie and opened the collar of his shirt. Then he walked out and shut the door behind him. He'd never be able to sleep in their bedroom again.

He knew one thing, though. He didn't want the baby. Every time he'd look at his son or daughter, he'd remember the child had cost him his wife. His mind made up, he picked up the phone and called Greg.

* * * * *

"What are you going to do?" asked Erin's younger sister, Sandy Daniels, the morning after Glenna's funeral.

"I can't have an abortion. I just can't."

"I told Greg that's what you'd say. Oh, Erin, I'm so sorry I talked you into doing this for the Tanners." Sandy used a soggy Kleenex to wipe away the tears that rolled down her cheeks.

"Don't cry. No one could have known it was going to turn out like this. When you told me your boss was looking for a surrogate mother for one of his patients and suggested that I apply for the job, it seemed like an answer to my prayers. A way I could manage for Timmy to have his surgery and still stay home to take care of him." When her sister's tears didn't abate, Erin took her hand. "I'm not sorry I did it. Look at how much better Timmy's doing now. The therapist thinks he may even be able to start using crutches in another month or two."

Though Erin tried to smile, the thought that she was likely to be totally responsible for this new life growing inside her scared her half to death. It was all she could do to cope with Timmy's special needs.

"You could always give the baby up for adoption." Sandy looked around Erin's shabby living room, as though she realized there was no way Erin could take on any more responsibility now.

"Wouldn't Mr. Tanner have to agree? After all, this is his baby as much as mine. More." After all, he was the one who'd paid for her to have his child.

"Yes. He would. But maybe he wouldn't mind. Greg said he was adamant about wanting you to have an abortion."

"Even if I wanted one, it would be too late. I won't do it. This baby is alive and I can't kill it—not for anyone, even its father. I have to talk to Mr. Tanner, Sandy. Make him understand how I feel."

"Greg's already told him he needs to talk to you, I'm sure. He feels as awful about this as I do. Anyhow, I'll have him relay your message to Glenna's husband."

"Thanks."

Sandy looked at Erin, tears still glistening in her eyes. "It'll be okay. Greg has known Mr. Tanner since they were college roommates. He says Mr. Tanner's a good man—that he'll come around and do what's right." She stood and picked up the key ring she'd set on the table. "I need to get back before Greg has the office turned inside out. Give Timmy a big hug from me when he wakes up."

Erin watched Sandy go downstairs and climb into Doctor Halpern's silver two-seater sports car, then went to Timmy's room. After straightening his blankets, she bent and kissed his pale cheek.

How could Blake Tanner not want his own child? If she hadn't had Timmy, she didn't know how she'd have survived the three long years since Bill's sudden death. Exhausted, Erin went back in the living room and stretched out on the sofa.

During the two weeks since Glenna's funeral, Erin had found it increasingly hard not to think of the baby inside her as belonging to someone else. More so now that she knew its father wanted it destroyed.

How could he? What sort of monster was he to have knowingly provided the sperm Greg Halpern placed in her body and paid her price to bear this child, only to demand, now that Glenna was gone, that it be thrown out like last week's trash?

No, this wasn't Glenna's baby anymore. It was her own, and Erin resented Blake Tanner. Hated him for what he wanted her to do. Ironically, though, she thought she understood some of what he was feeling because she'd grieved, too. She knew how crippling that emotion could be.

* * * * *

"I told you, I don't want anything to do with this baby," Blake repeated. "This was Glenna's idea to begin with. And she's gone."

"It will be your son or daughter." Greg got up, paced nervously around Blake's office. "The surrogate mother flatly refuses to abort it. Look, I know you're grieving, but think of Mrs. Winters. She's been carrying that baby for five and a half months. She feels it moving inside her several times each day. Frankly, I wouldn't think much of her if she were willing to have an abortion at this stage. If you weren't a lifelong friend and the circumstances weren't as they are, I wouldn't do it even if she were willing."

"What is she going to do?"

"Have the baby. She might be willing to offer it for adoption to another family, but whether she can do that is up to you."

"Goddamn it." Blake leaned back in his desk chair and rubbed his aching temples. "You know, I don't feel like anybody's father. Especially not of a baby whose mother I've never laid eyes on. Right now, all I feel is empty, and about all I can manage is to muddle along from one day to the next."

"Maybe this baby will give your life new meaning."

Blake appreciated his friend's having come here instead of making him go to his medical offices where this whole mess had started. Still he wished Greg would drop the counseling, however well meant. "Hell, you know having a baby was Glenna's obsession, not mine. Even before you told us she needed that hysterectomy, I'd resigned myself to not having children."

Greg leaned forward and rested his elbows on the corner of the desk. "Besides, you thought the surrogate arrangement was dangerous from the beginning." He paused. "Don't deny it. You told me how you felt about a woman offering to give up her child for money, and how you worried that she would keep making more and more demands to keep quiet about the arrangement. How could you not have had second thoughts? I did, and I'm not a lawyer."

"The legal uncertainties weren't what bothered me most. The whole thing seemed damn unnatural. The contract. Jerking off into a bottle in one of your examining rooms. Handing over fifty thousand dollars the day you told me she was pregnant. It all was so fucking artificial."

"I offered to let you collect the semen at home."

"And I told you no. I did it, damn it, but I wasn't about to use Glenna to help me get it up to fill up your container."

"Would you have rather done it naturally?"

"With Glenna? Yes." Blake felt a muscle twitch in his jaw. "With anybody else? Hell, no. Look, Greg, you can tell this Mrs. Winters I'll up the ante by whatever reasonable figure she asks for, and I'll agree the baby can be adopted when it's born."

"You'll have to tell her yourself, my friend. She's not talking to me since I relayed your desire for her to have an abortion."

Livid now, Blake slammed his fist onto the desk, welcoming the pain that shot up all the way into his shoulder. "I have no desire to meet the woman who rented out her body for fifty grand," he ground out. "Besides, she has to talk to you. You're her obstetrician."

Greg stood and glared down at Blake. "Like it or not, you're the father of that baby she's carrying. You owe it to her to meet her and say what's on your mind. Before you go making judgment about her character, you need to find out why she agreed to this arrangement."

"What the hell do you mean?"

"Only that maybe you've misjudged the lady. And that you need to see that baby growing inside her and realize it's as much a part of you as it is of her. I've got to go. I'm going to be seeing patients until seven o'clock as it is." Greg took a folded paper from an inside pocket of his navy blazer, pressed it into Blake's hand, and walked out without another word.

Chapter Two

Glenna's Ghost

❧

No, Blake. My poor, heartbroken darling, you can't mean you want to abandon our baby.

Glenna heard Blake talking with Greg as clearly if she had been standing at his side, but she had to strain in order to visualize the man she'd loved for longer than she could remember. His image was hazy now, but not so faint that she couldn't see the agony evident in his tear-clouded eyes and the burden he carried on those uncharacteristically slumped shoulders.

What have you done? What have you done to Blake? To our baby? To Erin Winters? And to me? Glenna's spirit raged at the twisted wretch who had ended her life with a single, barely audible blast. For a moment, she hated that faceless piece of humanity so much that, if she'd had the power, she'd have taken pleasure in turning his obscene little gun on him and blowing him straight to hell.

Then guilt washed over her. *That stranger pulled the trigger that took me away. But it was my obsession that has brought this awful grief to Blake, leaving him horribly alone yet responsible for the life of the unborn child in Erin's body.*

He doesn't want his baby now.

My poor, sweet baby.

And Erin. What is she thinking, carrying a baby whose father wants it destroyed?

My God!

Blake's image cleared in her mind so Glenna finally got a good look at him. His despair was palpable as he stared, unseeing, at a scrap of paper in his hand.

I've got to make this right. Can I come back? Just long enough to help them cope?

She felt a highly charged energy deep inside her, energy that transported her from the limbo of nonentity to Blake's office in a high-rise Dallas office building.

Blake. Her lover. Her friend. How well she knew her strong, earthbound anchor whose calm and analytical way of viewing life had always been a perfect foil for her own whimsical and often impractical nature.

They went back forever. Glenna's spirit lightened when she remembered the quiet, often solemn little boy who had vowed his undying love for her in first grade, teased her when they were ten, and asked her to be his wife the Christmas after they'd graduated from college. He'd always been serious, but she'd unearthed a sense of fun in him while he'd talked her out of the most impractical of her madcap schemes.

They'd been soulmates. She, raised by loving grandparents to enjoy life's every moment, and Blake, brought up by servants and imbued with a strong sense of responsibility and duty by his workaholic father, had been the odd couple whose lives had merged smoothly into one.

She'd love him for all eternity, but now she needed to convince him how precious his son or daughter would be. She wanted to hold and comfort him and tell him time would heal his grief.

More than anything, Glenna wanted Blake not to hurt anymore. She wanted him to see her, recognize her presence so she could tell him how sorry she was to have left him all alone. But she stopped short of making her presence known. She knew Blake as if he were her alter ego. He'd never accept her returning this way.

If he even allowed himself to admit he saw me, he'd run, not walk, and commit himself into the nearest psych ward.

No, she couldn't show herself to Blake, so she willed her spirit to drift away.

But I can work on Erin Winters. Glenna heartened at the thought that she might find an ally in the kind, caring woman she and Blake had hired to bear their baby. She recalled the sadness she'd seen in Erin's soft, dark blue eyes when they'd talked about the baby, that day they'd met for lunch. The gentle woman couldn't help but love the child she'd told Glenna she tried hard not to think about at all. Erin could be a real mother to their baby, not just a surrogate. If she would, she might heal Blake, too.

Yes. It could work. She'd go to Erin. Erin would love their baby, and with a little luck she could also heal Blake's grief. Taking a deep breath, Glenna gathered her strength for the long, hard task ahead.

Chapter Three

୬

For a long time, Blake stared at the paper Greg had given him. All it contained was a name, phone number, and address. The name was Erin Winters. He couldn't place the exact address, but from the zip code he deduced that it was in an area not too far from downtown Dallas, where the few residences that remained were pretty shabby and rundown. He'd have thought his fifty thousand dollars would have bought this woman a better place to live.

Was she on drugs? In trouble with the law? He raised the questions, but quickly discarded them. Greg was his closest friend as well as a damn fine doctor. He'd never have chosen a surrogate whose lifestyle would threaten the health of a child. Especially a child who'd belong to Glenna.

When he left the office, intending to drive home, Blake set the paper on the passenger seat. He didn't want to face Erin Winters, not yet. Before he realized exactly what he was doing, though, he found himself pulling to the curb in front of a three-story brick apartment building in a neighborhood that had definitely seen better days.

Go ahead, strip it if you want to, I don't give a damn, he thought when he saw a trio of teenagers eyeing his Mercedes sedan.

* * * * *

"Yes?" Erin's back hurt, her feet were swollen, and she barely had the energy to answer the door. Forcing her eyes to focus, she took in the tall, good-looking man standing in her doorway. The fact he had on a suit that probably cost more than she spent on groceries in a year made her doubt he was just another door-to-door salesman.

"I'm Blake Tanner."

She'd never seen eyes more bleak nor an expression more sorrowful. "Come in."

She led him through the front room, where Timmy was napping in front of their old TV set, into the kitchen. "Won't you sit down?" she asked, indicating one of the battered chairs at an old wood dinette table.

"What did you do with the money we gave you?" Blake didn't bother with even a cursory greeting. Erin watched his gaze shift from her shabby appliances to the tired-looking curtain she'd hung to block the view of the alley out back.

"I paid for my son's last surgery—at least for most of it," Erin said quietly, hoping Timmy wouldn't awaken to hear the bitter conversation she imagined would follow.

"Surgery?"

"Timmy was hurt three years ago in the accident that killed his father."

"Where is the boy?"

"In there. Didn't you see him?" She gestured toward the living room. "He fell asleep watching TV. That's why I brought you in here—so we wouldn't disturb him."

Blake stood and stared through the doorway, as if he needed to verify for himself the existence of her little boy. "How old is he?" he asked, turning back to Erin.

"Seven."

For a long time, neither of them spoke. Erin had wanted, needed to see her unborn baby's father, but now that he was here, she didn't know what to say. She'd been prepared to hate the man who had proposed that she get rid of his child. Now, having seen the depth of his grief, she needed to console him. Not knowing what to say, she stood at the counter, watching his gaze shift until it settled on her rounded belly.

"Would you like a drink? Tea? Or I could make some coffee," she said to fill the silence.

"No, thank you. You have no idea how happy you made Glenna when you agreed to have this baby," he said, his deep voice crackling with emotion.

"But not you?"

"I'd have been content to stay childless or adopt. You're carrying the result of my wife's obsession that our child must come from my body if not from hers."

Erin saw why Glenna had so desperately wanted this man's child. Even in his grief, Blake Tanner was devastatingly attractive. In happier circumstances she imagined he'd be almost irresistible.

His size—he had to be at least six-four—surprised her, since Glenna had been so petite. The conservative suit he wore didn't disguise his broad, muscular shoulders or lean torso. He had sable hair, darker than her own, conservatively cut but a bit shaggy, as if he was overdue for a trim. It gave him a boyish look, made Erin want to brush back the unruly curl that lay on his tanned forehead—the way she often did for Timmy.

His dark blue eyes looked dull, as though he saw nothing in which to take joy. They'd sparkle if he curled his sensual lips into a real smile.

What was she doing, practically drooling over a man who was nothing to her except her baby's father? She barely managed not to shake her head or laugh at the absurdity of that question. Of these circumstances that Miss Manners hadn't addressed when advising how to handle awkward social situations.

"This baby is yours." Now that she'd seen him, Erin had a good idea what the baby would look like. Its coloring would almost inevitably mirror his and hers since they both were blue-eyed brunettes. "What are you going to do about it?"

Blake looked as if he were trying to lift the weight of the world from his broad shoulders. "Would you want to raise it?" he asked, tunneling his fingers through his hair.

The baby chose that moment to kick Erin in the ribs. "Me?"

"You're its biological mother. Its only mother now." His words sounded harsh, as though it pained him to know he'd helped create the life inside her.

Erin imagined holding this baby in her arms. Then she thought of Timmy — of the series of surgeries still scheduled, the years before he'd be well enough that she could take a real job to care for them.

"It's all I can do to see to Timmy's needs." Did Blake think she lived in this shabby place because she wanted to?

"Do you want it to go to strangers?" His gaze pierced through her thin cotton maternity blouse as if he were looking at the baby.

Of course she didn't. It was going to have been hard to hand it over to Glenna, whom she'd known and liked. "What choice do I have?" she asked, unable to keep the bitterness out of her voice.

Blake's expression softened, as if he saw something or someone beyond her range of vision. He moved to the window and stared down into the alley.

"Mommy, I need to go to the bathroom."

When Erin bent to pick Timmy up, Blake nudged her away, slipping his arms around the little boy and lifting him with apparent ease. "Where's the bathroom?"

Later after she'd tucked Timmy in bed for the night, Blake was waiting in the living room. "He can't walk at all, can he?"

Erin shook her head. "Not since the accident."

"You shouldn't be lifting him," he said abruptly.

Who was this man to criticize her for doing what she had to do? "I'm not injuring myself or this baby."

"I don't agree. When you signed the contract with us, you promised to take proper care of yourself. It looks like you're running yourself to death taking care of Timmy. And don't tell me living here is conducive to anyone's good health."

"It's the best I can afford and pay for Timmy's therapy."

"Are you even eating right? I haven't seen the first bite of food since I've been here."

"We'd just had supper before you got here. Do you want to sample the leftovers?"

"I don't think so. But I would like to offer you a proposition." He stood, towering over her, saying nothing while he apparently gathered his thoughts.

"That baby inside you is mine. I can't ignore my responsibility to it. Or to Glenna. Here's what I think you should do. Move out of here, bring Timmy to my house, and let me take care of both of you, at least until after the baby's born. I'll pay for whatever you need."

"You want to keep the baby now?"

"I guess I do. I—I don't want it being raised by strangers. But what in hell am I going to do with it? My God! A baby needs its mother." Blake's hand tightened into a fist, and Erin worried that he'd slam it down and shatter her flimsy end table.

"A child needs its father, too," she said softly, reaching up to touch the taut skin on his cheek and give him what little comfort she could. Again, as in the kitchen, she watched his eyes glaze over and felt him mentally retreating.

After awhile, he sat on the sofa, taking her hand to pull her down beside him. "We're a hell of a pair, aren't we?"

She shrugged, sensing that he didn't expect a reply.

"You did this so you could get your boy the help he needs. I did it to make Glenna happy. Now, like it or not, we're both in one hell of a bind. You need money to take care of Timmy, and I need a woman to mother that baby you're carrying. We might as well make the best of it. Move in with me and we'll muddle through this mess together."

Chapter Four

∞

"Greg!"

"Yeah?" At the sound of Sandy's voice, Greg looked up from the accountant's report he'd been trying to decipher. He'd been thinking of Sandy anyhow, as he did every time he had to face the fact that unless one or both of his expensive ex-wives found another victim, he'd never be able to offer her the kind of life she deserved. Shit, he wished he'd met her long before there'd been one, let alone two former Mrs. Halperns bleeding him of damn near every cent he could manage to earn.

"You want to tell me what's going on between my sister and Blake Tanner?" she demanded, her voice rising with every word.

Surprised to hear Sandy screeching like his most recent ex so frequently did, Greg got up and reached out to stroke a strand of tawny hair away from her eyes. "Calm down, sweetheart."

"Calm down? You expect calm when my sister calls and tells me she's moving into Blake Tanner's house? What's going on? Damn it, I don't want Erin hurt. I'm the one that got her mixed up in this, and she's been through enough hell for three lifetimes as it is."

"Sandy. Please don't yell. This is the first I've heard about your sister moving in with Blake. I haven't talked to either of them since I went to Blake's office last week and asked him to go meet Erin. I've known Blake a lot of years, though, long enough to be sure he'd never hurt a woman."

"But Greg—"

"But nothing. Erin needs help. Taking care of Timmy's quite a job for any woman, let alone one who's six months pregnant. I ought to have suggested that he provide Erin with more help, although it seems I didn't need to."

"But putting her up in his house?"

"Why not? It's big enough. Half a dozen people could rattle around inside it and never see each other unless they wanted to. Look, sweetheart, I've got to go over to the hospital and check on Mrs. Slater. Come with me. We can eat out somewhere if she's holding on okay, and talk about this some more." He stashed the financial statements in his desk drawer and shrugged out of his lab coat.

* * * * *

"Do you really live in this great big house all by yourself?" Timmy yawned as he shifted awkwardly against Blake's chest.

Suddenly, pain washed through Blake at the little boy's reminder that now, he *was* all alone. "Not anymore, sport."

"Timmy, don't bother Mr. Tanner."

This move had her anxious, he knew, but she'd done a good job reassuring her son. Hell, he had his own doubts, too, but Erin was carrying his child, and that made her well-being his responsibility.

Blake forced a smile. "He's not bothering me," he said, looking over the child in his arms to meet Erin's gaze. "As a matter of fact, I think he's just drifted off to sleep. Shall I put him to bed?" He strode purposefully through the courtyard and pool area toward one of several sliding glass doors.

"I can do it," Erin replied, her voice quietly assertive.

"But you don't have to since I'm here." Dark circles under her eyes and fine lines around her sensual mouth bore witness to the fact that she'd been doing far more than a woman in her condition should. Blake laid Timmy onto the bed, then moved aside so Erin could hug him good night.

In the morning he'd talk to Mary and make sure the housekeeper knew to take over most of the physical aspects of

Timmy's care. "It's been a long day. Mary put your things in there." He gestured with one hand in the general direction of a connecting door.

His gaze settled on the rounded mound that held Glenna's baby. No, not Glenna's baby now. Glenna was gone. His baby. His and this soft-spoken stranger's. Her sad eyes seemed dark as the sky at midnight and hinted at suffering that must rival his own.

"Moving's exhausting. I think I must be almost as tired as Timmy." Erin set her purse on a chair. "Thanks for all your help. If you'll excuse me, I believe I'll skip dinner and make it an early night."

"Of course. There's a phone by your bed. Just press the button marked 'Intercom' if you need anything, and Mary will get it."

Much later, as he mentally crossed off the last of the details he had taken care of to ensure Erin and Timmy's comfort and well being, it struck Blake that he had gone several hours without being overwhelmed by the senseless, heart-wrenching realization of Glenna's death or his own emptiness.

* * * * *

Soft fuzzy apricots. That was what the floor looked like, Erin thought as she tried to focus her sleepy eyes. Vaguely she remembered coming in here last night after tucking Timmy into bed in his room next door, undressing, and collapsing between these cool, silky sheets.

She stretched, luxuriating in the warmth that came as much from dappled sunlight filtered through the leaves of a willow tree outside as from the quilted satin comforter she had burrowed into as if it were a cocoon.

Slowly she awakened and glanced at her surroundings. Last night she'd been too tired to notice much, other than that the room was close to being as big as the whole apartment she and Timmy had just vacated. Now Erin saw Glenna's airy touch in white art deco furniture and pristine walls warmed by the deep carpet and accessories in her favorite colors of aqua and apricot. The last time they'd met, Erin recalled, Glenna had mentioned how she was going to use those colors to decorate the baby's nursery.

I'm glad you're here.

Erin looked around for whoever just spoke. "Who's there?"

Nothing. Telling herself not to panic, Erin sat up and looked harder for her visitor. "Where are you?"

She thought she saw the sheer pale drapery framing closed French doors rustling slightly. But there was no one in the room. She had to be losing her mind.

Then someone knocked, and a beaming middle-aged woman pushed a tea cart through the door. "Mr. Tanner said you'd probably sleep late, but that I wasn't to let you miss lunch."

"Lunch?"

"Well, brunch, you might say. I'm Mary Malone, ma'am, and I've been running this house since Mr. Tanner was a boy. Will you be wanting to eat in bed, or here by the window?"

"I'll get up, thank you." Apparently Blake had failed to tell Mrs. Malone he'd rescued the surrogate mother of his child from a life that hadn't gotten her accustomed to hired help and breakfast in bed. He'd certainly neglected to let *her* know how opulently he lived.

She slid off the bed and waddled to the small table by the window where the housekeeper had already laid out silverware and a crisp linen napkin onto a snowy cloth.

The single rosebud in the center of the table gave off a spicy, sweet fragrance—almost as enticing as the smell that wafted up from the ham and cheese omelet when she lifted a silver cover off her plate. Erin sat, waiting until Mrs. Malone set out juice and a silver teapot before picking up a fork.

The sun looked high in the sky—too high for it to be very early. Erin looked around but didn't see a clock. "Do you know what time it is?"

"A bit past eleven, ma'am. After you've eaten, Mr. Tanner thought you might like to take a tour around the house and grounds." The housekeeper hustled around the room, making the bed Erin had just vacated and picking up the clothes she'd been too tired to put away last night.

"Eleven?" Erin pushed back her chair and started to get up. "Oh, no. I've got to get Timmy ready to go to the hospital for his therapy," she explained, washing down the last bite of her omelet with a swallow of tangy vegetable juice cocktail.

"Don't worry, ma'am. Mr. Tanner's got the therapist coming out here so you won't have to drive downtown." Mrs. Malone flipped back the napkin covering a small silver basket, tempting Erin with a flaky Danish pastry.

"But how? What about the equipment?"

"Why, Mr. Tanner's got a gym with more contraptions than a body could possibly need. He already had most of what that Ms. Michelle told him she'd need, and what he didn't have, the hospital supply people delivered yesterday."

Erin felt like Alice must have felt when she was tumbling down that dark hole into Wonderland. Yesterday she'd been struggling to find the energy to do everything that needed doing. Today Blake apparently had taken over. It felt weird, having no responsibilities other than to pamper herself and his unborn child. She had to do something productive, so she headed for the mirrored door she assumed hid a closet. She'd dress and go find Timmy.

She started to grab soft jeans and a cotton knit top, but changed her mind. Jeans didn't go with the softly elegant decor of the room where Blake had put her. Or with housekeepers in starched, black uniforms. Erin put the jeans back and chose a pale gray wool maternity jumper she'd found at a thrift shop. With a burgundy turtleneck shirt, black tights, and black flats, the jumper looked presentable. Good enough to wear to face whatever new surprises Blake had in store.

At least that was what she told herself as she brushed the tangles from her hair and pulled it back in a low ponytail. She wasn't so sure when she followed Mrs. Malone through the house. The place reeked of casual elegance, elegance she realized took not just money but class to achieve.

"This is the breakfast room," Mrs. Malone said as they entered a bright, airy enclosure with glass walls on three sides. As if denying the unseasonable bleakness of the cold, rainy April day, leafy plants abounded. Some grew tall and lush in glazed clay pots set on the Mexican tile floor. Others hung from the vaulted ceiling in baskets of wood, wire, and clay. Several orchids spilled cascades of delicate blossoms in all directions. "Mr. Tanner usually eats here unless he's having guests."

"It's beautiful." Erin took in the large round table surrounded with six matching captain's chairs, and the casual grouping of sofas and chairs. The table had been set for three. "Is Mr. Tanner here?"

"Why certainly. He stayed home, wanting to make sure everything was right for you and that precious little boy. Right now, I think he's talking with Timmy's therapist out by the pool."

The housekeeper motioned toward the wide expanse of glass, and when Erin followed she saw Michelle, Blake and Timmy by a large swimming pool. Her son's animated grin warmed her heart.

* * * * *

Blake liked Timmy.

He doubted he could endure the painful therapy he'd just seen the little boy accept without complaint. As it was, he'd barely managed to restrain himself from ordering Michelle to cease her torture and soothe Timmy's pain with a deep heat massage, or ultrasound, or maybe a healing soak in the Jacuzzi.

He'd wanted to grab Timmy and carry him away where no one could hurt him, not even in the name of healing.

Now Blake stood quietly while Michelle gave Timmy a massage, recalling patches of their earlier conversation.

"My mommy's going to have your baby," the boy had said when Blake asked if he'd mind letting Erin sleep a little longer. "Will he be my brother?"

"Half-brother or sister." At the time, Blake's reply had been technically accurate but meaningless.

"Mommy liked Ms. Glenna," Timmy had said then. "She died, like my daddy did. You must miss her a lot."

Timmy had come back off Blake's neutral reply with wisdom far beyond his tender years. "It's okay to cry when you hurt. Mommy says so. Sometimes I cry when Michelle moves my legs around. Sometimes Mommy does, too. She says it hurts her when Michelle has to hurt me."

"Hurt you?" The thought of anyone deliberately hurting Timmy—any child—had incensed Blake.

"Sometimes it hurts a lot. But Mommy says I'm lucky. They were able to fix my legs so they didn't have to cut them off, and if I work really hard, someday they ought to work almost good as new. I want them to work again."

From Timmy's comments and a serious conversation with Michelle when she'd arrived after breakfast, Blake had learned some of what Erin had gone through since the accident three years earlier that had cost her husband his life and nearly snatched away her only child. The knowledge strengthened his resolve to care for Erin and Timmy, while it helped him let go the bitterest portions of his own grief.

He felt Erin's presence before he actually saw her. Michelle had told him she came every day, and that she never left the room while Timmy had his therapy. Today, thankfully, Mary had kept Erin occupied while Michelle put Timmy through hell. Blake pushed himself away from the wall he had been leaning against and joined Erin next to the Jacuzzi where Timmy was soaking.

"This is too much," Erin said, looking around the gym.

"Most of it was already here. I don't want you having to drag Timmy all the way downtown to the hospital. Michelle assures me she can do his therapy here, and in the pool." Blake walked Erin over to the door and showed her the outdoor swimming pool where wisps of steam wafted up from its crystalline surface. "It's too cold today, but you can see that the heater's working now."

"You're heating that big pool?"

"Sure. I used to keep it heated all the time. It should be plenty warm for Timmy in a day or so, even if this cold front doesn't break." Erin's presence unnerved him, which surprised him since he fully enjoyed her little son's company.

Hell, it didn't take a genius to figure out why. His baby was growing inside her, and the disdain he'd originally held for one who would sell her body for his money had faded into admiration for the way she'd managed to provide for herself and Timmy under circumstances so dire he had trouble imagining them.

Damn it. Being around Timmy made him think of his own unborn son or daughter. He had no trouble picturing the baby, either. It would look like Erin. And him. His gaze raked the tall, dark-haired woman with eyes nearly the same shade of blue as his. His child would have none of Glenna's blondness, no chance to look at him from eyes like golden honey. Intentionally or not, Glenna had chosen a surrogate mother whose features mirrored his, not her own, robbing him of the possibility of a son or daughter he could think of as hers.

"Are you feeling more rested now?" he asked, forcing the sudden anguish from his mind.

"Yes. I'm not used to sleeping mornings away, though." Erin sounded a little annoyed.

"You needed the rest. By the way, I talked to Greg Halpern this morning. He and Sandy are coming over for dinner tonight, and he said he could do your checkup here so you wouldn't have to go to his office on Friday."

"Are you planning to keep me prisoner here?"

"Of course not. You're welcome to go and come as you please, just as long as you rest and take care of yourself. Greg said you probably shouldn't be making the long drive to the city, so if you want to go somewhere, let me know and I'll get Miguel to drive you, if I'm not available to do it myself."

"Thanks. I hadn't thought about the distance, not to mention the fact that I don't have the vaguest idea about bus service out here. I'll let you know if there's anywhere I need to go."

"Be sure you do. Let me get Timmy and we'll take him inside for lunch. I had Mary fix us burgers and fries. Hope you don't mind. Timmy picked the menu."

"I sort of guessed he did." Erin ran her fingers through her son's chestnut-brown curls, and Blake couldn't help remembering how gentle her hand had felt on his face the night they met, when she'd reached out to soothe his pain.

* * * * *

Later, after she'd napped and changed, Erin joined Blake in the breakfast room. It felt weird, sitting with the stranger who was her baby's father and trying to carry on a polite conversation.

From what Blake said, Timmy had taken him to the cleaners when they'd played his favorite video game earlier. Erin wished she could handle all the changes the way it seemed her little boy had. Glancing down at her navy-blue rayon maternity dress, the best in her limited wardrobe, she hoped she didn't look too out of place.

When would Sandy get here?

No sooner than she'd asked herself, the doorbell rang, and moments later Sandy and Doctor Halpern joined them. They were holding hands, like teenage boyfriend and girlfriend. Surely...no, Sandy had a case of hero worship for her boss, but—

Doctor Halpern took Erin's outstretched hand. "I hope you're getting your rest."

"Yes, Doctor Halpern."

"Greg. Don't make me feel like an old man."

Soon dinner was served. Thankfully neither Sandy nor Doctor Halpern—Greg—brought up her new living arrangements while they ate the delicious meal the cook had made. Erin listened to Blake's and Greg's desultory conversation, adding as little as Sandy, who looked as if she couldn't tear her gaze away from Greg for more than a few seconds at a time.

"Ready for a quick checkup, Erin?" Greg asked after they finished dessert.

"I guess so." For some reason, it felt strange, being in the presence of one man who had made her pregnant without ever having seen her and another who had examined her repeatedly and minutely in his role as her OB-GYN.

"In your room?"

"Oh. That's fine." At least Blake hadn't gone so far as to have an exam room set up somewhere in his huge, imposing house.

"Lead the way. Blake, where did you stash my bag?"

"In the coat closet. I'll get it."

Erin stood. Would Blake want to join Greg while he checked her blood pressure and listened to the baby's heartbeat? Would she let him if he did? When he didn't hand over Greg's medical bag, she assumed he planned to tag along.

She shouldn't mind. After all, she'd let Glenna join her in Greg's examining room to listen to the baby's heartbeat. Still her cheeks heated when Blake followed her in the bedroom and stepped back. Yes, he was out of Greg's way. But it seemed he definitely intended to stay.

Sandy helped her get off her panties and lift her dress, then pulled the top sheet up over her exposed belly. Greg quickly checked her blood pressure before lowering the sheet and gently probing at her abdomen.

"Want to hear your baby, Blake?" Greg asked.

Blake started to move toward the bed, but stopped in his tracks. "Do you mind?" he asked, his gaze studiously focused on Erin's face.

It's his baby. He's got a right to listen to it, realize it's alive.

"No. Go ahead." Erin tried not to notice the rapt expression on Blake's face as he listened to his baby's heartbeat through the stethoscope, but she couldn't help smiling at the way he jerked back from the tiny hand or foot when it poked against her taut skin.

"Does it hurt? Is that normal?"

Erin didn't know if Blake was directing his questions to her or to Greg. She was about to reply when Greg did.

"No, it shouldn't hurt, and yes, it's normal. It wouldn't be normal if the baby didn't move. Here. Feel." Greg grabbed Blake's hand and pressed it gently against the spot where the baby was pummeling her belly.

She was about to protest until she saw Blake's expression change to one of disbelieving awe. For the first time since they met, he let loose with a genuine grin. It lit his handsome face and brightened his eyes to the color of a clear, midnight sky.

"Does it move like this all the time?" he asked, his free hand joining the one already on Erin's belly to cup the other side of her abdomen just above where her hipbones used to be.

"Not always. Sometimes he sleeps."

Blake must suddenly have realized it wasn't only his unborn child that he was touching, because he jerked his hands away as if he'd been burned. "If you're done, Greg, come on and let Sandy visit with Erin while we have a drink. Erin, have a good night's rest," he added over his shoulder as he practically dragged his friend out of her room.

* * * * *

"Go on with them, if you want to." Erin watched Sandy kick off her high-heeled sandals before sitting Indian-style at the foot of the king-sized bed.

"And miss telling you I've fallen head over heels in love?" Sandy's eyes sparkled with happiness.

"You mean you've given up your crush on the much-divorced, alimony-ridden obstetrician you work for?"

"Don't even think that. Last night, I finally got Greg past his noble protests that he can't afford to fall in love again. And Erin, you wouldn't believe what a wonderful lover he is."

"I wouldn't?" Erin couldn't resist poking fun at her usually levelheaded sister.

"Never in a million years! How either one of those women he married could have even *thought* of leaving him, I'll never know. Greg is the gentlest, kindest, most caring man on earth, and I intend to have him."

Erin hoped Sandy wouldn't be too disappointed if her plans didn't work out. "What about the alimony and the teenage daughter? Didn't you tell me not a month ago that Greg was on the verge of bankruptcy from paying off his former wives?"

Sandy sighed. "I wouldn't care if we had to live in a furnished room. Besides, his apartment is nice, even if it isn't big and grand like this house. He took me there last night, after one of his patients lost a premature baby. Erin, Greg *cried*. He actually cried for that couple. It started out by me holding him, trying to give him comfort. Then, something happened. He started hugging me back, and then we kissed...and well, you know..."

"Yes, I know." It had been years, but Erin recalled that kind of passion—the kind that overruled reason and culminated in lovemaking that obliterated every obstacle to "happily ever after." She'd felt it with Bill, enjoyed it to the fullest before it burned itself out and left her with a marriage that had lasted until his death only because of their little boy.

"Erin, I want to have Greg's baby. He's so good with little ones, so kind and caring…" Sandy took in a deep breath and let it out slowly, and Erin saw the dreamy look in her bright blue eyes.

"Greg already has a daughter. Twelve years old, spoiled rotten, and singularly obnoxious, if I recall your description of her after you'd had to deliver her back to her mother," Erin reminded her sister in a futile attempt to bring her back down to earth. " Sandy, he's at least ten years older than you."

"I know. He's got baggage. I'm too young and he's too old. We're of different faiths. And he's got a profession that will always come before his relationship with a woman. Greg and I have talked about all of that. I'm sure everybody else will tell me, too. None of it makes a bit of difference in the way I feel about him."

Erin had always hoped her little sister would find love, but the love she'd envisioned for Sandy was simpler, without the complications Sandy would almost inevitably find in a relationship with Greg. Suddenly she felt very tired. "Good luck, little sister," she said quietly as Sandy was leaving to rejoin Blake and Greg.

* * * * *

What a day!

Sandy's suddenly changed relationship with her multi-divorced boss took a back seat to Erin's mild resentment at the highhanded way Blake had insisted on managing every aspect of her life.

More exhausted tonight from being bombarded with kindness and troubling emotions than she'd been yesterday from packing and moving, Erin struggled out of her clothes and collapsed in bed. Her anger grew when she thought of how Blake had suddenly taken her destiny into his own hands.

"I can't stand this...this silk and velvet prison," she muttered. "There won't be anything left of *me* if he has his way."

The room was comfortably warm, its windows and French doors securely closed against the late winter storm that raged outside. Still, Erin saw the curtains flutter and felt a slight draft pass across the room. At first she tried to deny the eerie feeling that there was some intruding presence there with her.

"I'm glad you're here for Blake now. He means well, Erin, and he needs you more now than you and Timmy need the material help he can give to you."

The voice was clear, soft, almost hypnotic in its tone. It was strange and otherworldly yet somehow familiar. Erin sat up suddenly, ignoring the baby's protest against her sudden movement, and strained her eyes to see in the pitch-black darkness of the room.

"Where are you?" She searched her memory for a name for that elusive voice.

"Here, by the window."

Erin looked in that direction but saw only the sheer, fluttering drapes. "I can't see you." She felt her panic rise with every second. "Am I losing my mind?" she asked, whether of herself or of the disembodied voice she did not know. "Tell me who you are."

"Glenna."

"No! You're playing an awful trick on me! Glenna's dead."

"Dead, yes. At peace, no. I've deserted Blake, and you, and the baby I wanted to the point of obsession, and there will be no peace for me until I've made amends."

"What? I can't believe this! Come on now, leave me alone. This whole situation may have me half insane, but I'm not far enough gone to believe I'm talking with a ghost." Erin forced her swollen body to move enough so she could flip on the bedside lamp. "Show yourself, or I'll scream for Blake," she threatened with more bravado than real confidence.

Suddenly, a burst of light drew Erin's attention to the other side of the room, where what looked like particles of shimmering dust gathered and materialized into a surrealistic female figure. Its features sharpened and solidified before her eyes, slowly but surely forming the substance of a woman. Glenna—or anyhow, a dead ringer for her.

"Why are you doing this? Is this some kind of macabre joke?" This had to be a high-tech trick, but she couldn't imagine who would want, to pull it, or why.

"Blake!" Erin screamed, but the yell she had intended came out as a muffled whisper as she felt an invisible hand clamp snugly over her gaping mouth. Terrified, she closed her eyes, as if doing so could erase her eerie tormentor's presence.

"Listen to me, Erin. I'm here to help, not hurt you."

When Erin found the courage to open her eyes, she saw Glenna perched on the edge of the bed. Her features, now, were clearer than before, clear enough that Erin could no longer deny her presence. "What do you want?"

"Listen carefully. I'm new at this, and I may float away at any minute. I want Blake to laugh again. I want his baby to have a loving mother as well as a daddy. I want you and Timmy to have a happy, secure home and plenty of love to go around. I want you to make Blake love you as much as he used to love me."

Erin nearly laughed out loud. "You must have heard me swearing at your precious husband's macho way of controlling everything. What on earth makes you think I'd want him—and if I did, what's to say he might be the least bit attracted to me?"

"That's just Blake's way. When you get to know him, you'll see he's really a big, lovable pussycat. Don't you worry about the other, either. He'll be wanting you, sooner than you think."

"I don't believe you. I don't believe *this*."

Glenna's image began to fade and disintegrate into the bright cloud of dust from which it came. *"Believe. Give our Blake a chance. I've got to go now, but I'll be back to help."*

Chapter Five

❧

The memory of her late-night visitor haunted Erin during the next few weeks. Sometimes she felt as if the whole scene had been a macabre dream, but at other times, she sensed Glenna's presence just beyond her consciousness. Though she was reluctant to admit it, Erin believed Glenna had come to her and that she'd return as she had promised.

When Blake was especially withdrawn or demanding, Erin could almost hear Glenna's voice, cautioning her sometimes to give him time and space, and other times to offer comfort and companionship. Tonight, Erin felt compelled to keep Blake company to try and ease the loneliness that surrounded him like a shroud.

"Thank you for spending time with Timmy this afternoon." If Blake felt like talking about anything, he would join in conversation about the little boy he'd come to care deeply for.

"He's a great kid. I enjoy his company. Are you feeling all right?" he asked, his attention focusing on the bulging stomach Erin didn't think could grow much larger in the next four weeks.

"He's worried about you. Say something funny."

"As fine as a watermelon can feel when it's getting just about ripe," Erin quipped. She must be going nuts, the way she'd started to heed the disembodied voice that popped into her head more often lately. But she couldn't seem to ignore it.

"That's the way, Erin, make him smile. He really isn't the stuffed shirt he tries so hard to be. Say something else to make him laugh."

It *was* Glenna, urging her to lighten up Blake's brooding mood. It had to be. Erin didn't quite know whether to laugh or scream.

Wondering for about the hundredth time if she was going quietly crazy, Erin looked at Blake to see if he, too, had heard that soft, smiling voice. Obviously he hadn't. If he had, he wouldn't have been grinning and sliding her way to place a gentle hand on her tummy.

"He's being quiet tonight?"

It was more a question than a statement. Blake sounded disappointed—probably because the baby hadn't chosen this moment to practice kickboxing against his hand.

Heeding Glenna's eerie advice, Erin searched her mind for another quip that might make Blake smile. "For the moment. But that could change." Just then, the baby kicked, and Blake followed its motion with his hand.

"I think I feel a foot here." Excited, he pressed a little harder at the right side of Erin's abdomen. "Or maybe it's a hand. How big is the baby now?"

"Big enough to come out, I think."

Blake smiled again. Erin wished he could always be cajoled so easily from the depression that often surrounded him like a dark cloud obscures the sun before a storm.

Blake was a paradox—unsure about his feelings for the baby Glenna had wanted so much, yet unable to squelch the feelings of awe and pride as he followed the development of that baby. Unmistakable sensuality, even a sort of sexual tension, passed between them more often now. Neither wanted it, but neither could discount its existence. The tension stemmed from the soon-to-be-born baby they'd created together, Erin guessed. However tenuous, a link was there and she couldn't ignore it. Most of the time, though, Blake's touch felt impersonal—detached from sexuality, affection, or any emotion at all.

"Keep trying, my friend. You know, I can't say it doesn't make me feel good that he loved me so much. But he has to get over the grief, get on with his life."

This time when Erin looked up, Glenna had materialized in the corner of the room. Erin glanced at Blake, but since his expression hadn't changed, she guessed he hadn't seen the pesky ghost.

She looked back toward to the spot where she had seen Glenna seconds earlier. But she saw only sunlight reflecting on that now-familiar haze of golden dust. Then the aura dissipated and there was nothing at all.

* * * * *

"I think Blake is going to make it after all," Greg told Sandy as they finished eating take-out Chinese in his apartment. He hoped so. He'd never seen anyone as devastated as Blake had been when Glenna died.

"I think so, too. Right now, though, I'd rather be thinking about us." Sandy reached out and stroked his forearm with a silky hand.

Greg grabbed her arm, giving her finger a playful nip before taking it gently into his mouth and sucking. "You taste better than the food, sweetheart." He got up from the table and drew Sandy into his arms.

"I love you." Her soft breath when she spoke tickled his ear.

He believed her the way he'd never thought he'd believe a woman again. He loved her too, and he wished to hell he had the right to tell her so. Maybe soon he would.

It had very nearly been worth spending his free afternoon without Sandy and letting his spoiled daughter cajole him for more money just like her mother always had, to hear Shana's latest gripe. It seemed her mother, his first wife, was about to sink her perfectly manicured talons into another, bigger fish. Greg hoped to hell that this time, Kay wouldn't let her victim slip away with any kind of luck he'd be freed of a big chunk of alimony. Alimony that would grind to a halt the day Kay remarried.

"Soon, sweetheart," Greg murmured. Maybe soon he'd be free to tell her how he felt. To ask her to share his life.

Meanwhile he wanted to seduce the only woman who'd ever made him feel ten feet tall and invincible.

He had a colleague taking emergency calls, no mothers threatening to have problems at the moment, a box of condoms in the drawer of his bedside table, and a burning need to see how many of them he and Sandy could use in the long, silent hours before morning. Tomorrow would be soon enough to see if just maybe he might have a future to offer Sandy along with his deep, abiding love.

"Come with me, sweetheart. I've got something in my shower I'm sure you want to see." He scooped her in his arms and carried her into his small, utilitarian bathroom.

"In here?" Sandy squealed when he set her down and started peeling off his clothes.

Greg reached in the shower and turned on the water. "Come, help me here. Get those clothes off. Haven't you ever had sex in the shower?"

"No. But it sounds like fun."

God, but she turned him on. More than any woman he'd ever had—including the two he'd married. Impatient, he slid her skirt and panties down her long, firm legs, bending to nuzzle the blonde curls that hid her sex.

"Oooh. Greg, that feels delicious. But aren't we supposed to go get wet?"

He separated her labia and blew gently on her clit, loving the way she was already glistening and wet, the way her clit tightened at the slightest stimulation. "Yeah, Come on. I want to lather up every inch of your hot little body." He lifted her against his chest and stepped into the warm spray. "I want you to touch me, too, all over."

"Oh, yes." Sandy skimmed her fingers over his chest, tangling them in the hair that narrowed when it neared his navel and fanned out to the bush that cushioned his cock. "You're a beautiful man." She punctuated her statement with a series of soft nips along his throat and down his body.

"Nah. You're the beauty. Damn, baby, what did I ever do without you?" He went to his knees, spreading her legs apart and taking her aching clit between his teeth.

Water sluiced over his dark, handsome face, making it glow in the fluorescent overhead light. Sandy threaded her fingers through his dark, wavy hair, pressing him closer as he worked his magic on her pussy. His tongue felt like hot wet velvet on her clit. So good. So intimate.

More intimate than his hands cupping her butt cheeks. The most intimate experience she'd ever had, and he alone had given it. The first time, when she'd perched on his desk after work one day, she'd been embarrassed. Now she loved it…loved the man who hadn't been her first lover but had been the first to coax out a climax.

Her pussy muscles clenched around his fingers when he found and massaged her G-spot. And when he opened his mouth over her clit and sucked her hard, she exploded in a hard burst of sensation.

"Like that, did you?" he asked, standing and holding her close. His hard sex throbbed against her belly, invited her touch. Suddenly she wanted to give him what he'd given her.

Sliding down his body, she cupped his velvety scrotum and ran her tongue tentatively over the plum-like head of his penis, tasting the salty drop of fluid that had gathered in its dimpled slit. She rubbed her cheek against his hard-muscled thigh, loving the feel of his crisp body hair against her own smooth skin.

"Please, baby. Love me." His voice sounded ragged, and he dug his fingers into her hair.

She could tell he wanted her to take him in her mouth. Surprisingly, she wanted that, too, though she'd never given head before. Could she take his long thick shaft that way?

She opened her mouth and took him in, her lips closing around the ridge and sliding down his shaft. "Oh, God, yeah. Like that." His fingers tightened at her temples, and she took more of him, swirling her tongue over his smooth, hot flesh.

"That's it. Swallow it. Take my cock all the way down your throat."

She swallowed, and he moaned. Again. Again. His grip on her tightened, and he pulled her away. "Feels so damn good. But you have to stop. For God's sake stop. I want to come inside you."

He shook with the effort of holding back but managed to roll on a condom after dragging Sandy to her feet. "Put your arms around me and hold on tight. We're going to take a hot, wet ride." With that he lifted her, impaled her on his pulsating cock, and wrapped her legs around his waist. Bracing her against the shower wall, he pounded into her hard, fast, triggering another shattering climax from her just as he shouted her name and gave in to his own explosive orgasm.

* * * * *

"Where's Sandy? This is the first time I've seen you without her in weeks," Blake commented the next morning when Greg walked into his office.

"At the office. This is between you and me—at least for now." Greg looked a bit chagrined, which wasn't unusual. He'd always been reticent about sharing his problems.

Blake couldn't resist needling him a little. "When are you going to make an honest woman of my baby's aunt?" Sure, he was kidding, but there was a grain of serious there, too because Erin worried about her sister and Greg's intentions.

"I'm going to ask Sandy to be Mrs. Halpern Number Three so fast it will make your head spin—that is, if you can get either of my lovely former wives to take a hefty reduction in their blood money. You might try Kay first. Shana said she's thinking about remarrying."

Blake leaned back in his chair and ran a hand through his hair. Greg had certainly managed to find two of the most grasping females he'd ever had the misfortune of meeting. Making another probably futile effort to extricate his friend from the alimony nightmares Kay and her successor had inflicted upon him wasn't high on his list of things he wanted to do.

"If Kay remarries, the alimony stops," Blake had hated family law in school and had taken Greg's cases in hand only because he pitied his friend for the way his original divorce attorneys had botched their jobs. "I'll look over the files again and see if there's any flaw I can use to justify asking for a review of the judges' respective orders. Does your accountant have current financial information put together?"

"Yeah. There's not all that much for him to record," Greg told him with a self-deprecating grin. "I'm serious. I'm barely surviving."

"Did you ever think of raising your fees?"

"I have. Regularly. I'm the most expensive damn OB-GYN in Dallas, unless Sam Harrell jacked up his prices again this month. Seriously, there's a limit to how much most people will pay to have a healthy baby — and insurance companies are squeezing us greedy doctors more with every passing day."

Blake got up and poured himself another cup of coffee. "You want some more?"

"No thanks. I have to get back to the office. What are my chances?"

"I'll let you know after I've taken a fine-tooth comb to the papers. Come on, I'll walk you to the elevator."

* * * * *

In the past week, Blake had read the four-inch thick file that documented Greg's two divorces in stilted legalese, several times. Now, though, he devoured each page in minute detail, looking for any irregularity he might have overlooked upon more cursory examination.

The yellow pad he'd used to note possible loopholes was pathetically close to blank when he finished his review and set the fat folder on the corner of his desk. Greg's best hope for relief from court-ordered poverty was that Kay Halpern would hook the fish Greg said she currently had on the line. In spite of his pessimism about gaining Greg relief in the courts, Blake picked up a cassette recorder and began dictating the petitions to reopen alimony and support hearings. He'd just finished dictating the first petition when his secretary, Sharon Raston, apologetically interrupted.

"Your housekeeper is on line two," she told him. "I wouldn't have disturbed you, but she sounds upset."

"I'll talk to her. Thanks, Sharon." Flipping off the recorder, he punched the blinking button on his speakerphone. "What is it, Mary?"

"It's Mrs. Winters. She twisted her ankle and fell, out by the pool."

"Is she hurt?"

"She says she's all right. I helped her up and into her room. She's lying down now."

It angered Blake that Erin resisted accepting most of the help he wanted to give her. Still, he admired her stubborn streak of independence. He doubted she'd admit being hurt unless she was at death's door. "How is she, really, Mary?"

"I think her doctor ought to check her out. It's awfully close to her time to have the baby."

"Then have Miguel drive her to Doctor Halpern's office. I'll meet her there."

Mary sounded distressed. "Miguel isn't here. This is his day off. Do you want me to call an ambulance?"

"No. She wouldn't appreciate that, not when she's insisting she isn't hurt. Just make sure she stays in bed until I get home. I'm leaving now."

"Shall I call Doctor Halpern?"

"I'll call him from the car." He snatched up his suit coat and bolted for the elevator.

"Will you be back?" Sharon asked as he strode past her desk.

"I don't know. You'd better cancel my afternoon appointments. I'll be in touch." Not waiting for Sharon to reply, Blake sprinted toward the parking garage.

If he ignored speed limits and got breaks in traffic, he figured he could cut a good ten minutes off his usual half-hour commute. When he pulled his powerful Mercedes onto the interstate, he watched the speedometer needle climb to ninety before setting the cruise control. Thanking fate for the light midday traffic, he tried not to dwell on the various tragic outcomes that ran through his head.

He wasn't having much luck, especially after pulling off the expressway and onto the narrow, winding road where he had no choice but to slow down. She could lose his baby. Glenna's baby…no, the baby belonged to him and the woman who now held it in her body. Had it been it just a few months ago that he'd wanted—no, demanded, he corrected himself with scrupulous honesty—that Erin destroy the life that had come to mean so much to him?

His lips moved, silently mouthing the words to prayers he hadn't thought about since childhood. He prayed for the baby, for Erin, and selfishly for himself, because facing the fact he might lose his child made him realize what an important part of his life that baby had become.

More important than anything except having Glenna back.

He wanted to see and hold the tiny child whose movement in Erin's womb enthralled him every time he felt and saw it. As he turned into the drive that led to his house, he made a silent pact with himself.

If his son or daughter was unhurt, nothing could keep him from giving that child the most secure, caring family that any child could want. He'd let nothing stand in his way, not even his own grief.

As he carried Erin to his car, and while he drove her sanely to Greg's office, plans formed in his mind to secure the life he wanted for their child.

* * * * *

"Greg didn't say I needed to stay in bed," Erin protested as Blake settled her in the center of her bed and pulled the covers up over her tummy. "He said rest, not confine myself like an invalid. I need to spend some time with my son."

"Timmy is polishing off the burgers we brought home for him, and practicing his letters with Mary. I told him that if he behaved, I'd join him later and we'd play some video games before he goes to sleep."

"Thanks for stopping by McDonald's. I'm sure it wasn't your first choice for lunch, but Timmy loves their burgers and fries. To tell the truth, so do I."

Blake shrugged. He'd felt downright foolish, going into the McDonald's near Greg's office, dressed in a suit and tie, and eating a Big Mac. "It was your choice. I thought we had something to celebrate after Greg said your fall hadn't done you or baby any harm."

"I told you all I hurt was my pride and the skin on my hands and knees. And I don't need to be put to bed like a half-witted child. You don't have the right to dictate every move I make."

"Give it up. Indulge me. Anyhow, I've been doing some serious thinking. We need to talk, and we may as well do it right here while you relax."

"All right." As if resigned to hearing him out, Erin adjusted the pillows behind her back and shifted onto her side. "This is about the only comfortable lying-down position I've found lately."

"I can imagine." Blake smiled. In the last week or so, it seemed she'd literally grown rounder every day.

"You wanted to talk?"

"Yes. I think we should marry."

Erin's eyes widened and her mouth gaped open. He assumed from her shocked expression that he'd have to present the arguments he'd mentally prepared to support this merger. He didn't doubt that the lady would put up a spirited defense.

He laid a hand on her belly. "Both of us care for this baby. We both want him or her to have a loving, stable home life. Who could provide a better home for our son or daughter than you and I, together?"

She lay quietly for a moment, as if considering what he proposed. "How does Timmy fit into this picture of domestic tranquility?"

"I'd like to adopt him. Whether I do or not, I'll treat him the same as if he were mine. It should go without saying that whatever Timmy needs, I'll see that he gets. I can't help loving your son."

Erin nodded. "And you believe you'll love this baby, too?"

"Yes. I hope you can forgive me for what I asked you to do after Glenna died." Knowing he'd asked Erin to destroy his child, even when he'd been crazed with grief, made him feel like a monster.

She laid her hand over his and gave it a sympathetic squeeze. "I forgave you the night we met."

He had no doubt as to her sincerity, and he wished he could forgive himself as easily as she apparently had pardoned him. "Thank you."

"What made you decide so suddenly that we owe it to this baby to tie ourselves to a loveless marriage?" she asked.

"Your accident. Knowing I might lose my child before it had a chance at life. Actually, I've been fighting what I've known since I first realized this baby deserved two loving parents. I reached that conclusion the night I came to you, intending to deny all but financial responsibility for my part in creating our child."

Blake moved from the chair to the edge of Erin's bed and stroked Erin's silky cheek. "We've got many reasons to marry, and very few reasons not to. Please don't debate them with me now. Just let me throw them out for you to think about. When I'm done, I'll leave you to consider what I have said."

"And when will you expect an answer?"

"Tomorrow morning. I'd say that time is of the essence since our baby is due in less than three weeks." Immediately, not giving Erin the opportunity to object, Blake began to make what he hoped was a compelling case for their marriage.

* * * * *

Long after Blake had left, Erin lay wide awake in the darkened room, her mind in turmoil. With skill she supposed he'd honed in courtrooms, he'd presented his position in ways she found difficult if not impossible to refute.

It takes two loving parents together to give a child a stable home.

Blake had hammered in that premise with every other argument he had given, and he'd woven in the probable trauma the baby would suffer if faced with the fact that its biological mother had borne it for money and rejected the opportunity to claim and raise it.

He'd reminded her of the joys of parenting, promising his full participation as the baby's father—and Timmy's. He pledged his financial support without qualification and his emotional sustenance insofar as he was capable of giving it. With a smile she'd thought was close to real, he'd promised he'd try to share control of their home and family with her.

Clearly, when he'd summed up his case, Blake thought he'd made her an offer she couldn't refuse. Perhaps he had. Tired emotionally and physically, she turned to her other side to ease the strain on her back and tried to unscramble conflicting thoughts that filled her mind.

"Yes, I want to be a real mother to you," she told her baby when it shifted in her womb. "And your father can't wait for you to be born so he can hold and love you, too. You ought to see him with your brother Timmy. I know you'd like to have your daddy and me living together, bringing you up together.

But little one, could we really make a happy home for you when all we have to hold it all together is you?"

Before Erin was done, she'd asked her unborn child all the questions for which she had no answers — answers she'd have to find tonight so she could give Blake her decision in the morning.

She hated to think she might be marrying Blake largely to provide for Timmy's future medical care. In her mind, doing that would make her a vulture just like Greg's grasping former wives apparently were if Sandy's frequent descriptions were accurate. On the other hand, how could she *not* consider her little boy and his special needs? Did her primary responsibility not belong with Timmy? And hadn't Blake specifically said he wanted to take care of him, adopt him if she agreed?

Blake seemed to think the arrangement would be fair. Erin would get a daddy for Timmy as well as their baby, all the financial support she might need, and some measure of control over her own life. What would Blake be getting, she wondered, beside a mother instead of a nanny for their baby?

She'd asked timidly if their marriage would be real. "Oh, it will be real enough in the sense that it will be signed, sealed and delivered. If you're asking me if we will be sharing a bed, the answer is no — at least not in the foreseeable future. I haven't wanted a woman since Glenna died. As of this moment, I have no desire to have sex with you or anyone else."

Living without sex wouldn't be a major problem for Erin. After all, the times she'd truly enjoyed making love with Bill during the last year or so of their marriage had been few and far between. The good, memorable sex had happened early in their marriage, when the bloom of love was still bright and full. She and Bill had been in love. That love had withered within the first six months after their wedding, replaced most of the time by indifference, but sometimes by downright dislike.

What chance for contentment would she have with Blake, starting out as they would be, with feelings best described as wary respect for one another? On the other hand, maybe a couple who made no pretense of loving each other might succeed better than a pair whose commitment was based on romantic love that was almost sure to fade. Unless one of them fell in love with somebody else, which would cause an awful dilemma.

She had to make the right choice. Should she or shouldn't she accept Blake's unemotional proposal? Exhausted and frustrated, she gave up when she found herself silently listing the same reason as justification for saying either yes or no.

Chapter Six

Glenna's Ghost

ဢ

You, marry Erin? Blake, how could you?

For a ghost, Glenna felt a mighty human burst of jealousy. Understandable, though. Blake had been hers since the beginning of time, would be hers as long as they lived.

It broke her heart to think of him alone and unhappy. Still, the thought of him pledging to love, honor and cherish another woman hurt so much more than she'd thought it would. She felt tears coming and reached up to brush them from her cheek.

Idiot, you're not alive anymore. Ghosts don't cry, and even if they did, they don't have hands to brush away imaginary tears.

She tried hard to force down the evil monster of envy she couldn't help but feel for Erin, who was alive and well and carrying the baby that should have been hers and Blake's.

You want Blake to be happy, don't you?

Happy? Glenna let out a tight, ironic chuckle. What Blake had proposed was a sterile merger, not a partnership between two caring and loving people. She wished she could reach down and shake some sense into the stubborn man she loved, the one who most of the time, infuriatingly, thought of everything only in terms of black and white!

He's proposing a marriage of convenience. He doesn't want to sleep with her.

Knowing that made her feel good in a purely human, feminine way. But it also made her sad. She'd believed until her dying day that Blake had been faithful to her all the time they were married, even though her illnesses and pregnancies had forced long periods of celibacy on them both.

Right! If I know Blake, he'll be wanting her soon enough. Glenna couldn't help resenting the fact that she was dead and the woman she'd set up to be her successor was very much alive. Blake was a healthy man, with strong physical needs. Someday soon, she knew, the sharp edges of grief would wear away and he would want the comfort of a woman's body.

That woman has to be Erin.

I set this all in motion when I insisted that we hire Erin as a surrogate. No matter how I wish I were still down there, loving Blake, I'm not. Erin is his baby's mother now, so it will be up to her to heal his heart and satisfy his sexual needs that won't stay dormant for long.

Glenna remembered what she'd told Erin on her first visit as a ghost. *"I want Blake to love you as much as he used to love me."*

Keep telling yourself that, Glenna. Maybe in time, you'll really mean it.

Glenna marshaled her strength to speak and be heard, to see and be seen. Soon she materialized for the second time in Erin's bedroom.

Chapter Seven

✍

"Erin. Wake up."

"Oh. What time is it?" Erin lifted a hand to cover her eyes in the room that had suddenly become as bright as day.

"About three o'clock. But we need to talk."

Erin forced her tired eyes to focus. "Glenna."

"You're going to marry Blake, aren't you?"

"I don't know. God, I don't know. Why did I ever agree to be a surrogate mother?"

"Fate. We must all bow to fate, Erin. Look at me. I wanted to bear Blake's children, but fate decreed otherwise. But we still had each other. It was fate, too, that I persuaded Blake to accept a surrogate arrangement so we could have the baby that meant everything to me — and that I was shot before I got to hold and love that child. Now, your destiny is to marry Blake so both of you can give your child a loving home." Glenna paused, as if going on were more than she could bear.

"He's a good man. Underneath that cool, clear logic and the grief I've brought him by dying, is a man who can love deeply and well."

Hearing Glenna — or rather, Glenna's ghost — talk so eloquently about Blake embarrassed Erin. "Why do you want us to marry?" she asked, wishing she could deny the surrealistic presence and escape into healing sleep.

"I told you before. I want to see good come from the situation I so unwittingly caused. I want Blake to be happy. I need to know the baby I wanted so much has a good, loving home. I have to know you and your little boy won't be hurt because I selfishly thought I needed Blake's baby to make my life complete."

The aura surrounding Glenna brightened more, making Erin turn her gaze toward fluttering curtains at the French doors she was sure she'd closed. "None of this was your fault." She could practically feel Glenna's pain.

"I was responsible."

"No."

"Yes. Erin, marry Blake. Give him time. He'll be a wonderful father, not only to his baby but to your little boy."

Erin trembled. That argument was the same one Blake had hammered into her, the one she couldn't ignore as she lay and tried to decide whether she should become the second Mrs. James Blake Tanner IV. "Is that enough reason for two people who don't love each other to marry?"

"Oh, no. But Blake will love again. His grief was talking when he said he was proposing a marriage of convenience. That won't last long. Blake needs affection, and he needs sex. He's also faithful to any promise he makes. He'll want you, all right — sooner than you think. And Erin, he's a wonderful lover, the ghost" added wistfully.

Erin blushed. "You're making me uncomfortable."

"Promise me you'll marry him," Glenna whispered as her image began to fade.

"I will."

Had she really said that? Had she meant it? Her late-night visitor disappeared into a cloud of golden dust as she had that first night, when the ghost had welcomed her into what had so recently been her own home.

Ironically, the ghost had become Erin's closest friend. There was something eerie, though, about having a friend who seemed to know everything you said and did. She wondered if Glenna was always lurking, whether she eavesdropped on every conversation. Had she been there earlier this evening, when Blake had argued that they should marry?

Erin laughed. Nerves, she told herself. For a minute there, she'd worried about Blake unknowingly hurting the ghost of his dead wife. Fat chance of that. She'd never forget his flat, sober expression when he said he didn't foresee wanting anyone but Glenna—that his heart belonged to her and always would. No, Glenna's death hadn't altered his commitment to her.

Her friendly ghost didn't seem to mind her husband's decision to acquire a mother for his unborn baby. As a matter of fact, Glenna had been even more persuasive than Blake in her insistence that marriage would be the best solution for them all.

She'd promised Glenna she'd marry him.

Suddenly the prospect of being Mrs. Blake Tanner, if only in name, seemed the only option that made much sense out of the muddled mess she, Blake and Glenna had so unwittingly created. "And I'm going to do it," she said before wriggling into a comfortable position and switching off the night-light.

* * * * *

"Have you made up your mind?" Blake asked Erin when she joined him for breakfast the following morning.

"Yes, I have."

"Well?"

"I'll marry you. I've thought it over, and I can't see any better alternative. Still, I have reservations—lots of them. Some conditions, too."

"Conditions?" Blake wasn't anxious to hear about Erin's reservations. He had plenty of his own.

"Timmy. I want him to believe this marriage is real."

"So do I. I'll do my part, if you'll do yours. What do you propose we do to accomplish this?"

Erin looked confused. Maybe she hadn't given the mechanics of making this farce of an arrangement look real any more thought than he had. "Do?"

"Exactly. Do we hold hands and kiss? Call each other pet names when the children are around? Sleep together?"

"I— I hadn't thought of *how*." Erin frowned. "But I don't want Timmy to think I'm marrying you because of him or this baby. Maybe, we should just forget it."

Blake met her concerned gaze. "You're absolutely right that we should keep the reasons for this marriage to ourselves—for both children's sakes. We can work out the details later." What the hell? Not only would they have to deceive a little boy and a baby. They'd need to put on a show-stopping performance for half of Dallas as well.

And half of Dallas it would be. When he paused to consider the situation, he realized that to keep Timmy—and eventually his baby—thinking his and Erin's marriage was a love match, they would have to fool their families, friends, and even casual acquaintances.

He looked away from the window with its view of lush grass and colorful flowers in full bloom this bright June morning, and settled his gaze on the ever-increasing girth of Erin's midsection.

Erin's question was small, reluctant. "When do you want—"

"As soon as possible, wouldn't you say?" He met her gaze.

"I guess so."

"I'll make the arrangements. Saturday afternoon, if I can find a judge who's free then. Do you have family you'll want to be here?" As far as Blake was concerned, the simpler, the better. Still, one needed some family present in order to make this look real.

"Just Sandy. Our parents died when she was a teenager. And Timmy, of course. How about you?"

Blake lifted his left hand to brush a strand of hair off his forehead. "My mother is out of the country," he replied. "Dad died a few years back." He watched Erin's gaze settle on his hand as it came back to rest on the tabletop.

"Do you intend to take that off?" she asked quietly.

Blake's gaze followed Erin's to the gold band that reflected the bright rays from the morning sun. He felt as if he were tearing out his heart as he slowly brought his right hand up to grasp the ring that had rarely left his finger since Glenna put it there, nearly fifteen years ago.

"Yes. I'll take it off. I've worn Glenna's ring since the day we married, but I obviously can't wear it when I'm about to marry you." He knew he sounded unnecessarily curt as he worked the wide gold band off his finger and put it in his pocket, but he couldn't help it. "I won't wear another wedding band."

"I didn't expect you would. I don't need one, either."

"You'll get one, anyway." This might be a loveless marriage he was entering into, but Blake would provide the bride's ring that society would expect. He made a mental note to have his secretary go out and buy it as soon as she finished making other necessary arrangements.

"Will you be home this evening?"

He got up and shrugged into the jacket of a tropical-weight gray pinstriped suit. "Yes. I'll let you know what arrangements I've made, at dinner."

* * * * *

"You've heard from the judge already?" Greg asked as Sandy stood back to let Blake into his office. "You must be damn good." It had taken months for his last attorney to write the alimony reduction petitions, much less get them acted upon.

Blake shook his head. "Hardly. I just filed the papers this morning. We should get hearing dates assigned within a couple of weeks. These things take time."

"Then what brings you here? I told you, Erin is fine. It takes more than a simple fall like the one she had to hurt a healthy baby."

"I need you to do a blood test."

"On whom?"

"Me. Erin, too, but I assume you've got her tests on record here."

"Go see your own doctor. My practice is limited to women. Wait a minute, my friend. What kind of blood tests? You certainly don't think you need proof that the baby's yours?"

"No. Damn it. We're going to get married. I just need whatever test the state requires to get a marriage license."

Greg stood and paced around the room while he wondered whether he should offer congratulations or commiseration. "You're going to marry her?" he finally asked to ease the silence.

Blake shrugged. "I'm about to become a father, as you know better than anyone, including the baby's mother. Don't you think it's reasonable that I provide my child with both its parents?"

Silently but fervently, Greg promised to avoid any future encounters with surrogate parenthood, as judiciously as Sandy kept him from accepting too many time-consuming charity cases.

Oh God. Sandy was going to pitch a fit when she heard this. His little angel was damn protective of her older sister, especially so since she'd been the one to suggest that Erin become a surrogate mother. "What about Glenna? I mean, isn't it awfully soon?"

"Of course it is. But what the hell do I do? Wait the usual time for mourning and let my child be born out of wedlock? This baby was Glenna's fondest desire come true. Since she's gone, marrying Erin now is the right thing to do. I'd rather let people think I'm a bastard for knocking up another woman while my wife was still alive, and an ass for remarrying too soon, than have my son or daughter labeled a bastard."

"When did you decide this?"

"I guess I've known from the moment I realized I couldn't turn my back on this baby. God knows I've fought doing it, but when I knew Erin was hurt and that the baby might be at risk, it hit me just how much I want this child. And how much the baby will need its mother."

"Congratulations, then." Greg figured Blake and Erin were going to need all the good wishes they could get. "Am I invited to the happy event?" he asked, forcing a grin.

"You're invited to be best man—again." Tears welled up in Blake's eyes when he added that last word.

Briefly, Greg recalled that other wedding, the one that had lasted through two of his own marriages and divorces. Glenna's and Blake's deep, loving commitment had made Greg hope that someday he might have a relationship as enduring and peaceful.

Then he smiled and patted Blake on the back. The last thing he needed was another glum face. "I'd be honored," he said. "When is this festive occasion?"

"Saturday. Seven o'clock, at the house. We'll have dinner afterward. Nothing fancy, just you, Sandy, the judge, Erin, and me—and Timmy."

"Good timing. Any later, and I might be attending for quite another reason."

Blake's laugh sounded forced, but he seemed at peace with himself and his decision. Greg hoped Sandy would take the news of this upcoming wedding with the same equanimity as it seemed that at least one of the two main participants was accepting it.

* * * * *

"I'm glad your last patient called and cancelled." Sandy set out salad and gazpacho from the deli as soon as they arrived at her apartment late that afternoon. "Sit down. You're about to enjoy my version of a home-cooked meal."

Her voice sounded strained, but she kept their conversation focused on the day's events at the office until after they finished their salad and gazpacho and settled on the swing in the corner of her tiny patio with root beer floats she'd made. Greg grinned as he recalled their discovery at the beginning of summer that they shared a passion for the frosty fountain drinks. Since then, Sandy had often fixed them instead of dessert when he came over.

"You know they're getting married, don't you?" Sandy asked, her manner quiet but serious.

"Blake told me."

"What do you think about it?"

Greg shrugged. "That they're both certifiable. But I see Blake's reasoning. That baby does need two parents."

"You think they're marrying just for the baby's sake? Erin gave me the impression there's some attraction between them, too."

Greg didn't just think it, he knew damn well they were marrying because of the baby— at least Blake was. "I got that impression. But then, Blake's the soul of good old WASP restraint. He doesn't let anybody, even close friends, in on his deeper feelings." Greg felt guilty, holding back his feelings about Blake and Erin's coming marriage, but he couldn't very well make Erin out to be a liar.

Sandy smiled. "I'm glad you're not shy about making your deepest feelings known," she said, moving closer to him on the old-fashioned swing.

Greg put an arm around her, letting his fingers rove over the silky soft skin of her bare shoulder. He loved the feel of her, the way she cuddled against his chest like a friendly kitten. He craved her when they were together, and even more when they were apart. In a few short months, she had become an addiction, one he had to have more and more of in order to survive.

"Want to know how I feel right now?" he asked, letting his hand wander down to toy with her soft, warm breast.

"Uh-huh." Her nipple beaded at his touch, burning into his hand through the soft, flimsy material of the T-shirt she'd put on when they got to her apartment.

"Horny." In the past three months, he'd been that way more than he remembered ever having been. Hornier even than when he was a studious teenager whose fantasies ran a lot hotter and heavier than his limited real successes.

"Want to do something about this?" Sandy lightly squeezed his hard-on through his slacks. "I could drag you inside this way."

"Promises, promises." Damn if she didn't make him feel ten years younger and as hungry for pussy as if he didn't have to examine dozens of them every day in the course of his work. Loving her the way he did was icing on the sex cake. "Come on, baby. I'll give you a ride you won't forget."

"Now it's you making rash promises." Sandy snuggled up against his chest and started unbuttoning his shirt. "Maybe this time I want to do the riding."

"Am I gonna have to show you who's boss?"

"Just how would you do that, Doctor Halpern?" She shot him a challenging look—but then she grinned. "Give me a spanking?"

He whipped off his belt and caught both ends in his fist. "Do you think you need one?" Hell, he didn't mind going along with her little game.

"I've been a bad, bad girl. All day I kept thinking how much fun we could have had if you'd just laid me up on one of your examining tables during a lull between patients and fucked me until I screamed for mercy." She giggled. "That would have shocked the pants right off prissy Mrs. Carlisle if she'd known."

"You're not supposed to talk mean about my nurse."

"I know, but it's so much fun to shock her." Very slowly Sandy lifted her oversize T-shirt and shimmied her hips as she pulled it off over her head. "Just imagine her walking in and catching us."

All Greg could imagine at the moment was getting his cock in Sandy's hot little cunt. "Just imagine me losing my license." Then he laughed. "You'd really fuck with me in the office?"

"Oh, yeah, Doc. Anytime, anyplace. I could always swear you were doing my annual checkup. You've got one hot cock, you know?"

"Not as hot as your cute little tush is gonna be." He shed his slacks and underwear, and sat on the bed, belt in hand. "Come here and bend over my knee."

"Oooh. Are you really gonna use that on me?"

He patted his knees. "You've asked for it, baby. Now you're gonna get it. And when I finish tanning your perfect little ass, I'm going to show you another use for it."

When she lay facedown across his lap, Greg bent and kissed her upthrust buttocks. "Are you going to stop thinking dirty thoughts, sweetheart?"

"Never."

"Then you're going to take a couple of licks with this." He dangled the belt menacingly before her face, then brought it up over his target.

"Please…"

He whacked her butt cheeks once, hard, then let the loop of leather trail across her reddened skin.

"…Please do it again. Harder."

Th-wack. The crack of leather on her firm, supple ass made his balls tighten with anticipation. He set down the belt and used his hand, sampling the heat that had risen from the belt strokes and her arousal.

"You ready to be good now?" Grabbing a handful of her bottom, he gave it a gentle squeeze. When she squirmed, the contact of her hip with his rigid cock made every muscle in his body clench with need.

"Oh, yessss."

As new to sex as Sandy was, she got off on every kind of play he'd ever tried. Now her puckered anus beckoned him, so he dragged his hand in the honey that flowed from her hot, primed cunt and ringed her puckered rear entrance with one finger. "Feel good?" He worked his finger slowly past her anal sphincter.

"Mmmm. Good." Then she gasped. "No, Greg. That hurts."

"Take some deep breaths. Relax. There, how does it feel now?" Once completely inside her, he gently probed with his finger, massaging her cunt through the thin wall that separated the two orifices.

"Different. Oh, that feels wonderful. But now I want your cock. Please. My pussy wants it now."

Carefully, he withdrew his finger, then gave her bottom a playful whack with his open hand. "My cock wants your wet little pussy, too. Get up and lie back on the bed, and I'll make us both happy." He reached in the drawer of the nightstand for a condom.

He loved how she rolled over on her back and opened herself for him. Kneeling between her firm, slender thighs after sheathing himself, he slowly sank into her wet, hot cunt. "How do you want it, sweetheart? Shall I fuck you real slow, make you beg for more?"

"Damn you. Quit talking and fuck me. Slow, fast. I don't care so long as you're inside me." She punctuated her demand by wrapping her legs around his waist and taking sharp little bites out of his shoulder.

"Okay. Hold on. Baby, you'll fuck me to death." But he loved being in her tight, hot cunt, feeling her squeeze his cock as if she'd never let him go. He loved her. Loved sinking deep in her hot, tight cunt and fucking her until they both collapsed in a sweaty heap of satisfaction.

Sweet and gentle or hot and fast, it was all good. So good he never wanted to leave her. So good he didn't know how much longer he could hold on.

She lifted her hips to meet his every thrust, squeezed his cock with her inner muscles. "Harder. Fuck me harder. Oh, yesss. I'm coming. Greg, I love you."

Her whole body shook. Her pussy flooded with slick, hot honey. She dug her nails into his back, her heels into his ass. Her spasming cunt milked him, dragged him along with her to a climax so powerful it left him drained.

Drained but supremely content. When he rolled to his side, Sandy came with him, snuggled against him, and dropped light kisses across his chest and neck. Unlike either of his former wives or the few other women in his past, she made him enjoy quiet times like these almost as much as the sex itself. He loved having a lover who made sex fun.

He sensed the love he felt for Sandy was the kind that could endure forever. Yeah, he loved fucking with her, but it wasn't only hot, wild passion like the fever that had made him marry Rhea, a woman he had barely been able to tolerate being around except when they were fucking.

And it was totally different from what he'd felt at first for Kay, whom he'd married right out of college largely because she'd been his mother's idea of the perfect doctor's wife. Greg smiled down at Sandy, so young yet more mature than either of the women he had married. He'd never let her go.

It felt right, lying in the dark with her while the night breeze from an open window cooled their sated bodies.

"I hope Erin and Blake find half the happiness that we've found together," Sandy murmured against his chest.

Greg seconded the wish he doubted would come true. "Me, too, sweetheart."

* * * * *

That day Erin had told Timmy, Sandy, and Mrs. Malone she and Blake were getting married, though Blake apparently had already told his household staff. Whatever else the man was, he was efficient—efficient enough to drive Erin crazy. She laughed. It was better to laugh than to cry. Here she was, planning to marry the grieving widower of a ghost—the same ghost who kept visiting her and nudging her toward Blake.

Nudged? Ha! Glenna's ghost didn't nudge, she pushed and shoved and badgered. Apparently she expected Erin not only to marry Blake, but to fall in love with him. And make him fall in love with her. What a joke!

No wonder they'd gotten along so well, Erin thought, not without a bit of malice. Both Glenna and Blake seemed to go after whatever it was they wanted with a singularity of purpose.

No one seemed particularly shocked or surprised when she told them about the wedding. Timmy took the news in stride. He liked Blake and thought he'd make a great daddy. And he loved living here and enjoying the luxuries that meant little to a rich man but a lot to the child whose life had been pretty lacking in material things.

Erin had expected shrieks and dire warnings from Sandy. But while her sister's feelings obviously were mixed, Sandy had agreed to witness the wedding. She'd even refrained from showing downright disapproval and offered to drive Erin to the stores tomorrow so she could find something to wear Saturday for the wedding.

A maternity wedding dress. That was how Sandy had put it. Erin laughed. How ironic it was that the first brand new dress she'd bought in more than three years would, of necessity, be one she could only wear for three more weeks.

Oh, well, there'd be plenty of money for dresses now. Blake had made it clear last night that he'd provide her with all the material things she could reasonably want. In practically the same breath, he'd assured her there was nothing left in him to give her, emotionally speaking. Suddenly Erin felt like giving in and crying.

"Cheer up. It's going to take some time, but he's got to stop grieving soon."

Glenna was there, somewhere. Erin had a feeling the ghost never slept, that she bore silent witness to Erin's every thought. She looked around in vain for the source of that bright, cheerful voice. "Where are you?"

"I'm here. Look, it takes a lot of energy to pop in where you can see me. There are times, like this, when I won't try. I've got a feeling you're going to need me more later than you do now. You looked like you were going to cry, though, so I thought you might need a friend."

"Are you always watching, listening?"

"Most of the time. I made a hell of a mess of your and Blake's lives. I can't rest until I get the damage repaired."

Erin glanced around the room, still searching for the source of Glenna's voice.

"I'm over here."

"Where?" Erin whispered.

"By the garden room door. By the way, I hope you're planning to buy something special for your wedding," the cheerfully disembodied voice continued while Erin tried in vain to see Glenna. *"You are, aren't you?"*

Apparently the ghost didn't always eavesdrop. If she did, she'd have heard Erin talking with Sandy about their plans to go shopping. Knowing Glenna sometimes made herself scarce didn't relieve Erin much, since she had no way of knowing whether or not the ghost was around.

"You met my sister Sandy. She works for Doctor Halpern. We're going to shop for dresses later this week." Erin glanced around the room to be sure there was no one around to hear her talking to herself. If there were, they'd think she was nuts.

The weird feeling that she was never alone didn't leave Erin as she went about her daily routine, playing with Timmy and getting more rest than any woman needed.

* * * * *

He'd enjoyed a busy but productive day. Blake mentally reviewed his plans as he pulled into the garage half an hour earlier than usual. He smiled when he saw Timmy waiting in his wheelchair, out beside the pool.

"Mr. Tanner."

"Timmy. How are you, sport?" Blake set his briefcase down and sat on a patio chair next to the little boy.

"I took six steps today. And Mommy says we're gonna marry you and live here with you and your new baby. Are we really?"

"Yes, we are." Blake paused, considering that the chance to be a father figure for this bright, brave boy was one big plus to his arrangement with the boy's mother. "Tell me about walking."

Timmy returned the grin. "Well, it's not really walking. But I held myself up between the bars and moved my legs all by myself. Michelle said I did good."

"I'm proud of you. Keep it up, and pretty soon you'll be good as new."

"Mr. Tanner, are you gonna be my daddy?"

They had to make their marriage seem real, for Timmy's sake. He and Erin had agreed on that, but Erin hadn't addressed his offer to adopt her son. Blake didn't like loose ends, and he resolved to tie this one up soon. "I'll be your stepfather, sport."

Timmy looked worried. "You mean like the wicked step*mother* in *Cinderella*?"

Blake reached over and ruffled his hair. "Of course not. At least I hope you won't ever think of me that way."

"I'd like to pretend you're my real daddy."

"I'd like that, too. Only you don't need to pretend. Your real daddy can't be here for you now, so I'll do my best to stand in for him." Blake placed the issue of adopting Timmy at the top of his mental list of things to be resolved.

"Are you and Mommy gonna sleep together? I remember when she and my—my first daddy used to let me crawl in between them in their bed on Sunday mornings." Timmy paused, and Blake wondered what was going through the boy's agile mind. "I guess I'm too big for that now," Timmy said wistfully.

"Yes. You certainly are getting big." At least the boy's last comment gave him an opening to avoid answering Timmy's first question. He hadn't considered that the boy would worry about his and Erin's sleeping arrangements. But then, he'd never have dared intrude on either or both of his parents' private spaces when he was a boy, so he supposed his lack of foresight was understandable.

Timmy grinned. "You think our baby's gonna be another boy? I sure hope so, don't you?"

"We'll have to wait and see, sport. A boy would be nice, but so would a little girl." Relieved at having been able to defer Timmy's other line of questioning, Blake ruffled the boy's hair.

"A girl. Yuck. I don't like girls."

"Sure you do. What about your mom? And Michelle, and Mary, and your Aunt Sandy?"

"They're not girls. They're all grown up." For a minute, Timmy stayed quiet, his brow wrinkled as though in deep thought. "Do you like girls?"

"Yes, I do. Little ones as well as grown-up girls."

"You must like my mommy a lot, since you want us to marry you and stay with you and our baby." Timmy made a statement, but the inflection in his voice made it sound more like a question.

Blake could handle that one. "Sure. I like both of you a lot," he said, getting up and motioning toward the house. "I promised your mom we'd talk when I got home, so I'd better head on inside now. Would you like a push?"

"No thanks. I can do it myself. Michelle taught me how. What am I supposed to call you after you and Mommy get married?" Timmy asked as he rolled along beside Blake on the sidewalk that led to the back door.

"I'd like it if you wanted to call me 'Daddy,' but if you'd rather, you can just use my name."

"Blake? Like Mommy calls you?"

"Yes."

Timmy rolled along quietly for a few seconds, before announcing that he thought he'd like to think this over for a few days. Though he hadn't considered sleeping arrangements before, Blake considered Timmy's assumptions. Perhaps he needed to have Erin's things moved into the master suite before they married.

* * * * *

Blake didn't talk with Erin right away. Instead, he had Mary serve their dinner on trays so they could watch a movie with Timmy on the giant screen TV in the family room. After helping tuck the sleepy little boy into bed at nine o'clock, he walked Erin to her room.

"Get ready for bed."

After having stayed awake most of the previous night worrying about what to do, Erin was too tired to bristle at Blake's terse command. When she emerged from the bathroom in her oversize T-shirt and lay back on the bed, he was still there, apparently waiting to pull the sheet and light blanket over her legs and tummy.

"I'll be right back," he said once he'd tucked her in. "We need to go over some things."

He was back in a flash, his black leather briefcase in hand. "I think I've taken care of most everything," he said, settling on a chair next to her bed and fishing out several neatly typed sheets and some kind of a legal document bound in stiff, blue paper. "Here, these are for you."

If Blake thought he had arranged every detail, he probably had. "What do I need to do?"

"These are the arrangements for the ceremony. All you need to do is go with me to get the license and go buy whatever you'd like to wear. The license, we can get late tomorrow afternoon. I thought Miguel might take you shopping first. Then he can bring you to meet me at the courthouse around four o'clock."

"Sandy said she'd take me shopping. It would save her from having to drive me back here if she could just drop me off at the courthouse. If you wouldn't mind driving me back?" Erin had agreed that Blake's house would become her home, but she couldn't think of it as such, at least not yet.

"I planned to." He smiled, but then his expression sobered. "Erin," he said after a long pause, "you said you wanted Timmy to believe this marriage would be real. And I agreed. Don't you agree that if we're going to succeed in this little deception, we're going to have to become a lot more comfortable with each other?"

"What do you mean?"

"He means, you're going to have to get close if you're going to pull off this without folks asking a lot of embarrassing questions," interjected the familiar ghostly voice.

Blake shrugged. "I mean, we're going to have to be together occasionally without Timmy there as a buffer. More than occasionally after the baby is born, because if we don't do things as a couple, people will think there's something strange about our marriage. We need to be friends, even if we're not lovers."

"But we hardly know each other." Blake certainly had shown no interest before in becoming pals.

"You'd best be getting acquainted, Mommy. You two are going to spend a lifetime raising that baby, you know."

When Blake smiled, his deep blue eyes seemed to brighten. "You're right. My point is, we need to get to know each other. After all, we're going to be married. And we'll be parents in less than a month. We're going to be sharing one big master suite if not one bed. I won't bite."

"All right. By the way, it was nice of you to suggest we all watch that movie together."

"I enjoyed it. You know, I don't think my parents ever spent a whole evening with me, just relaxing at home."

"*He's right, Erin. Like I told you before, his parents were something else again.*"

"I kn—I mean, really?"

Blake raised an eyebrow at her inadvertent slip, but he apparently chose to ignore it and give her another bit of his life history. "Really. My father lived and breathed the law, and Mother's world still revolves around whatever her jet-setting friends are doing. I'm going to need a lot of guidance, but I intend to be the best parent I can be to my children."

Blake sounded matter-of-fact, but Erin imagined a lot of turbulent emotion lurked behind his simple declaration. Of all her doubts—and there were many—one was not that Blake would be anything but a caring father for his child. "You'll be a wonderful dad."

"Are you ever going to relax around me?" Blake asked suddenly. "Look at you, you're as strung out as an embezzler caught with his fingers in the till."

He'd be strung out, too, if he had a ghost popping in and nudging him nearly every time he turned around. Realizing she'd clenched her fists, Erin released them, though she imagined the strain of being here alone with Blake and the omniscient but invisible ghost of his dead wife showed plainly on her face. "I'm sorry. I can't help feeling vulnerable, lying here undressed with you there, fully clothed, handing down ultimatums."

"Would it help if I took off my shirt?" Blake set the blue-bound papers on the bed and attacked the second button of his pale yellow dress shirt. His grin told her he was joking now.

But she wasn't. The sight of his hard-muscled chest, dusted lightly with dark brown hair, made her mouth go dry and her heart beat in double time. How could he not affect her when he shot her such an irresistible smile?

"Stop it." Frantically, Erin searched the room, searching for that golden aura that usually surrounded Glenna's ghost.

"*Uh, I think it's time for me to go. I'll be back,*" Glenna whispered as Erin watched a trail of golden dust float through the closed patio doors.

She looked back at Blake quickly, but not soon enough to keep him from giving her a very puzzled look. "What's wrong?"

Erin hesitated. Part of her wanted to tell him about the ghost, until the saner portion of her brain intervened. If she hadn't seen Glenna, she wouldn't have believed. There wasn't a chance in the world that she could make Blake believe in the ghost's presence. Finally she found her voice. "Nothing. What is this?" She picked up the blue-bound, official-looking document Blake had set on the bed and leafed through it.

"It's a form we both need to sign, rescinding the surrogate arrangement." Blake stopped unbuttoning buttons and met Erin's gaze. "I don't want this baby ever to know you agreed to have it and give it up for money."

He still thought what she'd done was wrong.

Erin's hurt must have shown, because he reached out and touched her—not her hand or face, but the round, hard mound that defined their child. "I understand why you did this. And I respect you for it, but you're going to be this baby's real mother now. Do you want him or her to find out some day that you originally intended to have him for someone else?"

No, she didn't. But to sign another paper? It had been hard enough to sign the first one. "Why can't we just rip up the original contract?"

"Because copies have been filed with the family court. These papers rescind the permission you gave for me to adopt our child at birth. I'll get the original papers back when I present these to the judge. Then we can tear them up. We can even burn them if you'd like," he offered lightly.

"All right."

Glenna had told Erin last night that Blake was a good man who could love deeply and well. Erin knew that was true. Knew she could easily love him if she let herself, and that he'd love his child. But she doubted Glenna's assessment that he would someday be ready to love a woman again.

"I'm going to go now, let you get some rest. I'll meet you tomorrow afternoon so we can get the license. Other than that, you won't need to do anything except be in the garden room at seven o'clock on Saturday. Here, I almost forgot. You'll need these if you're going shopping. I don't want you worrying about the costs." He pulled some credit cards out of his pocket and set them on the table.

It ruffled Erin's fierce sense of independence that Blake should pay for her wedding dress, but she didn't protest. Her depleted checking account currently boasted forty-eight dollars and some odd cents, not enough to go very far toward decking her out as a blushing if very pregnant bride. Besides, she imagined she should save arguing with Blake for something that mattered more than a bit of tattered pride.

Chapter Eight

ဆ

"Keep away from that sale rack," Sandy cautioned when Erin headed toward the sign that advertised another fifty percent off already-reduced prices.

"Yes, do. And put that dreary navy-blue thing back. Where do you think you're going? To a funeral?"

Erin looked around. Glenna couldn't be here, in this little out-of-the-way maternity boutique where the clothes all wore discreet designer labels and even more discreet but obscenely expensive price tags. But there she was, perched on the corner of the antique desk that served as a cash register, so dainty and pretty she made Erin feel like a circus elephant about to be fitted for a new tent.

"Do you like this one?"

Erin turned to her sister, who was holding up a pale pink organdy dress with a white linen collar.

"Only if it comes with a matching outfit for one's little girl."

Erin laughed at Glenna's observation. The dress, with its short puffed sleeves, Peter Pan collar and the gathered skirt that billowed from a yoke complete with lace insertions, did remind her of a giant version of a child's party dress.

"What's so funny?" Sandy asked.

"Oh, nothing." Glenna grinned, Sandy looked perturbed, and Erin felt as though she might go stark raving crazy before she got out of this place. "I don't think that will do." Erin shook her head at the offending garment and pulling another dress off the rack.

"Too somber." Sandy was apparently not impressed by the tiny white flowers on a background of black cotton. "And not dressy enough."

"She's right. If I know Blake, he'll be wearing one of those gray pinstriped suits and a somber tie. You don't want your wedding pictures to look as though color film hasn't been invented yet. Here. Try this one."

Erin reached out quickly to grab the garment that almost leaped off the rack at her. It was pale blue, gauzy silk, with a low-scooped neckline and a skirt that fell in soft, wrinkly pleats from the empire bodice. For a maternity dress, it was gorgeous. Then she looked at the price tag and gasped, putting it back on the rack with a sigh of regret.

"I like that one," Sandy said. "Go try it on."

"It's too expensive." Determined to find something that would please both her sister and her ghostly friend, Erin flipped through the size eight selections on the sales rack. "Here, this should do." She held up a silvery gray jumper whose black silk blouse would lend a slimming effect to the ensemble.

"This is not a funeral. Lord knows, we've had enough of them."

Erin whirled around and looked at Glenna, shocked.

"What? I can't say that? We can't ignore it. It happened. Now put away that outfit and go try on the one I found for you. So what if it's expensive? Didn't Blake tell you not to worry about the cost?"

The dress practically fell into Erin's hands again. "I guess I'll try this one on after all." If she did, and if she looked like Dumbo the Elephant, then she'd have an excuse not to buy it.

"You look gorgeous," Sandy said with wonder when Erin stepped out of the dressing room.

"I look pregnant. Very, very pregnant." Erin felt huge but pretty in the soft, blue dress.

"But it's his baby. He'll think you're beautiful."

"Sandy, this dress costs almost a thousand dollars." It felt good, though. Erin ran her fingers over the crispy, crinkled silk that formed a calf-length skirt.

"*Every one of Blake's suits cost more than that. And when I died, he donated a closet full of my clothes that cost fifty times the price of that dress to charity, just to get them out of his sight. You've got to put things into perspective. Get the dress. It's gorgeous, and so are you.*"

Glenna slid off the corner of the desk and moved to a display of jewelry. "*I want to pick out something, just to you from me. Here. See this necklace and earrings. They will look beautiful with that dress.*"

"Are you going to get it?" Sandy paced around Erin, looking at her from all angles. "The cut must be what makes it so expensive. It makes you look radiant, not blimpy. Come on, Erin, buy it. You can lend it to me someday when I'm expecting Greg's baby," she added, a dreamy look on her face.

Erin felt pulled toward the locked display case Glenna had indicated. "I'm going to get it, but it's insane to spend this much. Even if Blake *can* afford it." Then, she saw the jewelry that had caught Glenna's eye.

There were three roses crafted of gold, with shiny blue dewdrops that looked like sapphires. The smaller ones were earrings, and the larger one a pendant on a fine gold chain. The workmanship took Erin's breath away. She loved them, but after noticing the smile on the clerk's face as she opened the case, she realized they must cost as much or more than the dress.

"*You like them, don't you? I knew you would. Go ahead. Take them. Our Blake isn't much of a jewelry man — I had to buy most of my own trinkets when we were married.*"

Erin recalled the simple string of creamy cultured pearls Bill had given her the day before their wedding, regretting for a moment that she'd sold them to raise money for Timmy's first, long hospital stay. Blake had said he'd be giving her a ring, but she imagined it would be the only token she'd get to remember this very practical, unemotional union.

"I'll take these, and this dress," she told the clerk. "Sandy, do you think we'll have time for me to find a pair of shoes?"

"Sure. There's a store two doors down."

As Erin gathered her packages and prepared to leave the boutique, she saw Glenna surrounded by that golden haze that always seemed to herald her arrivals and departures. She could almost swear Glenna gave her the thumbs-up sign along with an exaggerated wink.

* * * * *

The next afternoon, Erin recalled Glenna's farewell gesture and felt she could use some cheering up, even if it did come from a ghost. Timmy had gone with Blake to get a haircut. Mrs. Malone was busy with getting things ready for the ceremony and the meal that would follow.

Erin had been ordered to nap, but sleep wouldn't come. For a little while, she tried to conjure up Glenna in her mind. When that didn't work, she let her mind wander to another day, another wedding.

Had she ever been that young and that I? Erin pictured herself at twenty-one, starry eyed as she'd walked slowly down the aisle. Her dress had been traditional—white lace on satin, with a chapel train. Her veil had obscured her view of Bill's handsome, smiling face. And she'd been the traditional bride, ready to love, honor and cherish the young man who became her husband for as long as they both might live.

She tried to picture Bill, to recall how he'd looked and what he'd said when they cut the three-tiered wedding cake at her parents' home after the ceremony. She thought hard, trying to recreate their wedding night in a small hotel on the beach in Galveston. Those memories had faded to a sepia glow. Unfortunately the ones that still lay heavily on her mind weren't nearly as glowing. Erin couldn't help the feeling of sadness that swept over her.

They'd shared good times in spite of time and circumstances that dulled the joy of first, young love. She'd stayed home while Bill worked his way up the corporate ladder at a small electronics company. He'd been the original party animal, and until Timmy's birth, they'd enjoyed constant sensual adventures.

It was impossible for Erin not to compare Bill's initial distaste for fatherhood with Blake's wholehearted enthusiasm for his coming child. Bill had adored Timmy from the day he was born, though. He'd been a good dad until that rainy Saturday nearly four years ago when he'd run his financed-to-the-hilt silver Porsche into a tree, killing himself and crippling his little boy.

Now, as she prepared for her second wedding, Erin told herself this rational, logical union would work out. Better than her first marriage that had begun with two kids in love and ended in a mass of twisted metal on a highway outside Dallas.

By the time Sandy arrived to help her dress, Erin had a mask of calm, cool assurance firmly in place. It was only inside that she was shaking, praying silently that she was doing the right thing for Timmy, this new baby, Blake, and herself.

* * * * *

Blake was having similar feelings after he left Timmy with Mary and made a final inspection of the room where Erin would be sleeping from now on. In another two hours, she'd be his wife, and that thought brought on sharp, agonizing pain. He saw the room not as it was today, but the way it used to be, reflecting Glenna's presence in every whimsical detail she'd added through their years together.

Every item had commemorated a special time. The woven Navajo rug Glenna had bought while they camped in Arizona because its colors reminded her of the desert sunrise…that glistening rough-cut blue topaz they'd found in the wilds of Panama… Even the massive four-poster bed he'd commissioned from a famous Appalachian craftsman while they vacationed in Gatlinburg had brought back memories…

He'd ordered Mary to get rid of all the tangible evidence of those memories, but they were as vivid in his mind as if they were still here, waiting for Glenna to come back and restore them in fact as well as in his heart.

How she'd teased him about that bed! Once she decked it out like a harem couch, in crimson silk instead of the crocheted lace that usually cascaded from heavy square posts that nearly reached the twelve-foot ceilings. She'd seduced him handily, he recalled with more agony than the ecstasy the moment had brought.

Reality, within the same walls of the same house he had lived in all his life, was this bland, correctly furnished suite of rooms he could just as easily have found in any of a hundred luxury hotels.

And reality was the woman downstairs who soon would be the mother of his child—his wife even sooner. Banishing the bittersweet memories as best he could, Blake went into the odd-shaped office he had outfitted as his own sleeping room. After laying out his clothes, he set about methodically to shower, shave, and dress.

* * * * *

Adjusting the tie he'd randomly selected, Blake made his way across the courtyard. He felt strangely detached, as if it were someone else's wedding he would be hosting within the hour.

"Blake."

He strode into the morning room and joined Greg. "Where's Sandy?"

"She's helping Erin dress—or so she said. Want a drink?"

About a dozen. "Sure. Whatever you're having will be fine."

Blake watched Greg pour two fingers of Jack Daniel's into a highball glass over a few cubes of ice. "Here's to liquid courage," Greg said as he handed over the glass.

"To courage."

"Want to talk about it?" Greg sat back down and sipped his drink.

"What is there to discuss?"

"Whatever's on your mind that you'd like to share. I've had more experience at this than you. I'll be happy to offer advice, if the price is right, of course." Greg grinned.

Blake couldn't help smiling. "Advice? Remember, I'm the guy who's trying to dig you out of the alimony poorhouse with two ex-wives. By the way, Si Abrams called me yesterday. Kay apparently is amenable now to giving up her monthly checks in return for a lump sum settlement. I told Si to forget it."

"For God's sake, Blake! Why?"

"For one thing, you can't afford the amount she and Si have in mind. For another, you say she's about to marry again. If she does, the monthly payments will stop without you shelling out any more than you already have. Trust me. Negotiating settlements is what I do for a living, even if most of the disputes are between oil companies and the agencies that regulate them."

Greg shook his head, but he still was smiling. "I know. Damn it, though, I wish something would happen fast. I feel like hell, not being able to offer Sandy anything except a mountain of debt along with the dubious honor of marrying a two-time reject fifteen years older than she."

"You've asked her to marry you?"

"Not yet. But I want to."

Blake didn't know Sandy all that well, but he had enjoyed the questionable pleasure of close acquaintance with both of Greg's former wives. Though he wished Greg the best, he wasn't at all certain his friend had finally found a woman who could and would share a harried lifestyle that revolved around his work. "You're sure?"

"I'm sure. For Sandy I'd fight the devils in hell. I'll even fight my exes, and talk my mother into moving in with her sister out in Phoenix, if that's what it will take to make Sandy happy."

"Sandy doesn't meet with Mom's approval?" Blake imagined Sadie Halpern's dislike would be a formidable obstacle. Not that he didn't get along fine with Greg's mother. He'd even called her "Mom" at her insistence since Greg started taking him home for holidays when they were in school.

"Too young, too *shiksa*, but she's a sweet, sweet girl, for a nice boy her own age," Greg said with a grin, mimicking his mother's distinctive speech pattern. "I don't care. Mom will come around. Anyhow, she liked both Kay and Rhea, and look how things turned out with them."

The doorbell rang, and Blake got up to answer it. It was Judge Adkins, who joined them for a drink while they waited for the other members of the bridal party.

"Are you having one ring or two?" the judge asked, apparently planning the ceremony mentally while they talked.

"One." Blake reached into his pocket and withdrew a small, flat box.

Maybe he should take a look since he hadn't done so when his secretary had set it on his desk. Blake opened the box and glanced at the wide, plain gold band. "Not bad," he commented.

"I'll hold it," Greg offered.

"Blake!" Timmy rolled into the room, Mary scurrying along behind him. "Look at me. It's fun dressing up. Doctor Halpern, how do you like my new suit?"

Greg smiled. "Looks just like one of Blake's. You sure you didn't borrow it from him?"

"Blake took me to the store and got it just for me. A bunch of other clothes, too. Who are you?" he asked the judge.

"Judge Adkins. You must be Blake's new stepson, young man."

"How'd you know? My name's Timmy. I'm supposed to tell you Mommy and Aunt Sandy will be ready in just a few minutes. Mommy looks real pretty."

Greg wandered over to the stereo and picked up a stack of compact discs. "Background music, anyone?"

"Pick out something appropriate and turn it on," Blake suggested.

"Certainly not *this*?" Greg barely restrained his laughter as he held up a disc.

"Why not?" To Blake, one classical piece was pretty much the same as the next.

"I think we'd all find a soprano screeching in Italian a little distracting, don't you? This is an opera, some heartrending tragedy if I recall correctly," Greg explained, holding up the cover that featured a geisha girl and identified the disc as a sound track of *Madame Butterfly*.

"Cut out the comments and just find some music that will do. That's all the classical music I've got."

Greg set the offending selection down and dug through the discs, finally settling on one that he inserted in the CD player. A moment later the room filled with soft, unobtrusive harmonies.

"Where's the wedding going to be?" Timmy maneuvered his wheelchair closer to Blake.

Blake smiled. "Over there by the windows, in the little alcove Miguel made with the plants and flowers."

"Are you going to give Mommy a ring?"

"Yes."

"And flowers?"

Flowers? Blake had forgotten that among other things, he was supposed to have sent Erin some kind of bouquet or corsage. Oh, well, it was too late now. "No, sport, just the ones we've got in here."

Timmy looked around. "But Blake, these are the same flowers that are always in here. They're just all scrunched up in that whatever you called it over there."

"Alcove."

"Yeah. Oh, boy, here come Mommy and Aunt Sandy."

Blake's gaze went to the doorway, where Erin's tightly controlled smile hinted this was going to be as hard for her as for him. She'd done well with her shopping. He couldn't help liking what he saw, from dark, simply arranged hair that curled around her shoulders to slender feet shod in low-heeled sandals. Her pretty, light blue dress veiled but didn't conceal his unborn child. He made himself smile.

"Here, Mommy, you need a flower," Timmy said, plucking a fat yellow rosebud out of an arrangement on a low table beside a chair and handing it up to Erin.

Embarrassed that he had overlooked the necessary detail of flowers for his bride, Blake picked another rose from the vase. "For the maid of honor," he said lightly as he handed Sandy the flower.

He glanced at his Rolex and stifled the sense of longing that seeing Glenna's gift always evoked. "It's time," he said, taking Erin's hand and walking slowly across the room to the alcove where they would formalize their new arrangement.

* * * * *

For the second time, Sandy watched Erin repeat marriage vows. This time, she knew what it should mean to make those hopeful, solemn promises. She was twenty-three, not twelve, and the man she loved was standing across from her, looking handsome and relaxed as he, too, paid close attention to Erin and Blake's mutual pledge.

"Do you, Blake, take this woman to be your lawfully wedded wife? Do you promise to love her, honor her and cherish her as long as you both shall live?"

Blake answered, but it was Greg that Sandy imagined making those solemn promises to her. Then, when it was Erin's turn to make the same vows, Sandy was repeating the pledge of lasting fidelity to Greg. Her gaze settled on his solemn face, and her heartbeat accelerated.

"Do you have the ring?" Judge Adkins asked, and Greg dug into his pants pocket and pulled out the band Blake would be putting on her sister's finger. Smiling, he handed it to Blake, then looked back at Sandy.

"Repeat after me, 'With this ring, I thee wed.'"

Sandy watched Greg, and Greg watched Sandy as Blake repeated the judge's words in a hushed, halting voice and slipped a wide gold band onto the ring finger of Erin's left hand.

"With the power vested in me by the State of Texas, I pronounce you man and wife."

Blake hesitated, just for a second, but Sandy caught the pause. Then, he lifted a hand to cup Erin's chin and brushed his lips briefly over hers. It wasn't a kiss of passion. It wasn't even one that indicated warmth and caring. Sandy's heart went out to Erin, because she was certain now her sister had entered into this marriage for reasons having little to do with emotion, less to do with love.

The mood was somber as the bride and groom accepted hugs and good wishes, casting a pall on the beautifully served, sumptuous meal that followed the short cocktail hour. The table was immaculate, covered with snowy linen edged in hand-crocheted lace. Dark blue candles flickered in silver candlesticks, casting soft light on an arrangement of multicolored roses and some lacy white flowers Sandy couldn't name. The food tasted great, too, from a tangy fruit soup appetizer to the perfectly prepared Chateaubriand and crisp, buttered vegetables.

She couldn't fault a thing, not really, but it bothered Sandy that, except for crystal flutes to hold the imported champagne and a small white-iced cake trimmed with fresh flowers, this could have been any company dinner at Blake Tanner's big, fancy house. Blake was hospitable but subdued, Erin obviously was faking the gaiety that made her laugh nervously at everything anyone said. Even Greg seemed on edge. Only Timmy and the judge seemed to be enjoying themselves on what should have been a festive day.

"I'd like to propose a toast," Greg said after Mrs. Malone and her helper had cleared the table, served the cake, and poured champagne. He stood and smiled, first at her and then at Erin.

"To Erin. May your future be as beautiful as you are today." The conventional toast held none of Greg's usual exuberance.

Blake got up next. "To our happiness," he said simply, lifting his glass in Erin's direction before taking a sip.

"May I?"

Blake's expression warmed when he turned to Timmy. "Sure," he said, smiling.

"Can I make a wish for all of us?"

"Go ahead, sport."

Timmy looked first at Erin and then at Blake, who sat at opposite ends of the big dining table. "To our whole family," he said gravely, lifting his glass of sparkling grape juice and taking a sip.

Judge Adkins cleared his throat and gave his own good wishes. "To a bright future for this wonderful family. Blake, your grandpa Jimmy would have been proud of all of you today," he added before excusing himself.

Sandy felt Greg's gaze before she realized that she, too, was expected to propose a toast to the newlyweds. "Be happy, you two," she said, wondering as she did whether that wish would ever come true. For Erin, or for herself.

Why couldn't relationships be simple? Baby or no baby, why had Erin just married a man who'd just lost his much-loved wife?

Sandy didn't know, any more than she knew why she'd fallen in love with Greg. No woman in her right mind would have picked a guy with two greedy ex-wives, a spoiled-rotten daughter who'd wrapped Daddy around her twelve-year-old finger, and a mom who determinedly tried to run his life. But she loved Greg. She couldn't help loving him.

"Sandy?"

She and Greg were the only ones left at the table. Timmy had gone with Mary to get ready for bed, and Erin and Blake were saying good night to Judge Adkins. Sandy stood and followed with Greg to the door.

"I think we'll call it a night, too. Thanks for letting us be a part of your wedding. Best wishes to you both," Greg told the newlyweds.

* * * * *

On the way home, Greg stopped the car at a small park and turned to Sandy. "They'll be all right. Let's get out and take a walk."

He held her hand, and they strolled down a well-lit path. The air smelled sweet from the honeysuckle vines that snaked around the trees.

"What's wrong? You're awfully quiet tonight."

"It almost seemed like they were signing a contract instead of getting married," she said sadly.

"Marriage is a contract, sweetheart."

"It is? I thought people got married because they love each other."

"That, too. But think about it. In the old days, *yentas* used to match up couples who'd never met. They'd negotiate detailed marriage agreements, usually with the bride's and groom's parents. First time the couple laid eyes on each other was at the wedding. Most of those marriages must have worked out fine, because as Mom points out every chance she gets, hardly anybody used to get divorced."

"You didn't—"

"No, I made my own mistakes. 'Fraid I can't blame a *yenta*. Greg stopped and pulled Sandy into his arms. "Honey, don't worry. Erin and Blake will do okay."

She stroked his lean, muscular cheek. "What made you fall out of love, then?"

"I'm not sure I ever loved Kay or Rhea. I know I didn't love them the way I love you. They both required a lot of maintenance I didn't have time to provide. Bottom line was, I guess, they didn't like coming second to my patients and I didn't care enough to give either of them the kid-glove sort of care they expected."

Greg just said he loved her. Her worries about her sister forgotten, Sandy suddenly felt like dancing with happiness. "You know I love you, too," she said, and then she threw her arms around his neck and dropped kisses all over his face and neck.

"Easy, sweetheart. All I could think about tonight when Blake and Erin were saying their vows was that I wished we were the ones getting married. I want to marry you, wake up with you every morning and go to sleep with you in my arms. I want us to have a couple of kids while I'm still in good enough shape to teach them to swim and play tennis and so on. Most of all, sweetheart, I want to know you're going to keep loving me like I'll be loving you, as long as we live."

"I'd marry you tomorrow."

Greg put an arm around her, and they walked back toward his car. "Not tomorrow, love. But soon, I hope. I won't even ask you until I've worked out something so that I can support you. "

He seemed unusually quiet when they drove on to his apartment. She didn't mind. The lack of conversation gave her time to savor knowing he loved her and wanted her to be his wife.

"We could start planning our wedding now," she said suddenly, visions of white lace and silk illusion drifting through her head. "I'd like something more traditional than Erin and Blake had."

"As long as it's legal, whatever you want will suit me just fine." He paused for a minute. "We can't have a religious ceremony, but we can do as big and fancy a civil wedding as you want."

"Oh." Sandy hadn't thought of that. "Won't your mother and sisters be upset?"

Greg shrugged. "Probably. But I wouldn't ask you to marry outside your faith, any more than I'd expect you to want me to say the most important vows of my life outside of mine."

"Greg, do you really believe circumstances are going to change with…with your alimony situation? I don't want to wait forever."

He nodded, but didn't say anything as they walked up to his apartment.

"I wouldn't mind living here and keeping on working like I do now. You wouldn't have to pay me if we were married," Sandy said when she'd kicked off her high heels and padded to the kitchen for a glass of water.

"Sweetheart, I couldn't support you on what I pay you for managing my office." Then he laughed, as if he suddenly realized the absurdity of what he'd just said. "That is, I couldn't afford to support you the way I want to. Come here and let me love you."

"Here?"

"Why not? You want to check out my examining rooms. Why shouldn't I get to check you out on my kitchen counter? I've been planning this all week long." Lifting her easily, he set her on the edge of the counter between the stove and sink and fished out a condom and the brand-new Pyrex butt plug he'd stashed in a drawer after sterilizing it the other day. "Look what I found."

Sandy saw the toys and grinned. "More play toys?"

"Uh-huh. You have no idea how hot I got, imagining what I'm gonna do with them. With you."

He bent and gave her a quick, hard kiss. "Come on, spread 'em for me. That's my girl. What do we have here? Stockings and a garter belt? And could it be a bare pussy under that thong bikini? A bare, wet, hungry little pussy wanting my cock?"

Giggling, Sandy slid to the edge of the counter, spread her legs, and propped her feet against Greg's narrow waist. "Better get your instruments out if you're gonna do an exam, Doc. Want some help?" Teasing him, she reached for the nearest drawer and started to open it.

"Only other instrument I need is in my pants. Go on, unzip me."

She gave his cock a playful squeeze before loosening his belt and tackling the snap and zipper. "Better than one of your cold, hard speculums any day," she purred, loving the warm, pulsing flesh she drew from his pants and rubbed against her clit. "Want to put it in me, Doc?"

"Oh, yeah. But first I want you to relax. You're gonna like this. Oh, baby, I love you. Love how wet you get for me." He tickled her clit with the cold, hard toy before sliding it in her dripping pussy and along her slit until she felt him press it gently at the entrance to her rear passage. "Breathe deep. And think how full you'll feel.

"This is as close as you're ever coming to a threesome, 'cuz I'm greedy and I don't share what's mine. Feel good?" Slowly, while working her clit, he worked the plug past her anal sphincter, past the pain that made her gasp. Deeper, until its base rested flush against her body.

"Feels...full." She wiggled, brushing his swollen cock head over her clit. "I want this in my pussy. Now."

He paused, rolling the condom over his straining erection. "My pleasure, sweetheart. Here, take it all."

When his hot, throbbing cock rammed into her pussy, a thousand stars burst in her head. She'd never felt so full. All her feelings centered between her legs. God! When he moved in her, his cock head got her G-spot every time. Her ass vibrated around the plug every time he moved in her pussy. Even the nerve endings in her labia prickled at the delicious contact with his satin-skinned ball sac.

"Oh yesss. Greg, I love you. Love how your big, hard cock feels in my pussy. I love how you love me. Damn, I love everything about you."

"Feels good, doesn't it?" He lifted her legs over his shoulders, changing the angle of his thrusts. Brushed her swollen tingling clit with gentle fingers.

"God, yes. Fuck me harder, now. I'm on fire. Burning. Oh, yesss."

Her pussy convulsed around his cock. Sensation spread through her body, all the way to her fingers and toes. She'd never come so hard, so long. His shuddering climax fed hers, as though they were a single quivering mass of mind-blowing sensations.

As Sandy snuggled closer to Greg's warm, hard body later that night, her mind wandered back to Erin. Was she sleeping peacefully beside her gorgeous new husband, or lying alone in her room, married in name only?

Sandy couldn't imagine them in bed together. They'd acted like everything but loving newlyweds. Sandy imagined Greg's first impression of Blake's and Erin's reasons for marrying had been correct. They married for the baby's sake. Any emotional attachment, any other motive they might have had for marrying, hadn't been evident this evening.

* * * * *

Standing, shoulders slumped, under a bright moon that reflected off the pool, Blake felt anything but detached. Tremors that had threatened all during the wedding and simple reception were coming with a vengeance now. Unable to stand any longer, he sank onto a patio chair, not caring that the night dew was soaking through his pants. Elbows braced on his thighs, he supported his head between shaking hands.

There'd been part of him that had wanted to embrace the quiet, pretty woman who carried his child beneath her heart, to thank her for the gift she was giving him and offer her far more than the sterile vows he'd made. But no. He hadn't been able to offer more than cold material security to Erin and Timmy, and he hated himself for shortchanging them.

He felt guilty as shit.

Having wished he could have meant those promises made him feel even guiltier, because he owed his loyalty to Glenna.

By getting married, had he and Erin set Timmy up for more hurt? Blake hoped not. The little boy had seen such loss and pain in his short lifetime; he deserved joy, not more distress and loss. Erin had done nothing, either, to deserve the loveless life she'd just committed herself to.

She was a good woman, worthy of emotional support Blake could no longer give. He'd touched her, kissed her, because it had been expected. He imagined he would have to make public displays of affection from time to time, to reinforce the I that the marriage they had entered into was real. Hell, he felt guilty about that, too.

God. He'd had to touch her, look at her. Damn it, Judge Adkins would have thought it was mighty fishy if he'd treated his bride like a leper. He had to marry her, had to provide a mother for his unborn child. Why, then, did he feel guilty?

He knew why. Glenna was everywhere, in every nook and cranny of this house where they'd lived together for fourteen years. It was as if she'd taken a trip and would soon be home. But she'd gone and left him here with a life as sterile and empty as the walls of that master bedroom he'd stripped of every sign of her.

"Damn you, Glenna. You wanted this baby, I didn't. But now it's almost here and very much alive, and I've found that I do want it after all. You're gone, I have to carry on, and who could be better to mother my child than the woman who is giving it life?

"Do you remember the night we sat in the garden room, watching the snow come down last winter and listening to those old pop songs you liked so well? How you laughed and teased me about how I was loving you while another lover like the one in that song was carrying my child? Do you remember the way I teased you back, singing along with the line that said the other lover could never have the part of me I gave to you or something like that?

"Well, my darling, now I've got a hell of a problem. I gave all of me to you. There's nothing left for me to give the woman I just promised to love, honor and cherish. I stood there and perjured myself in front of our closest friend and a judge who's known and respected my family since long before I was born. And it's all your fault!"

He stopped, thinking he'd heard someone come out of the house; then, he continued his tirade, cursing Glenna for her obsession to have a baby, the idiocy of getting in front of a bullet meant for someone else, and the tyranny of leaving him alone, without his heart.

Deep, wracking sobs came from deep in his chest, making it impossible for him to go on railing against the woman he loved. She was gone and beyond his fury, but her presence was with him in every breath he took.

He heard a door close, but placed no importance on it as he let loose the tears that had refused to come when Glenna died, or even on the rainy February day when the workers had lowered her casket into the icy ground.

* * * * *

In the silence of the newly furnished master bedroom Blake had insisted she occupy to make the world believe their marriage was real, Erin curled up on an overstuffed lounge chair covered in navy-blue silk damask and stared at the lonely looking king-size bed. She wrapped her arms around the massive bulk of her abdomen. And she cried.

Chapter Nine

Glenna's Ghost

ဆာ

"You hurt her, Blake, not me," Glenna whispered, feeling more inclined to admonish him for causing Erin's tears than to refute the angry accusations he'd hurled at her.

She wanted so much to go to him, ease his anguish and tell him she had never meant to hurt him so. But she couldn't. She'd let him go. He had to fight his own demons to tell her goodbye, and if he came to hate her in the process, maybe that would make his personal war less painful.

Might Blake be right? Glenna counted back, realized it had been more than four months since she'd died. So far he'd shown no signs that he was beginning to recover from the shock of losing her. Would he ever?

He had to. She couldn't bear the thought of floating in limbo forever, watching Blake suffer endlessly because she'd gone before him. She needed peace, the eternal peace of angels that could not come until she knew she had righted the pain she'd unwittingly caused Blake — and Erin.

Their wedding had been so small, so sad, with Erin's little Timmy looking hopefully on while Erin held the rose the child had given her when Blake had forgotten that small but telling detail. Greg had looked as if he'd like to have been saying those vows to Erin's young sister instead of witnessing Blake's antiseptic recitation. And Sandy had seemed to make her own silent pledge to Greg. Blake had said and done all the right things at the right time, with all the emotional involvement of a robot programmed to act the happy bridegroom.

It was Erin's sometimes hopeful, sometimes desolate expressions that had affected Glenna most. She'd pushed Erin so hard to take Blake's wounded soul and try to heal it with her baby's love. Had she doomed them all to a life of living hell, and herself to eternal death without peace?

In Glenna's troubled mind, Erin's tears mingled with Blake's anguished cries in a cacophony of sounds. She hoped his tears were cathartic, and that his healing had begun. Erin's quiet, solitary sobs were worse. Hearing them continue for what seemed like hours in the darkness of the night moved Glenna to gather the last of her strength.

She had to go to Erin, try to ease the hurt Blake's anguished words had caused.

Chapter Ten

ဆ

Erin tried to think logically, calm herself. What had she done tonight? What had she been thinking when she married a man whose grief was so intense that it filled his life so nothing and no one else could find a place there?

She shifted in the chair, not willing to lie down and let the whole night pass while she shed bitter, silent tears. Then, at the patio door, she saw a brilliant golden haze—and Glenna suddenly appeared.

"How could you?" Erin tasted the salt of her own tears, the bitterness she felt toward the woman who'd caused her new husband such anguish. "Why couldn't you just conjure yourself up to him and do your own comforting, instead of selling me on stepping in and trying to be the wife he doesn't want?"

Glenna's image wasn't as clear as it had been when she'd appeared before. She seemed nearly transparent. Her features were recognizable but through them, Erin saw the flickering golden aura that before had only surrounded her.

"Don't you have an answer?" she asked harshly.

Glenna's image flickered, then strengthened. *"Do you think I wanted to die?"* she asked, her expression tortured as Erin had never seen it before. *"Or that I want to wander formless on this earth now, seeing the trouble I've caused but not being able to make things right?"*

"Then why not go to Blake? He's out there, suffering like no one should ever have to suffer. Only you can ease him. You know that, don't you?"

Erin thought she saw sparkling golden tears falling down Glenna's pale, translucent cheeks, but she tried to squelch pangs of sympathy for the ghost. She recalled how, earlier today, she'd wished Glenna would have come to ease her own well-placed misgivings about the marriage she now was positive had been conceived in hell.

"I can't. Don't you think that if I could, I'd have Blake with me now, in whatever plane of existence we might have to live? Yes, I could go and try to comfort him. But that's your place now."

"He loves you. He has nothing to give me or anyone else. I'm sure you heard him say he had given all of himself to you if you were hovering, watching the misery you've brought on us all."

When Erin saw Glenna trembling, noticed her image fading then brightening as if by some supernatural act of will, she wished she could take back some of her accusations. The ghost's voice wavered, but she managed to whisper clearly enough for Erin to hear.

"Blake is going to heal. And he will love again. What he's going through tonight is a good sign. Do you realize this is the first time he's cried? The first time he's truly opened himself up enough to suffer? For months, he's been blocking the truth from his heart, trying to tell himself our love had never been and therefore could not be lost to him."

"How do you figure that?" Erin shifted in the chair to ease the strain on her back and twisting the engraved gold band Blake had managed to get onto her swollen finger earlier.

"Look around this room. What do you see?"

What was she getting at? "Just a room. A huge, luxurious room with lots of angles and glass, and a curved wall behind the bed. Nice, comfortable furniture that looks brand-new. Nothing personal. It's as though no one ever lived here."

"Precisely. Would you believe it if I told you that four months ago this suite looked completely different? That every piece of furniture, every accessory held special, loving memories for Blake — and me? Would you believe Blake emptied it out of everything, and that he ordered new furniture, carpeting and drapes without even going in person to pick them out?"

Erin looked again around the luxurious but sterile-looking room. "Yes, I guess I would. I wondered why the rooms in this wing seem so cold and impersonal, when the rest of the house has all the caring touches that make it seem like a home."

Glenna's image faded, then brightened. *"Think,"* she said, her voice faint but clearly audible. *"For four months now, Blake has done nothing except deny his sense of loss, try with every trick he could think of to put my dying out of his mind. Tonight he faced it for the first time. What you heard was the guilt and anger finally coming to the surface of his mind. I've got to go now, Erin, but believe me, Blake will heal."*

"Will you be back?"

"Yes..."

With that last, faint promise Glenna's image disappeared, leaving Erin looking at rapidly disseminating golden dust and thinking about what the ghost had revealed.

* * * * *

For the first two weeks after their wedding, their lives went along pretty much as they had before. Blake got up and went to his office, apparently unaffected by his tortured self-revelations on their wedding night. Timmy had his daily therapy, Mary ran the household, and Erin divided her time between playing with her son and resting while she waited for the baby to be born.

Glenna's ghost was silent, but Erin sensed she was around, observing and replenishing her strength. Sometimes Erin even found herself searching through the house for a glimmer of Glenna's golden aura, and she rarely managed to put the ghost and her futile hope of matchmaking out of her mind.

While Blake said she could make whatever changes she wished to the master suite, Erin hadn't found the energy or the self-confidence to add accessories that would have made the sterile rooms seem more like home. She had, however, begun to furnish the empty, oddly angled room next to her bedroom as a nursery.

She ignored the small voice inside her that said she should fix the baby's room the way Glenna described it that day when they'd met and talked over lunch. Instead, she deliberately set about making the nursery a small statement of her own taste.

A trip with Mary to an attic storeroom yielded an old oak crib and changing table that Miguel cleaned and polished, and calls to the infant department at Saks resulted in the delivery of linens and baby clothes. Erin set the antique cradle Greg and Sandy brought her in the alcove by a padded window seat.

The following morning, Erin was looking around the nursery, checking for necessities she might have missed, when Blake stuck his head inside the door. He'd come from the pool, she guessed, because he was wearing brief navy racing trunks and had a big striped towel draped around his broad, muscular shoulders.

"Don't you need some toys or something in here to brighten the place up?" he asked. "I heard somewhere that babies respond to primary colors almost as soon as they're born."

"I've read that, too. I guess I could call and order some pictures and toys. I'd thought I would wait until I could go pick them out myself." Blake had been adamant that she was not to endanger herself by going shopping so late in her pregnancy. Understanding his fear that would have seemed unreasonable if she hadn't known its cause, she'd accepted the constraint.

"Would you mind if I picked up a few things?"

His hesitant manner surprised her. "Not at all. But do you have time?"

"I've arranged my case load so I won't have to go to the office for a few weeks," he said, eyeing her at what used to be waist level as if trying to guess how much longer it would be until she exploded.

"You mean you'll be here most of the time?"

Blake smiled. "Yes. I'll be working on some legal matters I've taken on for Greg. Will my being underfoot disturb you?"

Erin didn't know. It certainly bothered her to see him there, looking like he could model for a Chippendale calendar and making her wish he cared half as much for her as he did for their unborn child. "No," she said, realizing she'd been standing there staring at him like a half-wit.

"I thought I'd keep Timmy occupied so you can rest. Maybe he'd like to go with me to find some baby toys."

"Yes, I'm sure he'd like that. He's still talking about how much fun he had when you took him out to get his suit. Thank you, Blake." She felt remiss for not having thanked him adequately for all the attention he was lavishing on Timmy.

"I enjoyed it as much as he did." He glanced down at himself, as if he just now realized how nearly naked he was. "I'd better go change, before I drip all over the carpet." He turned and disappeared into what she guessed had been his office/hobby room in the master suite until he turned it into a combination bedroom and study.

Later Erin rubbed at the aching spot at the small of her back, then wandered out by the pool. She longed to jump in and cool herself in the crystal-clear water, but contented herself with watching Michelle put Timmy through his exercises. Her recent conversation with Blake ran through her mind, and she wondered what kind of work Blake was doing for Greg—and why Sandy hadn't mentioned it.

* * * * *

"Doesn't Sandy know?" Blake asked Greg when he confirmed an appointment for them to meet with Kay's attorney late that afternoon.

"No. Why?"

"Because Erin seemed surprised when I told her I was taking care of some legal matters for you. I assumed she'd know, from Sandy, what we're trying to accomplish."

"I haven't said anything to Sandy because I don't want to raise her hopes in case your efforts don't bring results. I guess

I'll tell her now, though, before Erin does." Greg sounded stressed, but part of the reason could have been the difficult delivery he said he'd just finished before returning Blake's call.

"I didn't mention what kind of work I was doing," Blake assured Greg. "Anyhow, I doubt Erin will say anything. Since I've been home, she's spent most of her time resting. How long is it going to be, anyhow?"

"Before you're a father? Any day. Do you want to see your baby being born?"

Blake hesitated. "I'd like to. But it's going to feel damn strange, considering the circumstances. I doubt Erin will want me there."

"She said she didn't mind if you wanted to be in the delivery room. Before you ask, that's a standard question I ask all my expectant moms."

Her reaction surprised Blake. As uncomfortable as she seemed when they ran into each other in varying states of undress around the suite they shared, he'd assumed she'd hate the idea of him seeing her as intimately as he assumed he would when she gave birth.

"Then I want to be there."

"Okay. Since you haven't done the prenatal classes, I'll bring a couple of tapes for you to watch so you'll know what to expect. You said Si and Kay would meet us at your house at five?"

"That's right. You're welcome to stay and have dinner after we're done with the meeting."

Greg chuckled. "Will I feel like eating after the meeting?"

"I have no idea. But I'll see you in another couple of hours." Blake hoped that Greg would come alone. He wanted nothing to upset what he hoped would be a reasonable discussion about reducing Greg's alimony burden.

When Greg arrived, still wearing wrinkled scrubs with an equally disheveled lab coat, Blake noted Sandy's conspicuous absence.

"How's my favorite patient?" Greg asked as he pulled up a patio chair and joined them.

"Getting anxious. Where's Sandy?"

"At the office, working. It's only four-thirty, and I'm an evil taskmaster."

Blake stood abruptly. "Since this isn't a social call, we'd better go inside. The other parties will be here shortly."

He hardly had time to brief Greg before Mary came into the study and announced that Mr. Abrams and his client had arrived. "Send them in," Blake said, and then he reminded Greg to keep his sometimes acerbic tongue in check.

"Si. Kay. Thank you for coming here instead of downtown." Blake knew he hadn't inconvenienced them at all, since Si's office was less than two miles away.

Kay laughed, a brittle, tinkling sound that matched the brilliant red of her linen suit and pale, bright tone of her short curly hair. "I wouldn't think of having you leave your brand-new bride so close to her delivery date."

"You always were considerate, Kay," Greg said silkily from his seat on the sofa in the corner, while Blake bit his tongue to keep from replying to Kay's pointed dig.

Kay turned on Greg. "I see you're dressed for work, as usual. Are you planning to deliver Blake's baby here and now?"

The tension was building. Somebody needed to diffuse it, and it seemed that his colleague was content to sit back and watch the show. "Greg came straight here from the hospital when I told him you were willing to negotiate the alimony. He wants Si and me to help settle the matter, not referee a verbal war between you two. Let's cut out the childish sniping and get down to business."

"Right." Si opened his briefcase and drew out a sheaf of papers. "Kay realizes you're paying more than you can afford in alimony, Doctor Halpern. Are you aware that three weeks ago, I conveyed her offer to give up future payments in return for a lump sum settlement?"

"He's aware, Si. Your offer was unacceptable. Kay, is it true that you plan to remarry shortly?" Blake asked.

Kay nodded, letting her bright blue gaze drop noticeably to the headlight of a diamond on her left ring finger. "That's why I wanted us to get together. I won't be getting alimony after this month, anyhow, but I thought I'd offer you a small present in celebration of my remarriage."

"Let me," Si said as Blake sat back, wondering what would be coming next and trying to plan his line of attack. "Kay is marrying a wealthy man. He dislikes the idea of his wife's receiving what he considers an excessive amount in child support. We've all talked this over, and we feel a thousand dollars a month should be adequate to take care of Shana's needs until she's of age."

Blake mentally reviewed the numbers Greg's accountant had provided. Without the alimony he was paying Kay, Greg could easily afford the court-ordered monthly child support. "Greg hasn't contested the child support, Si. Just the alimony. He wants to support his daughter."

"Of course he does. But if he isn't having to pay so much in support, he will have more to give her the little extras every girl wants." Kay sounded so sweet, Blake knew there had to be a catch to her offer.

Greg spoke up. "Who do I have to kill to make this happen?"

Kay faced him, her features serene. "Why, no one, darling. All you have to do is take temporary custody of our daughter for six months or so while Abe and I take an extended honeymoon. That's a trip, like the ones we never took while you buried yourself in the hospital caring for every woman in the world except me, and I got stuck vegetating in a tiny, cramped apartment I hated."

"That's all?" Greg sounded incredulous.

"That's all, and I'll even waive child support for the time Shana will be spending with you. Of course, you will have to buy a house and hire a housekeeper. I won't have my child living in that tenement you call an apartment building."

Blake studied the papers Si had handed him that spelled out Kay's proposed agreement. "It seems to say exactly what Kay has told you," he said as he worked his way through the last page.

"Then I'd be a fool to turn it down."

Then Blake came to a clause that gave him second thoughts. "Could I speak to my client alone before he makes a decision?"

"You think Greg won't like the clause that says he can't carry on with women while Shana's with him? Blake, my friend, you don't know my former husband at all. He'd rather deliver babies than make them." Kay shot him a dirty look. "Obviously unlike you."

"Kay, let's keep this businesslike." Si laid a hand on Kay's arm, as though to restrain her.

"Yeah, Kay, try to hold in those talons before you draw blood," Greg drawled. "Go ahead, Blake, explain my lovely ex-wife's terms right here. I'm sure she can withstand the embarrassment."

It was Blake's turn to be embarrassed. What, he wondered, had gone on between these people who'd seemed to be in love when they married fifteen years ago?

He reread the clause and handed the unsigned agreement to Greg. "What it says is, you're not to expose Shana to any of your relationships with women."

"What the hell? Kay has obviously exposed Shana to this guy she's about to marry. Shana told me about him months ago. I don't go having indiscriminate flings, and Kay damn well knows it. I am seeing one woman, and Shana already knows her." Greg had stood during his diatribe and now was pacing restlessly around the room.

"All I want is to be assured you won't be 'seeing' your little nymphet right under our daughter's impressionable nose, Greg.

Certainly you have adequate time to dally with her at your office."

Blake saw Greg getting ready to explode. "Sit down and calm down," he ordered quietly but firmly. "Si, we need to revise this clause. Like Kay, we want to ensure Shana's safety, both physical and emotional, but we feel that contractually prohibiting Greg from seeing a woman friend while in his daughter's company is absurd."

Si leaned over and studied the offending words. He checked with Kay and made a counteroffer. Blake studied the new wording and consulted with Greg. Blake thought they would never reach agreement, but finally they did. Greg was about to be freed from one albatross. Now all Greg had to worry about was Rhea.

Blake got up and walked Si to the door while Kay and Greg indulged in one last shouting match. He was damn glad he didn't deal in this kind of legal dispute every day.

When Kay stormed past him, Blake felt like throttling her for the snide comment she'd tossed his way. If he didn't have the feeling it would only make things worse, he'd have broadcasted the aborted surrogate arrangement. But it would. What the hell could he do to keep his baby and Erin from being hurt by mean-spirited shrews like Greg's former wife?

* * * * *

There wasn't to be a whole lot of time to form a line of defense against what friends and acquaintances were going to think. When Blake and Greg walked into the garden room, Timmy was rolling toward them in his wheelchair, wide-eyed and obviously scared.

"My mommy's sick," the little boy said. "Doctor Halpern, please help her."

Blake stayed and tried to calm his stepson while Greg went to examine Erin. It didn't help much that he was as frightened as Timmy, if not more so. Still he managed to keep his hands from shaking and to explain a little discomfort was normal when a mommy was getting ready to have a baby.

"Well, Timmy. Before long you're going to be a big brother," Greg said when he came back a few minutes later. Then he turned to Blake. "It's time, my friend."

"Should I call an ambulance?"

"Not necessary. We've got plenty of time. Mrs. Malone is helping Erin get dressed. When she's ready, you can drive her to the hospital. I'll meet you there."

Blake watched, dumbstruck, while Greg walked away. "Wait. Don't leave her."

"Calm down. Your baby's big, and Erin's barely started to dilate. We're going to have a long night. And I need to call Sandy." With that, Greg left, punching numbers on his cell phone as he walked out the door.

"I'm scared." Timmy clutched Blake's arm with his thin hand.

Blake ruffled his hair. "Your mom's going to be just fine, sport. I'm going to take her to the hospital so we can get our baby."

"But she was sick," the boy repeated stubbornly.

"Trust me, I won't let anything bad happen to your mom. Go on, get Mary to fix you a hot fudge sundae, and tell her I said it's okay for you to stay up and watch a movie on the big TV. Then you get a good night's sleep, so you can go to the hospital with me tomorrow to meet your new brother or sister."

Blake was petrified when he remembered Greg saying Erin wasn't dilated and the baby was big. He'd also assured Blake that Erin was healthy and able to have this child without complications, but Blake wasn't placing a lot of credence in that prediction at the moment.

He was trembling when he helped her into the car, and her soft moans did nothing to reassure him. "Go ahead, scream," he told her between clenched teeth as he gunned the Mercedes into the center lane of the interstate and sped toward the hospital where he hoped to hell Greg was waiting.

Erin let out, not a scream, but certainly at least a yelp, and clutched both hands to her heaving abdomen.

"Jesus, I'm sorry," Blake muttered, sweating now. How much farther was the damn exit?

Erin's voice sounded strained. "It's not your fault."

Yes, by God it was, and he hadn't even given her a lover's pleasure to make it happen. "Like hell."

"I'll be fine," Erin managed between groaning and writhing pitifully on the front seat.

Blake wished he believed that.

"Stay with me," she said, clutching his hand.

"I will." Blake swerved into the exit lane and moments later pulled into the hospital's emergency entrance. Tossing the keys to a security guard and ordering the man to take the car and park it, he scooped Erin into his arms and bolted through the double doors.

A nurse accosted them. "You'll have to go to Admitting," she told Blake as she tried to get him to set Erin into a wheelchair. All Blake could think of was that he had promised not to leave her. And that he suddenly was scared to death of losing her, too.

"Send a clerk upstairs. We're supposed to meet Doctor Halpern in the labor room."

"I'll take your wife to him. You have to stay down here and take care of admitting her. Then, you can go upstairs." The nurse assumed what she apparently thought was an uncompromising pose.

"I promised not to leave her. So you can damn well send an admitting clerk upstairs or do without the formalities. Where is the labor room?"

"Third floor," the nurse said sullenly as Blake headed with Erin for the elevators.

Blake did have to leave Erin, but only for as long as it took for him to take off his slacks and shirt and don a set of shapeless blue scrubs. Then he joined her in a labor room painted in cheerful tones of blue and yellow.

She was writhing on the narrow bed, turning from side to side as pains wracked her body. "Is there anything I can do?" Jesus, he'd never felt so helpless in his life. Or so damnably responsible for someone else.

"You can sit down over there and hold her hand while Jessica starts an epidural," Greg said as he came into the small room with a plain but pleasant-looking woman Blake assumed must be the anesthesiologist. "Here now, Erin, you'll be feeling better soon."

"You're going to put her to sleep?"

The anesthesiologist smiled. "No, this will keep your wife comfortable during labor. I will place this tiny catheter into the epidural space so that medication can be administered as needed. Is that all right?"

"Yes." The last thing Blake wanted was for Erin to suffer unnecessarily.

For what seemed like days even though he knew it was only a few tension-filled hours, Blake sat with Erin, rubbing her back and shoulders, wiping the sweat from her forehead with a cool, damp cloth, and simply being there in case she needed him. He felt he should be talking to her, but damned if he knew what to say. He wanted to tell her he cared for her...that he couldn't wait to see their baby. But guilt kept him silent. Guilt for feeling at all when he'd buried his emotions with Glenna.

"It's time for the big event," Greg said jovially as he straightened up and adjusted the sheet over Erin's lower body for at least the tenth time since they'd been here. "Come on, Blake. Erin, sweetheart, let these pretty ladies get you ready, and we'll meet you in the delivery room."

Like a zombie, Blake followed Greg out of the labor room as two nurses prepared to move Erin to this other room where their baby was to be born.

"Do you need the neonatologist to stand by?" the nurse asked.

Greg grinned. "Not tonight, unless Bernie's got nothing better to do. Do you have some caps, masks and shoe covers for us?"

"Delivery room three is ready for Mrs. Tanner," another nurse called out.

Another doctor came in and began to scrub up while Greg and Blake were soaping their hands and forearms. "Want a consult, Greg?" the older man asked jovially.

"Sure, after I finish here. Sam, this is Blake Tanner, who's about to become a daddy for the first time. Blake, Sam Reed."

Reed greeted Blake with a sympathetic smile. "If anyone can get a problem baby here safely, this young man can. Good luck, son."

Blake swallowed hard. Had Greg not told him something he should know? "Damn it, Greg—"

"Not to worry. Erin's fine." Greg turned to his colleague. "Blake and I were roommates in college. Tonight we're anticipating an uncomplicated delivery. What's the consult about?"

"A thirty-eight-year-old brittle diabetic. Her seven-month fetus died *in utero*. I'm going in now to take it."

Greg let out a low whistle. "Doesn't sound good. Any other kids?"

"A daughter, sixteen." Reed shook his head sadly. "She remarried a couple of years ago, and she's damn near obsessed to have his baby."

"You want me to see her today?"

"Not her. Her records. See if you can offer any hope for them. If you can't, maybe you can help me persuade her husband they mustn't try again."

A feminine voice broke Blake's morbid fascination. "Mrs. Tanner's ready," she said from the entry to the scrub room.

"I'm here." He stood beside Erin, grasping her cold hand and trying not to shiver in the room that was damn near freezing cold despite hot, blinding lights that focused on Erin from all directions.

He watched a nurse adjust a large, round mirror above Erin's head. "Here, now you can see," she said before moving to a small stainless steel table where she arranged some evil looking instruments on a towel-draped tray.

Greg sat on a stool at the foot of the table and murmured his approval. "You're doing great, sweetheart." Blake hoped to hell Greg's confidence wasn't misplaced. "Come on now, give this baby a little push. Look, can you see? He's got lots of dark hair."

Blake listened to his friend coax and cajole. "Hey, little one, you've got a mommy and daddy just waiting to spoil you rotten. I bet you've already got more toys than lots of kids see in a lifetime. Again now, Erin, push!"

Blake was listening to Greg when he heard an indignant howl. His baby was born! He took two long steps to stand beside Greg and watch firsthand while the wet, wriggling mass of humanity emerged from its mother's body.

"What is it?" Erin asked excitedly.

"A baby. A furious, squalling little baby," Blake exclaimed, enthralled as he watched Greg gently turn the baby's shoulder so he could work its body free.

"It's a boy. Congratulations, Blake, Erin." Greg held the red-faced, squalling baby, gently suctioning mucus from his nose and mouth. Then he turned to Blake. "Here, take him over and get him weighed, and show him to his mom while I finish up down here." He handed Blake his naked, screaming son and turned his attention back to Erin.

Blake had never felt such pure, heady adoration as came over him when he held his baby. He hated relinquishing the squalling little guy long enough for a nurse to weigh and measure him. When she handed the baby back, wrapped snugly in a blue receiving blanket, he examined the infant's features with wonder and love. Then he took Erin their son.

"Meet our little boy," he told her, tears running down his cheeks. "Thank you." Gently he brushed away tears that stained her flushed cheeks, wishing he could have shared her pain. Wanting to give her more than empty words. Acting before he could change his mind, Blake bent and kissed her gently on lips parched from her ordeal.

Blake was awestruck. Seeing this woman he had never lain with giving birth to his child was the most intimate yet innocent experience of his life. It was sweet, yet erotic beyond anything he could recall.

As if it were his perfect right to do so, he brushed aside the loose, worn cotton of her hospital gown to bare one full, firm breast. Carefully, he laid his newborn son down and guided her rose-tipped nipple to his avid little mouth. As he watched, his long-dormant sexuality emerged, and his cock began hardening beneath the baggy scrubs.

He could have been there for seconds, or it could have been hours when Greg stood and told the nurses they could take Erin into the recovery room. He watched as they rolled her and their baby separately away before following followed Greg out another door.

"Thanks, my friend," he said when they finally sat down in the lounge with cups of what had to be the strongest coffee he'd ever tasted.

"My pleasure. What's his name?"

Blake shrugged. "You mean you can't guess?"

Greg chuckled. "The Fifth? What I meant is, what are you and Erin going to call him?"

"Erin can decide if he's going to be James, Jimmy, JB, Blake, or some other nickname. After all, she went through hell, getting him here."

"Not really. She had a fairly easy labor and delivery." Greg refilled his cup from the urn on a small, crowded counter. "You didn't have the chance to look at those videos I brought by, did you?"

"Hardly. What happens next?"

"Erin will be in recovery until the epidural wears off. She's probably taking a well-deserved nap. Meanwhile, John Kaplan will be coming sometime within the next few hours to give The Fifth a thorough exam— that is, unless you have another doc you'd rather use. I called John because he's Timmy's pediatrician."

"He knows what he's doing, doesn't he?"

Greg shrugged. "Clinically, he's one of the best. I've always thought his bedside manner with parents and colleagues left a good deal to be desired, but from all I hear, his little patients love him."

"Then he's fine with me. The baby's all right, isn't he?"

"The little slugger looks healthy as a horse to me. He's damn near as big, too. Nine pounds, three ounces—biggest baby I've delivered for a long time."

Blake grinned. Then he thought of the ordeal Erin had just gone through to deliver his lusty, bouncing baby boy. "How is Erin?"

"Fine. She'll be tired and sore for a few days. I could probably send her home tomorrow, but I'd rather keep her here for two or three days. Hell, you can afford the extra assurance that she and The Fifth are okay."

Blake grinned, now fully reassured no problems lurked on the horizon. Suddenly he remembered the meeting he and Greg had earlier, before Erin had gone into labor.

"I seem to recall you're in the market for a house." He voiced a thought that had been lurking in the back of his mind. "There's a place down the road from me that's just gone on the market."

Greg laughed out loud. "Really? What bank do you suggest I rob to pay for an estate in the most expensive damn area of Dallas?"

"It's not an estate, just a small house and pool on less than an acre. From what I hear, the Campbell's heirs are anxious to unload it."

"How small?"

"Four or five thousand square feet, I guess. It used to be a guesthouse for the Trayne estate. During a recession back when I was a kid, they got in a bind and sold off this place and several other small parcels of land."

"Hmmm. Suitable for my little princess and cozy enough that I just might be able to swing buying it, you think?" Greg asked thoughtfully.

"It's a possibility."

"Maybe I'll make an appointment and take Sandy over to see it tomorrow. Oh, my God. Sandy. I promised I'd call her the minute we got out of the delivery room." As if he'd been shot from a cannon, Greg bolted up and grabbed the phone on the counter.

Blake got up and headed for the door. "I'm going to stop by the nursery and look at my son again. Then I've got to get home and let Timmy know he has a baby brother. Will I see you tomorrow?"

Greg nodded and waved as Blake hurried out of the lounge.

* * * * *

Blake seemed to have glued himself by her side while she and baby Jamie were at the hospital, and Erin had thought he was just trying to make the world think theirs was a normal marriage. Now that she was home, he showed no inclination to re-establish their relationship as polite strangers. In fact, Blake was even more attentive now that he wasn't hindered by nurses and doctors who dictated the amount of time he could spend with his baby.

He hadn't stinted on the time he spent with Timmy, either. Instead, he'd gone out of his way today to make her son feel he was just as important as the new baby in the house. Maybe Glenna had been right when she'd said that with time Blake would set aside his mourning and want to build a real family with the boys, and her.

Off and on, Erin found herself searching for signs of Glenna. She felt the ghost's presence, but wherever the ghost was, she apparently wasn't ready to show herself. As Erin was about to nod off to sleep, Blake strode into her bedroom, their squalling son cradled securely against his bare, muscular chest.

"He's hungry." A sappy smile lit his face while he watched her prop herself up with several pillows and adjust her nightgown.

"Here, I'll take him." When Blake brushed his callused fingers against her bare breast, Erin tingled clear down to her toes. How would those big, strong hands feel if he touched her with passion? Would he be gentle...forceful...suddenly she wanted to know. She'd most likely never know, but the way he'd looked at her a few times today, and in the delivery room, made her wonder. Chastising herself for fantasizing about how it would feel to have him make love to her, she forced her attention to her nursing baby. Her sudden burst of purely feminine fancy must have resulted from hormones that apparently had kicked into high gear after Jamie's birth.

She hoped Glenna's ghost hadn't picked this particular time to pop into this dimension and read her mind—almost as much as she hoped Blake didn't share his dead wife's penchant for discerning her thoughts.

"May I stay?"

Blake's question forced Erin to meet his intense, indigo gaze. "Of course." It surprised her that he asked, because while she was in the hospital, he'd shown no reticence at watching her nurse Jamie. Here in the home he'd shared with Glenna, she supposed he might feel more deeply the boundaries he'd defined for their marriage.

One thing Erin knew, Blake adored Jamie as much as she did. His love showed in awed expressions and in the endearing way he wanted to take part in every aspect of the baby's care. When he lifted the sleeping baby out of her arms and gently admonished her to get a good night's rest, she lay back, content to let him have time alone with the baby they had made together, yet separately.

Chapter Eleven

Glenna's Ghost

ဢ

I knew you'd love him.

For the longest time Glenna hovered out of sight, watching Blake stand by the crib, staring with adoration at his sleeping baby. It was all she could do to keep from joining him there, sharing the moment she'd waited so many years for.

Finally, he bent over and gave Jamie one last tender pat on his upthrust little backside before leaving. Instantly Glenna materialized in the spot where Blake had been standing, and she, too, stared down into the antique crib with wonder and awe.

My God, how long have I been standing here, staring at this child?

Glenna reached out and stroked the baby's velvety-soft, dark head as he slumbered undisturbed. *"My baby. My sweet, precious angel Jamie. I'm glad they decided to call you that now, but I bet you'll be JB by the time you get to school."* Her fingers drifted down to trace Jamie's plump, ruddy cheek.

She choked back an almost human urge to weep. *"You'd have been mine. And I'd have called you JB from the start."* Glenna soaked up every detail, from his fine, dark hair and long eyelashes to the determined way he clenched his tiny fists—so like his daddy in so many ways. Gently, she eased back the yellow and dark blue blanket that didn't quite go with the things she'd planned to use in JB's room.

It pleased Glenna that Jamie was robust, nicely filled out, and already stretching his blue sleeper. He'd be a big man, like Blake.

"You're your daddy's baby. And hers. There's nothing of me in you, my angel."

Glenna felt like screaming with the unfairness of it all. This baby, the one she had wanted and waited for years to get, wasn't hers at all. He was Blake's—and Erin's. She'd never hold him, never dry his baby tears, never beam with pride when he hit his first home run or won a prize at school. She was gone. Dead. It wasn't fair. Erin had Timmy. Now she had Jamie, too. And soon she'd have Blake loving her.

This baby was not and never would be hers. Even the nursery that she'd planned in her mind, down to an aqua padded rocker and the whimsical porcelain clowns she'd picked out but never had the chance to buy before she died, contained nothing of her.

Dispassionately, she took in pale yellow walls, antique oak furniture, and accents of indigo and royal blue. Erin must have fixed up the room with Blake's favorite colors in mind. A fierce wave of jealousy swept over her, but she struck down that uncharitable but human reaction and focused her attention again on Blake's son.

He belonged to Blake all right. Jamie was the son she hadn't been able to give him. Memories of the babies she'd lost flooded her mind as she watched Jamie's eyelids flutter and his little fists unclench and tighten again around a section of blanket.

The last one would have been sitting up by now, exploring her small world with eager enthusiasm. *Would she have been big and dark-haired like you, or little and blond like me? Oh, Jamie, I wanted her and the others so, so much. I wanted you, too. Would you have filled the empty spaces they left in my heart?*

Jamie stirred again, as if he had heard her thoughts. As he uncurled his fingers, Glenna wished she were alive, so she could feel him curl a trusting, curious hand around her own finger.

Being a ghost had its downside. She wished, just once, she could become flesh and blood again so she could feel the joy of loving and being loved. But that wasn't going to happen. She couldn't come back, and she couldn't have the joy of raising

Blake's baby as her own. But, being a ghost, she could do her best to see that Jamie had two parents who loved each other. Allowing herself one last look, Glenna willed herself to fade away so she could guide Blake, through Erin, back into the light.

Chapter Twelve

ဢ

Blake kicked off his tennis shoes and sat on the bed to strip down. He'd have to get the hang of positioning a towel or something over his shoulder while he held his son, although he didn't mind that Jamie had burped all over the collar of his shirt.

Loving the little guy as he did, Blake knew he'd have adored the babies he and Glenna had lost, but somehow they'd never seemed as real to him as the living, breathing baby across the hall. Yeah, he'd hurt every time Glenna had miscarried—but that pain had focused on grief for her loss more than for his own. The lost babies hadn't seemed real. Hadn't seemed as much a part of him as Timmy.

This afternoon, he'd been thrilled when Erin's son had called him Daddy for the first time. And damned if he didn't feel like a father, not only to Jamie but to the little boy whose life had begun with the passion of another man.

Blake also felt horny. For the past three days his cock had stayed half hard most of the time, and the constant state of unrelieved arousal was driving him nuts. He couldn't will away the hard-on, and that annoyed the hell out of him, too. Determined to work off his frustration, he wrapped a towel around his waist and headed for the pool.

Not once in the nearly five months Glenna had been gone had Blake felt the slightest twinge of desire until three nights ago, when he'd first watched his newborn son nuzzle up to Erin's ripe, full breasts. It happened then, and every time he punished himself by watching Jamie nurse. Hell, he was even getting hard now, just thinking about how creamy smooth they'd feel and taste and…

"Come off it, Blake. You've never been a breast man, anyhow," he muttered. "Not to mention, most folks would tell you you're a certifiable sex maniac to be lusting after a woman who gave birth three days ago." Unfortunately, his cock didn't listen. Shedding the towel, he dived cleanly into the tepid water, determined to force his inconveniently restored libido into submission.

Twenty laps later, he hauled himself out of the water. Cursing the heat of the night and the fever inside him that wouldn't subside, he strode back into the house.

In the sterile confines of the study he'd turned into a monk-like cell, Blake lay in the dark. The soft sheets brushed his naked body, made his balls tighten.

Shit. Grasping the base of his cock in his fist, he started to jerk off. The unthinking, mechanical action reminded him how he'd sat in Greg's office and collected that sperm sample. And that made him think of Erin again. He visualized her full, inviting breasts that nourished his son…her long legs and caring smiles and…

Blake tried to picture Glenna but couldn't see her beloved face. When he concentrated on recalling the *Playboy* centerfolds who'd helped him come that day in Greg's office, nothing happened. Nothing took his mind off the woman across the hall. Damn it, she was his wife.

Fuck it. He tightened his fist, increased the pressure, milked his flesh until it hurt. He refused to concentrate on anything but getting off. He wasn't fantasizing about fucking Erin. He wasn't. Maybe if he kept repeating it in his head he'd start believing it. If he didn't, he'd lose his mind. He'd never manage to squelch the inappropriate, ill-timed yearnings for the woman who had brought him to this state.

He wasn't fantasizing about tasting the milk that nourished his son, or imagining it was her slim hand instead of his own taking care of the hard-on that didn't want to cooperate and come.

The hell he wasn't. Knowing he'd regret it later with renewed guilt and feelings of disloyalty, he imagined being on her, in her, sinking into her hot, moist sheath. His balls tightened and his cock throbbed against his fist. His mouth watered, needy to taste her milk…her honey.

Finally he felt it coming, the orgasm he wished he were giving her. When the musky, heated essence of him spurted onto his own naked flesh, he saw Erin. Not Glenna. Moments later, when he stepped under the warm, pulsing jets of water in the shower, he tried hard to wash away the persistent wanting along with the guilt that wouldn't go away.

He'd always taken pride in his ability to analyze and evaluate the feelings of others accurately and incisively. Why, he wondered, was he now suddenly unsure about his own agenda? And why was he acting so out of character?

He'd vowed never to open this drawer, yet here he was, rifling through it and cradling the photo he'd swept off the desk at his office the day after the funeral. Glenna. This had been his favorite picture of her, taken about six years ago when they'd just learned she was pregnant the second time.

Glenna was dead, damn it. And it was her own fault. "You had to have a child, even if it killed you, and by God it did. It wasn't enough that you had me, was it? My loving you wasn't enough to fill that need—that obsession—inside you. You left me alone. Damn you, you should have stayed home. You didn't need to buy out Neiman's for a baby that wasn't even close to being born."

But Jamie was here now. And Blake loved him.

He'd wanted a child as much as any man would. But he'd wanted Glenna more. Suddenly he wondered if that had been the truth. Had he somehow made Glenna believe he had to have a child of his own to experience the sort of elation he'd felt when Greg handed him his newborn son?

Blake searched the still, smiling face in the picture, then replaced it in the drawer and turned the key. Glenna had been his safe anchor, his emotional harbor. Now she was gone, and he was adrift. He loved Glenna. He'd always grieve for her. Yet he exulted in the knowledge that he had a healthy, beautiful son across the hall.

Fuck it, he lusted after his son's mother, too. That made him feel guilty as hell.

How did Greg do it? Blake lay in bed and pictured his friend's uncomplicated, joyful relationship with Sandy—a relationship that seemed unaffected by the love Greg once must have felt for two other women who'd shared his name and life.

* * * * *

"I think we'll like living here," Greg said, stretching his bare legs out and ogling Sandy, who looked like a water nymph against the backdrop of flowing water and natural stone that dominated the smallish backyard. "I hope Shana will like her room."

"I'm sure she will."

Sandy's tone reminded him his daughter's choice of a pricey, avant-garde-style bedroom set still rubbed her the wrong way, but Greg didn't quite know what to do about it. "I'm sure Shana will settle down once Kay gets married and she comes here to live with us."

"Live with us?" Sandy sounded horrified.

"Just for a few months, sweetheart. While Kay and her fish take a prolonged honeymoon. Don't tell me you're afraid of a twelve-year-old."

Sandy sank onto a patio chair, one of the set that was the first furniture purchase they had made together for their new home. "Shana doesn't like me. I'd hoped we could get to know each other…more gradually."

Obviously Sandy wasn't happy, and Greg was feeling her stress. Hell, he knew his daughter could try the patience of a saint. Still, he loved Shana and hoped this time with him and Sandy would restore the closeness he missed. "Shana doesn't much like anybody who tries to tell her what to do. From what I've heard, most kids her age are like that. I'll bet you gave Erin and her husband some rough times when you first went to live with them."

Sandy smiled, a nervous little motion of her lips that didn't reach her eyes. "I guess. I don't know how to be a stepmother." She wouldn't look at Greg.

The way she stared at the spa and pool that looked like a natural feature of the back yard landscape made Greg very nervous. "You'll learn, love. And I'll be here to help smooth over any rough spots." He wished he felt half as confident as he sounded.

"But you're away so much at night, and I'll be here with her all by myself. Greg, what if I can't make her like me? I already loved Erin when I moved in with her and Bill."

"Hush. I've hired an associate, and he'll be taking call every other night. Besides, you took my office in hand and you've made it run like a top. Handling one little girl half your age should be a piece of cake."

"All right." As if determined to put the prospect of becoming a full-time stepmom out of her mind, Sandy got up and came to Greg, letting out a sexy little whimper when he pulled her down on his lap and tweaked her nipples through the flimsy material of her red string bikini top.

Her fingers tangled in the hair on his chest when she searched out and teased his nipples as he was doing to hers. He groaned when she shifted around to face him fully, wrapping her legs around his waist and lining up his suddenly burning erection with her warm, moist pussy.

"Interested, are you?" Her tongue darted out and moistened her inviting lips as she looked down at his cock as it rose against the confines of his tight, black swim trunks. He shuddered and grew even harder when Sandy slid his suit down, exposing his cock head and stroking it slowly with a teasing finger.

She had a way of making him feel like he was the only man in the world. And of erasing everything from his mind but the need to fuck her until they both collapsed in a sweaty, satiated heap. "Don't stop there, take it all the way off."

Once she had him naked, she bent and lapped at his cock with her tongue. If she didn't stop, he'd explode. As it was, he was so hot he could barely breathe.

Desperate to get lost in her hot, wet cunt, he clasped the warm, naked skin of her buttocks. She might as well not have bothered with the tiny T-back scrap for all it covered. It easily slid aside, exposing her sopping pussy to take his hard, fast thrust.

She was so hot and tight...so wet. "Oh, yeah. Squeeze my cock. That's it. God, you feel so good. How could I have gotten so lucky?"

He forced his eyelids not to close. Looking at Sandy when they were making love was worth the effort of holding back, teasing her with long, lazy strokes. Damn it, he loved the way she writhed against him. Loved feeling her cunt tightening around his cock like a vise. Even the sexy way her mouth slackened and she cried out his name when she came made Greg feel ten feet tall. Not until he felt her jerk and constrict around his cock for the third time did he close his eyes and let go, thrusting one more time and giving himself up to a shattering climax.

"I love you, baby." He held onto her silky thighs, not wanting to give up the pleasure of being deep inside her even after the fire inside him had been doused.

"Baby?"

"Yeah. You're my sweet, loving baby."

Sandy nuzzled at his neck like a friendly kitten. "I'm your woman, not your baby. Shana's your baby."

"Shana, and the ones we're going to have together. Still, I'll call you my baby if I want to." Greg felt himself hardening again. It had never felt so good, so natural, before. He had felt her hot, welcoming wetness ease his way, enjoyed the feel of their body fluids mingling when he spilled his seed deep into her womb.

He hadn't protected her.

"We may have one of those babies sooner than we planned, honey," he murmured as he lifted her off him and adjusted their bodies to fit side by side on the generously wide chair. "I forgot to use a condom."

"I know."

"And you didn't say anything?"

Sandy reached out and caressed his cheek. "I think I said please."

Greg met her gaze and felt the love he had been searching for since he was a boy. "Please knock me up?"

"I wouldn't mind if you did. I want your baby. Several of them. By the way, it's the twelfth day of my cycle."

"In that case, it's my professional opinion that you should start planning your wedding, then, Ms. Daniels." Greg laughed, but he was only half joking.

He wouldn't worry about how the two women he loved would get along, living for a time in the same house. Life was too short for agonizing over details. He'd let each day take care of itself. Maybe he was overoptimistic, but he had a feeling that while he, Shana and Sandy would have to adjust to being a family, everything would work out.

* * * * *

Every day over the next month, Blake gave Erin conflicting signals. One moment he would be warm, friendly, and teasing. The next, he'd turn cool and distant, but only with her. Since Jamie was born, Blake had doted on the baby and Timmy, whose finalized adoption papers Blake brought home to her yesterday afternoon.

More important, Blake had suddenly started springing surprises on her, such as his love for horses that he hadn't indulged for years. Tomorrow they'd fly out to his great uncle's ranch to choose a few to have shipped home for them to ride. Excited, because riding had been her own childhood passion, Erin stepped into the stable at the back of Blake's property, anxious to see the results of renovation work that had been going on since last week.

"I'm glad you ride. It always made me feel bad for Blake that I was scared to death of horses. You know, this is the first time I've ever been inside the stable."

Erin recognized Glenna's voice at once, although it took a few minutes for her to find the ghost hovering behind a half-closed storeroom door, as if afraid of the horses that weren't there.

Why had Glenna come here? It was painfully obvious to Erin that this must be the last place the ghost would have chosen to go. "I've always liked to ride. It's been years, though, since I've been on a horse."

"Blake, too. He got rid of his horses when he realized how much they frightened me. His dog, too."

Erin smiled. "I wondered if Blake would mind Timmy having a puppy. After his next surgery, that is."

"He won't mind. He'd go as nuts over a dog as he has over the boys. Well, maybe not quite that nuts, but close." She shot Erin an impish grin.

"I don't know what to make of Blake. Sometimes I think you're right, that he's giving *us* a chance to have a real marriage, but then he clams up and won't let me in to help him heal."

Glenna glided close enough that Erin almost felt her ghostly aura. *"Those times when he shuts you out are going to get shorter and farther apart. Hang in there. As much as I hate to admit it, you're going to be a better match for Blake than I ever was. What you need to do now is get back to the house and set a scene. It's your baby's one-month birthday, in case you forgot. Celebrate with Jamie. Then start seducing Jamie's daddy."*

Erin's mouth dropped open. "It's too soon for that." Not to mention that talking to Glenna about seducing the ghost's widower struck Erin as bizarre. And incredibly awkward.

"Maybe for the main event, but not for a preview of what you two can look forward to in another couple of weeks. Don't kid yourself. Blake hasn't had sex for months. He can't help being horny. So—seduce him. Make him so hot that when Greg gives you the go-ahead, he won't be able to resist. I would, if I were still alive."

Erin mulled over Glenna's outrageous suggestion as she watched the ghost fade out of sight. Why not? The idea of seducing Blake wasn't all that outrageous when she considered it had been not months but *years* since she'd had sex. Suddenly Erin was starved. And her husband-in-name-only looked good enough to eat. Literally.

After taking one last look around the stable she strolled back to the house and started to make preparations. Later that afternoon, Erin thought she heard Glenna murmur her approval at the menu she asked Mary to serve in the small sitting room in the master suite.

Erin went about her business, picking out linens and dishes to set the table. Maybe those dark blue pottery plates. There was nothing romantic about them. Well, maybe that would be best. No use being blatant about seducing him. Still, she hesitated.

"Use them. They used to belong to Blake's grandmother. He likes them because they'll hold a huge hunk of steak. Might as well find his mother's gold-plated silverware and use it, too. I hated it, so he hasn't seen it for years."

Obviously Glenna wanted this seduction to work, which unnerved Erin. Still, if the ghost wanted to help who was she to object? She selected a pair of crystal wineglasses. "Will these do?" she asked, barely whispering for fear Mary would hear her and think she had gone over the deep end.

The stemmed glasses levitated out of Erin's hand as if by magic and returned to their places in the china cabinet. As she stared, aghast, two glasses made of jewel-toned carnival glass came out of the cabinet and nestled in her hands. *"Use these,"* Glenna commanded sweetly.

When Erin had finished setting the table, Glenna badgered her into going to the attic, where she found a pleasant landscape and several accent pieces. Once she'd hung the picture and set a trio of colorful glass decoys on the mantel, the sitting room reflected a personal touch that had been missing from the coldly elegant bedroom and sitting room.

"He'll like it – and you," Glenna said as she floated away.

Good. Two hours left before Blake would be home. She'd use the time to pamper herself now that Jamie was fed and in the capable hands of Theresa, his nanny, and Timmy had settled down with Mary to help with dinner. Looking forward to the evening, Erin rifled through her limited wardrobe, settling on a body-skimming caftan woven of dark blue cotton shot with metallic threads of gold. She assumed Blake would like it since he was the one who'd brought it to her in the hospital, the day after Jamie was born. Maybe tonight, it would appeal to him more, since she'd shrunk down to her pre-pregnancy size — almost.

She rifled through her underwear drawer, pushing aside plain white nursing bras and matching panties. There they were, the sexy-as-hell navy satin-and-lace thong and matching bra that Sandy had given her before her wedding. When she held the miniscule bra up against her swollen breasts, she laughed. No doubt she'd look far sexier than the bra's designer had intended. Good. Even if Blake never knew that beneath his tasteful, luxurious gift was underwear that ought to raise the interest of a dead man, Erin would know.

Luxuriating in the ritual of beautifying her body, Erin methodically waxed her legs. She'd always hated the feel of razor stubble, so much that she hardly felt the sting anymore when she jerked off each strip of hardened wax. Next she dumped fragrant oil into the tub while it filled with water, breathing in the damp, sweet air that permeated her skin while she shampooed her hair and applied a light cleansing mask to her face. Then she climbed into the tub.

"You're going to knock him clear off his feet." Glenna laughed when Erin reflexively crossed her hands across her breasts. *"What's that fragrance?"*

"Something Sandy got some free samples of at *La Parfumerie*. The bath oil came out of that tube over on the makeup table."

Glenna reached out and lifted the tiny sample container. *"I don't believe this! Erin, this is an omen."*

"What do you mean?"

"Do you know what this is?"

What was Glenna getting at?

"It's *La Mer l'Été*. It means 'Summer Sea'. Just like it says on the package."

"Blake bought me a huge bottle of the perfume once, after he smelled it on a woman in the shop. He loved it. On her. Unfortunately, when I put it on, I smelled like a scared skunk. He was awfully disappointed."

"You don't think I should wear it?"

"Oh, yes, you definitely should wear it. You should run out and buy the biggest bottles you can find of the stuff. It smells the way it's supposed to on you. Blake won't be able to keep his hands to himself, not that he would for long, in any case."

"You really think so?"

"Yeah. I do. Relax and enjoy your bath. I'm going to make myself scarce." With that, Glenna faded away, leaving Erin to her bath and her reading.

Half an hour later, the timer's shrill buzz brought Erin from the fantasy world she had found in her book, an erotic romance with a tall, dark, gorgeous hero who reminded her a lot of Blake. She set the book down and climbed from the warm tub to subject herself to icy needles of water that pulsed from four jets in the separate shower.

Rough-soft terry cloth soaked up the water from her skin, leaving a faint, sweet smell of lemon, flowers and herbs. Beginning with her toes and working all the way up to her neck, she massaged cool lotion into her skin, strengthening the fragrance just a bit. Finally, she took up the tiny vial that held pure essence of *La Mer l'Été* and dotted drops of it between her breasts, at each elbow, and on the hollows behind both knees.

Pampering did wonders toward making Erin feel pretty and sexy. Her tummy still looked a little convex above the tiny thong bikini, and her legs could use a bit more firming exercise, she allowed as she looked critically in the mirror. All in all, though, she liked how she looked. If Blake saw her naked for the first time tonight, he shouldn't be too disappointed.

After all, he saw her breasts almost every day, when he watched her nurse their baby. He'd seen her pussy, too. Erin's cheeks grew warm when she recalled he'd been there watching when Jamie had emerged from her straining body. Not a sight to set a man's blood boiling, she thought ruefully.

She glanced at the clock. Blake would be home soon, and she wanted to be ready. Hurriedly, she dried her hair, applied light makeup, and slipped into the caftan, noting with satisfaction how it emphasized her new slimness with a subtlety that belied the frankly sexy way she felt inside. As she stepped out of the dressing room, she heard Blake's voice from Jamie's room.

* * * * *

"Would you like to bring Jamie in the sitting room?" Erin asked a few minutes later when she joined Blake in the nursery. "He could join us while we enjoy his birthday dinner."

Blake regarded his sleeping baby. "Maybe we should let him sleep. I brought him a pony." He reached into the crib and showing Erin the black and white stuffed animal. "It's got a music box inside." Before setting it down he wound it up, and a tinkly version of "Home on the Range" began to play.

"You're spoiling him. And we have dinner waiting."

"Where?"

"In the sitting room."

At least it wasn't in her bedroom, where Blake knew damn well he wouldn't be able to keep his thoughts off what he'd like to be doing in that big new king-size bed. "I'll wash up and join you in a minute." As they left the nursery together, he tried to recall where he'd smelled that incredibly erotic perfume before.

He should have brought Jamie in here. Timmy, too. But Blake doubted anything could take his mind off Erin...and the fact they were alone together, in shouting distance of a bed his cock was practically screaming to break in. That scent of hers...he tried to put it out of his mind but couldn't.

The food tasted great, but for all the enjoyment Blake got from eating it, the prime New York strip steak might just as well have been old shoe leather. Try as he might, he couldn't take his eyes off Erin. She'd always been attractive. Tonight, though, with her shoulder-length dark hair loosely curled around her face, Erin took his breath away.

Her blue eyes sparkled when she looked at him. And her beautifully shaped lips tempted him to taste them. The long dark blue cover-up he'd brought her in the hospital skimmed slimmed-down curves his fingers itched to explore. God, how she and that elusive, airy scent she was wearing turned him on. Blake wanted her badly, and from the looks she gave him, he was pretty certain she wanted him, too.

What could they talk about? Before they finished their steaks, they'd exhausted the subject of the trip, and they'd praised Jamie's and Timmy's various accomplishments over salad. Blake was desperate to keep the conversation going, if for no other reason than to keep his mind off what he knew he shouldn't have. Couldn't have, at least not now.

"Greg bought Sandy a ring today," he told her as he sank a fork into a piece of apple pie. "What would you think about our giving them an engagement party three weeks from this Friday?"

Erin's smile nearly took his breath away. "Sandy would love it. She told me yesterday that she wished she could give a small party, so she could show Greg off to her friends from school. It won't be too expensive if I have her keep her guest list small. I can handwrite the invitations, and we can serve cake and maybe some simple sandwiches."

Blake held up a hand. "I'm not worried about the cost. Greg's one of my closest friends, and Sandy's your sister. Besides, the party will be a good setting to introduce you as my wife," he added, recalling Kay Halpern's snide remarks the day Jamie was born.

"Oh. How many people are we talking about?" Erin asked warily.

"A hundred or so, plus whomever you and Sandy want to invite, give or take. A cocktail dance would probably work best for that many guests, don't you think?"

Erin raised her eyebrows expressively. "I think that's an awfully big party to put together in three weeks' time. I suppose I can do it, though." The long, slender fingers of her left hand tapped out a nervous rhythm on the smoked glass tabletop.

"You'll have plenty of help," he said, wanting to allay her obvious discomfort at the thought of hosting such a large gathering.

He felt her smile all the way down to his gut and beyond. His balls tightened painfully, so painfully he wanted to leap across the table and drag her off to bed. "Sharon will do the invitations and make most of the arrangements," he said, trying to focus on anything except Erin's soft, infinitely kissable mouth.

"Sharon?"

"What? Oh, Sharon's my secretary. Remember, she came to visit while you were in the hospital."

"Oh. She won't mind? I don't imagine planning parties is part of her job description." Erin's blue eyes twinkled when she teased Blake, and that only made him want her more.

"Actually, it is. She's always planned personal as well as business entertaining for me. She likes doing it. How long will it take you to get together a list of people you want to invite?"

"I can get with Sandy after we get back tomorrow, and give you names and addresses in a day or two. We're going to need every bit of space we can find to accommodate such a big crowd. Do you think the weather will still be nice enough to use the patio as well as inside?"

Blake forced a smile. He and Glenna had hosted many a glittering party here, and the house was plenty big to entertain two hundred or more people in comfort. But there were too many memories. "I want to have the party at the country club."

"Why?"

Because he wasn't ready, didn't know if he'd ever be ready to laugh and be happy in the home he shared with Glenna. "Because it will be easier for you." He didn't want that soft, pleased expression to vanish from Erin's lovely face. He couldn't bear the thought of hurting her. He wanted…

Abruptly, Blake stood and stepped around the table. Grasping Erin's shoulders, he pulled her to her feet and held her at arm's length.

"Oh, hell," he muttered, drawing her close enough that he felt her warm, moist breath against his chest. "This is what I want, and you've been telling me all evening with those sweet, soft looks that you want it, too."

When she didn't protest and he felt her pulse quickening against his fingers, he bent and took her soft, inviting lips. Gentle at first, Blake soon unleashed the fierce desire that had been riding him for weeks. His tongue sought and found entrance, and he drank in her sweetness like a man long starved.

It was heaven, holding her. Hell, knowing he couldn't fuck her pussy the way he was fucking her mouth with his tongue.

Still he sought more torture, tugging down the zipper of her caftan and stroking the satiny fullness of breasts barely contained by some silky scrap of a bra.

She smelled like flowers and musk and woman, he thought as he laid a path of open-mouthed kisses down her neck. When he reached her bra, he nuzzled it out of the way and closed his lips around a tight bud of a nipple he'd been dreaming of for days. With his tongue, he teased at the pebbly nub until it rewarded him with a sweet, hot taste of the milk that sustained his son.

He was so hard he thought he'd die. She wasn't helping the matter, either, the way she pressed her hips to his and rocked back and forth against his throbbing cock. He'd die if he didn't bury himself inside her now. His movements urgent, nearly desperate, he scooped her in his arms and headed for the bed.

"We can't," she said when he laid her down and stood back to get rid of his clothes. "It's too soon. The baby…"

"I know."

What had he been thinking? Fuck, he knew exactly what he'd been thinking with, and it certainly wasn't his brain! "I'm sorry." Blake sat on the edge of the bed and reached for Erin's hand.

"It's all right." Her face was flushed, her expression dreamy. She'd obviously wanted him as much as he wanted her, if that was possible.

He held her gaze and rubbed his thumbs across the palms of both her hands until he found his voice. "I know I told you before we married that I didn't want a sexual relationship—in the foreseeable future, was the way I think I expressed it. Well, in case you haven't already guessed, I'd better tell you I foresee wanting one damn soon."

Her hands curled and tightened around his. "All right," she said, her voice low and husky, and sexy as the devil.

Suddenly he pictured Glenna's face, and he drew his hands away. "I hope that doesn't bother you half as much as it's tearing me up inside with guilt." He'd whispered, barely loud enough for himself to hear, but when tears welled in her beautiful eyes, he realized she'd heard — and she hurt.

"Damn it, I'm sorry. Please don't cry. Look, I've got to go now." When Blake walked out, he began preparing himself to face another hard, lonely night alone.

* * * * *

"Blake was the one who thought of our having this party for you and Greg," Erin said when Sandy began thanking her effusively. "Don't ask me what made him think about it in the first place, but he brought up the subject last week while we were having dinner to celebrate Jamie's one-month birthday."

"I wouldn't have believed your husband had a romantic bone in his gorgeous body." Sandy grinned.

"I don't know that he does." But Erin hoped the new, friendly way Blake had been treating her lately might mean he was thinking about her with more than just the physical attraction he'd reluctantly confessed feeling that night. Needing someone to talk with, she told Sandy about the dinner and what had followed.

"I worried about Blake after he stormed out of my room, but by the next morning he seemed to have shaken off whatever remorse he'd been feeling," Erin concluded. "For the most part, he's acted like a different man than before." Erin lifted a deceptively plain black silk dress that looked almost like a floor-length slip from a Neiman Marcus dress box and put it onto a padded hanger in her closet.

"Different how?" Sandy asked, her eyes bright with excitement as she reviewed the list of guests who had accepted invitations to the party.

"Nothing specific. He just seems more open. I don't know. It just seems that once he took the boys and me to his great-uncle's last week, Blake has been easy to be with. Fun. Would you believe, he looks even better in tight jeans and cowboy boots than he does in his suits?"

"I believe that."

"You would. I never would have thought Blake loved being outdoors the way he does. Until we went to get the horses, the only exercise I'd seen him doing was pumping iron in his gym and swimming. But he rides like a rodeo champ, and I can almost feel his excitement when he's around the horses. I believe Blake would be as happy being a rancher as he is practicing law."

"How many horses do you have? And how long have they been here?"

"Three. A black colt, a dappled gray pony, and the chestnut mare he picked out for me. They arrived Monday in an air-conditioned horse trailer."

"You must be thrilled. I remember how much you used to love to ride." Sandy set aside the guest list and curled up on the love seat in Erin's bedroom.

"I am. I was shocked when I found out Blake loves horses as much as I do. I probably never would have if I hadn't gotten curious and asked why he kept that big field behind the house fenced in, with nothing except grass growing in it. After he showed me the stable and told me about the horses he'd always had when he was a boy, I admitted that riding used to be one of my favorite pastimes."

"So he just decided, like that, to go get some four-legged transportation?" Sandy shook her head.

"Basically, but he arranged to have the stable fixed up, first. That took two weeks. Then, last weekend, he loaded Timmy, Jamie and me into his plane and flew us to his great uncle's ranch outside Lubbock. He picked out the horses there."

Sandy sighed. "I don't suppose he'd let my future stepdaughter ride one of them. On top of everything else I've got to do, Shana has decided she has to ride every day after she comes to stay with Greg and me. Guess who gets to take the princess to her riding club? It's twenty miles, one way, so I'll be stuck there for two hours every evening while she has her lessons."

"You can ask him." What few comments she'd heard him make about Greg's daughter hadn't given her the impression Shana was one of his favorite people.

"I will."

Erin smiled. No one could accuse her little sister of lacking nerve. She hoped that spunk would keep Sandy going when dealing with her husband's daughter became a fact of her daily life.

* * * * *

When she watched Sandy greeting friends and strangers at her engagement party the following weekend, Erin couldn't help feeling an almost motherly pride. Her baby sister was all grown up, poised and sophisticated in a forest-green silk halter-top gown. She'd had chosen well. The deceptively simple gown and her upswept chestnut curls accentuated her beauty and made an elegant backdrop for Greg's engagement gifts, a beautifully cut diamond solitaire and the modest diamond studs she wore in her ears.

As she stood with Greg and his mother, Sadie, greeting their guests, Sandy radiated confidence Erin was trying hard to emulate. From looking at the three of them, no one would guess Sadie's approval had come grudgingly, or that Shana's absence from the receiving line had been a subject of much dissension. The picture of unity belied the ripples of one-upmanship the three women played in the game of jockeying for first place in poor Greg's life.

Erin shuddered. She'd hate having to tiptoe around Sadie Halpern. Never mind that the woman was currently beaming and chattering her approval of her son's coming marriage to everyone she greeted. Beneath Sadie's disarming smile lurked a mother whose major function in life apparently was trying to manipulate her only son.

"Where's Shana?" Blake whispered during a lull in the stream of arriving guests.

Erin smiled up at him. "Over there. She decided to skip the receiving line."

He looked toward the sullen preteen whose expression of studied boredom would have done justice to a jaded thirty-year-old. Erin thought of Sandy at that age, when she had come to live with her and Bill, sweet and eager to please despite having just lost her parents. The comparison made her furious. Shana was doing her level best to make Sandy's life, and Greg's, hell on earth, for no reason Erin could see except perhaps that doing it amused the kid.

"I don't envy Sandy or Greg, either, having to deal with the little monster Kay has created," Blake muttered under his breath, sliding his hand up a little on Erin's back and massaging the bare skin above her waist with a circular motion of his thumb. "Judge Adkins. You've already met Erin," he said heartily to the elderly man who'd performed their wedding. "Erin, this is the judge's granddaughter, Julie."

"She's a lawyer with the district attorney's office. Tried that mass murderer last year." The voice of the ghost came out of nowhere into Erin's ear.

"I'm glad to meet you, Julie. I followed the Harvey case on TV. It must have been exciting, working to convict him."

Julie smiled, apparently pleased Erin had connected her with the case.

Suddenly Blake bent his head and whispered in Erin's ear. "Oh, God! I didn't realize we'd invited them."

"Whatever you do, don't compliment this one on her dress. You'll never get rid of her. She'll tell you who designed it, why she wore it tonight. If you let her she'll even tell you who designed and why she didn't wear everything else in her closet."

Glenna's ghost was driving Erin nuts with her helpful asides, but as the evening went on, she noticed Blake smiling when she used Glenna's information to set another guest at ease. Finally they disbanded the receiving line and adjourned to a big, round table at a corner of the dance floor.

The volume of the music from a small band increased almost imperceptibly. Waiters scurried around to keep the buffet tables filled and drink orders flowing from three bars.

This was a cocktail buffet? Erin stood at the serving table, her plate poised in one hand while she tried to choose from the cold roast beef, turkey, cheeses, raw vegetables and dips she'd suggested, along with a selection of hot dishes that came as a complete surprise. There were meatballs, croquettes, and several savory-smelling casseroles. Erin counted five different shapes and varieties of rolls in huge silver baskets. She selected some food and went back to the table.

"My mom has a diamond three times as big as this," Shana was saying after lifting Sandy's hand to inspect her ring. "The ring Dad gave Mom was bigger and better than yours. She had it made into a pendant, you know."

Greg had gone to fill Sadie's plate, and Shana was on the attack. Glancing at Sandy with sympathy, Erin suppressed an urge to shake Greg's daughter until her bright, silvery braces popped out of her head.

"Shana. That's enough," Sadie said sharply before turning to Sandy, whose mouth was trembling. "Sandy, dear, don't mind her. Every little girl is jealous of the women who attract her dad's attention."

"Here you go, Mother." Greg set a plate down in front of Sadie and took his seat between her and Sandy. "What's the matter, princess?" he asked Shana, whose pout let everyone know she wasn't happy.

"None of my friends are here."

Erin could have reached over and kissed Blake when he spoke up. "Whose fault is that, young lady? Sandy and Erin both asked you who you'd like to invite. And my secretary spoke to you again before the invitations went out. Come on, relax and be happy for your dad."

The conversation warmed, and Erin could see Sandy relaxing again, basking in Greg's obvious adoration. She was watching Sandy float gracefully around the dance floor in Greg's arms when her ghostly friend appeared in a haze of pale gold dust on the other side of the room.

"Ask him to dance," she mouthed, inclining her head toward Blake before her image faded away.

Blake looked surprised when Erin tapped his shoulder and gestured toward the dance floor, but he rose politely and held her chair. Taking her hand, he led her onto the highly polished dance floor and took her in his arms.

"You look beautiful tonight," he murmured as they swayed in time to a sweet, romantic tune.

"You, too." Blake looked good enough to eat in stark black formal attire. When he'd come to her room, ready to take her to this party, Erin had nearly drooled. She hadn't wanted to stop looking at him, had barely managed to keep from wrestling him to the bed.

"Sandy and Greg make a good couple."

Erin sighed. "I hope they can survive adjusting to Shana." When Blake tightened his arm around her, she leaned closer, and her nipples tingled at the contact with his warm, hard chest.

"And Mom Sadie. She may be a help with Shana, though, because she won't put up with the kid being outright rude."

"I noticed." Erin glanced over at the table where it seemed Shana was getting a talking to from her grandmother.

"Do all kids get obnoxious when they get to be her age?" Blake pulled Erin closer, nudged her belly with his hardened cock.

Erin tilted her head so she could look up at him. "I hope not," she replied, smiling.

"Me, too. Come on. It's time to make some toasts." He squeezed her waist. "Time for me to show off my wife."

Blake's arm felt good around her as he made the formal announcement of Sandy's engagement. She felt herself flush with pleasure when he ad-libbed, "And for those of you who haven't met her yet, this is Sandy's sister—my beautiful bride, Erin."

The next time they danced, Blake did the asking. He held her a little closer. She felt the rush of his warm breath against her hair and the insistent pressure of his erection against her aching body. A sweet hope began inside her that he might feel more for her than friendship, more than the lust he seemed to be fighting with all the weapons at his command.

"Do you know what you do to me?" he growled when they danced the night's last dance together. He held her close—both his arms wrapped like tender tentacles around her waist. His fingers played havoc with her senses as he rubbed them softly over her bare back, and his arousal scorched her belly.

"I think so." Erin knew exactly what she was doing to him, because he was doing the same thing to her. She was warm and wet and needy, longing to take his hard, hot cock into her body and end the long nights of wanting...dreaming.

Would he act tonight on the desire he couldn't hide? Her heart beat faster as they rocked slowly to the rhythm of a slow, sensual love song.

Chapter Thirteen

ဆ

"I'll see you in the morning," Blake told Erin brusquely after they'd checked on Jamie. He practically ran from the nursery into the room where he slept, because he knew that if he didn't, nothing in the world would keep him from betraying his wife and making love to the woman who had him so hard and aching he could hardly stand up.

Erin wanted him to stay. He knew from the look in her beautiful dark eyes that his abrupt departure hurt her. God, he didn't want that, any more than he wanted to indulge his body while subjecting his mind to the worst kind of guilt he could imagine.

For a long time, he sat on the edge of the bed in his study, staring into the darkened hallway. He tried to picture Glenna, but Erin filled his mind.

"Damn it to hell!" Frustrated, he got up and started to undress. He could take care of the throbbing ache in his balls the way he'd done several times this last month and a half. Why didn't jerking off appeal one tenth as much as tossing away his misgivings and fucking the night away with the enticing woman across the hall?

His wife. The mother of his son. No, sons. But Erin wasn't really his wife. Glenna was. And Glenna was dead. When the nursery door closed, he glanced into the hall and looked toward the pale, yellowish light from Erin's room that cast its shadow on the wall.

Her hair was loose, wild, and windblown now, when at the party it had rippled against her shoulders in soft, ordered curls. In slow, tantalizing motion she raised her arms and lifted off that clinging, satin gown that left the supple skin of her back bare.

He held his breath for her to peel off black panty hose, so sheer they hinted at the ivory skin beneath them. No, by God, they weren't pantyhose at all but thigh-high stockings held up by skinny, black lace straps, he realized when her sheer black half-slip slid down those long, long legs. Her bra followed, and she stood there in plain view, her body backlit by that soft, diffused light, wearing nothing but those stockings and the flimsy black garter belt that held them up. His cock damn near burst out of his pants.

He ought to quit torturing himself, look anywhere except the nest of soft dark pubic curls where he longed to bury his face. But he'd denied his body's needs for months, and now it was determined to have its way. Almost as if she'd bewitched him, Blake took that first step toward Erin.

By the time he reached her door, he had his cummerbund off and cuff links loosened. When he stopped three feet away from her and met her gaze, he'd worked loose all but two of the onyx studs that secured his shirt. In the time it took for him to walk into her outstretched arms, he managed to toss his suspenders and shirt carelessly onto the floor.

"Witch." He took her mouth and tongue-fucked her while he stroked her throat, her shoulders...the tender small of her back that tantalized him all evening long. He cupped her firm, shapely ass cheeks, warm naked skin and textured lace garters.

Garters that pressed against his palm and reminded him how damn hot and hard he had gotten, watching her strip off that slinky black satin gown.

She had her hands on him, too, her touch timid at first, becoming more ravenous as he deepened the kiss, dragged her so close they might as well be fucking standing up. When he felt her unbuttoning his tux pants, he damn near came on the spot.

"Some other time, honey," he rasped out as he captured her questing hands and brought them to his lips. "Your little strip tease has me about ready to shoot my load. I don't trust myself to let you touch me." With more haste than finesse, he finished unfastening his pants and shoved them down with his briefs.

"Oh, my."

"Oh, what?" Blake was in a hurry, and his socks didn't seem to want to cooperate.

"You're…"

"Horny. Very, very horny. Do you like what you see?" The second sock finally came off, and Blake threw it in the corner before dragging Erin down onto the bed and covering her body with his own. "I asked you, honey, if you approve." Rolling onto his side, he cupped her breast with one hand and bathed the nipple with his tongue.

"Uh-huh. You've got a great body."

"So do you." He splayed his hand across her flat belly and felt a few faintly raised, spidery lines that reminded him she'd borne his son just seven weeks ago. His son had marked her, and knowing that heightened his desire. "Is this okay for you?"

"It's fine."

She nibbled at his neck, then dropped kisses on his chest. Her hands wouldn't stay still. She stroked him, from the back of his head where her fingers gently tugged at strands of his hair, down his back, tickling the indentations at the base of his spine. She wiggled her hips and slid a hand between his legs to stroke his balls. She was driving him to the brink of insanity.

"Tell me how you like it, honey. I'm not going to last very long," he murmured against the velvety softness of her breasts.

As if in answer, she opened her legs, inviting a more intimate touch. Because she'd just given birth, he stroked her hot, damp slit slowly, gently, pausing to circle her clit before inserting first one finger, then two, inside her sopping cunt.

"There's a condom in the drawer," she told him breathlessly as he withdrew his finger and knelt between her legs.

For a moment, he just stared at her. Why would she worry about *that*? They were married. Then, unwilling to spoil the moment with conversation or wait longer to fulfill his body's aching need, he reached over and dragged out a small foil packet.

"May I?" she asked, propping her head up with one hand.

His hands shook. He wanted her so badly, he'd never get the thing on by himself. On the other hand, if she touched him, it just might be all over. He handed her the packet and muttered between clenched teeth, "Be my guest. Just hurry."

By the time she sheathed him, he'd lost his sanity. Without finesse, he rolled her over and entered her in one long, hard stroke. She shuddered, and he wondered through a fog of mindless passion if he had hurt her. Then when she wrapped her silk-clad legs possessively around his waist, he knew it was desire, not pain, that drove her.

He wanted to bring her pleasure. But it had been so long, and her cunt felt so damn good around his cock! He gritted his teeth and tried to hold back, but when she tightened around him and milked him when he partially withdrew, it was too much. He couldn't stop himself. He pounded into her with short, hard thrusts and seconds later, he buried himself to the hilt and came.

* * * * *

He seemed completely drained. Erin held Blake against her breasts and stroked his silky hair off his forehead. Drained, not satisfied. For the first time since their sad, separate wedding night when he'd sobbed alone, she'd seen Blake lose control.

He was a magnificent specimen, she decided as she watched him in the dim, seductive light that neither of them had bothered to douse. He didn't have a lot of body hair, but the light dusting of silky, dark curls that shadowed his muscled arms and chest emphasized his masculinity. He'd shaved before the party, but now, just hours later, she made out the stubbly beginnings of a heavy beard. Her breasts tingled, as if they liked the prickly feel of his cheek as much as she'd relished it while they were making love.

Remembering the sterile terms of their marriage agreement, Erin tried to tell herself that what had just happened was just pure and simple sex. A man and a woman put in close proximity, giving in to the demands of their hormones. But she was afraid that, for her, there was much more to it than that.

Just then, Blake stirred, his lips making contact with her nipple and teasing it to attention. "Again?" she murmured as her hands moved to stroke his hard, flat belly.

"I always try to give as good as I get, honey," he told her sleepily as he moved lower, grazing her belly with a rough, pebbly tongue...nuzzling at the damp curls between her legs before placing gentle nips on the inside of her thighs. Then, he sucked her clit into his mouth and tongued her.

She'd forgotten how good sex could be. How fantastic it was to feel the rasp of beard stubble, the incredibly arousing but soothing swipes of a tongue against her clit. Damn it, Erin couldn't recall sex ever having felt this good. "Mmmm," she whimpered when he paused and nibbled her inner thighs.

"You want more?" When he looked up at her, she saw his pupils were dilated, the muscles of his neck and shoulders constricted.

Erin lowered her gaze and found his cock swollen, throbbing. He was more than ready to take her again.

"Yeah, I want you, too," he growled. "Reach over and get another one of those damn things if you want me to use one this time."

She reached down instead and cupped him in both hands. "Greg didn't want me to take the Pill while I'm nursing Jamie." Unfortunately. She wanted nothing more at this moment than to feel his cock inside her with nothing between then. It was big and hard and beautiful, and for the moment, it was hers. "You don't want to take a chance on another baby so soon, do you?"

Blake scowled, but the softness of his voice belied his expression. "I just don't like it. The guy who said using condoms felt like taking a shower in a raincoat had a point," he teased as she smoothed the soft, pliable latex over his throbbing flesh.

This time, their loving was slower, more tender. But not a bit less explosive. When Blake sank into her, grinding his hips against her clit and tweaking the G-spot that had lain dormant so long, her body sang. When he groaned and told her how sexy he found her, she felt cherished. And when she raised her hips to meet his needy thrusts, Erin realized she'd gone and fallen in love. She clenched his cock, as if she could hold him inside her forever, and when her pussy began to convulse around him, he tightened his hold and let go with another explosive climax. They'd come together, something that had never happened to her before, and she felt sleepily content.

"G'night," Blake muttered, his head half covered by a pillow. Then, he sat up as if stunned. "Oh, my God!" he said, and Erin didn't know if he was praying or swearing.

"What's wrong?" She reached out to touch him, but he moved out of her reach as if she were poison.

He picked up one of the gossamer sheer black stockings he'd skimmed down her leg an hour earlier and crumpled it in a trembling fist. It seemed to Erin that he was groping for words to express whatever it was he was feeling.

Finally, he spoke, his voice hardly more than a whisper. "Glenna's dead. She's hardly been gone six months, and here I am having sex with you. What's more, I enjoyed every minute of it. I could do it again right now, and several times more before the sun comes up."

Blake paused, his fingers loosening around the stocking he had crushed into a tight, wrinkled mass. He met her gaze before going on. "I'm not over Glenna. I don't know if I ever will be. Every time I touch you—hell, every time I look at you and want you, I feel this awful guilt. I'm not being fair to you when I feel like this. Damn it to hell, I feel as if I'm being unfaithful to her!"

Silent tears rushed down Erin's cheeks as she watched Blake storm out of the room. She'd had thought she could make him care for her. The ghost of his dead wife had believed she could. But they both were wrong. Glenna's hold on Blake, even in death, was so strong it would never let him go.

And Erin realized she'd fallen in love with Blake—deep down, head-over-heels in love. She curled up where they'd made love moments earlier and pictured a long, miserable life ahead, tied by love for her children to a man to whom she would never be more than a friend—and maybe occasionally a sex partner, when his libido overruled his heart.

* * * * *

Blake didn't want to be alone, yet he couldn't stay with Erin and not want to touch and taste and devour every square inch of the body that turned him inside out and made him forget he'd always belong to Glenna. Still naked, he went into the nursery and scooped his sleeping baby gently out of the crib.

For a long time, he just held Jamie, rocking back and forth in the old oak chair he vaguely remembered from long ago, when any one of several faceless nannies had soothed his childish dreams and given him the affection neither of his parents had time for.

That affection had been paid for by the hour. Blake hadn't known honest caring until he was five, when a tiny blond angel had befriended him, he reminded himself while he absently stroked the baby's back through the soft material of his sleeper. He choked back a cry.

As if he felt his father's anguish, Jamie began to stir against Blake's chest, his little mouth open and searching. "That's one thing I can't do for you," he said, his melancholy lessening as he deftly changed a soggy diaper and stuffed the baby into a clean, dry sleeper.

In the weeks since Jamie's birth, Blake had taken him to Erin countless times. Tonight, though, he hesitated at the door he'd closed behind him when he left her bed. At the sound of the baby's impatient howl, he pushed aside his reluctance and strode into Erin's room.

"He's hungry." His statement was unnecessary, because Jamie was making that fact abundantly clear.

Erin's head emerged from under the embroidered navy blue sheet. Had she been sleeping, or hiding from the hurt he must have inflicted on her earlier with his abrupt attack of conscience? Blake thought he saw the remains of tears on her smooth, soft cheeks, but he couldn't be sure because she turned away when he laid the baby in her arms.

"Do you want a gown, or something?" he asked, noticing that she wore nothing except the precariously draped sheet.

"Don't you?"

"What? Oh, yeah." Blake scooped up his briefs from where they'd fallen and jerked them on. Ironic, he figured, how he couldn't get his pants on fast enough now when just a few hours ago, he'd broken speed records getting them off. Self-conscious, he practically ran into Erin's dressing room and rifled through drawers to find something, anything to shield her luscious body from his gaze.

"Here." He thrust the first garment he found at her. "Put this on. I'll hold Jamie." He scooped up the baby and turned to stare out the window toward the pool.

He knew from the soft rustle of cloth that Erin was putting on whatever he'd brought her, but he wasn't going to watch. He couldn't. Jamie cried, and Blake tried to soothe the indignant baby who suddenly wanted nothing except his mother.

"I'll feed him now."

Blake didn't want to face her, but he walked to the bed and deposited Jamie in her arms. The sadness he saw in her solemn gaze flooded him with yet more guilt. "I'm sorry about tonight. Truly sorry. I know we need to talk, but can we do it later?"

"All right."

Blake fought to ignore the urge to take Erin and kiss away the pain he'd caused. His feelings were too ragged. Too jumbled. "I'm not very good company, I'm afraid. I'll see you in the morning."

He left her to nurse their baby. But he couldn't make himself close the doors between their rooms.

Chapter Fourteen

Glenna's Ghost

&

No, Blake!

It was all Glenna could do to stay in the shadows, restrain herself from materializing and giving him a piece of her mind.

Glenna sighed as she settled back in a dark corner of the hall that connected the rooms of the suite she'd once shared with Blake. She'd expected to feel jealousy tonight, for all the brave words she'd spouted to Erin about wanting her and Blake to have a real, loving marriage together.

There was a twinge of envy, I'll admit. But mostly I felt relief. Relief that Blake was finally coming out of the darkness I inflicted on him and getting ready to live again.

And anger! Now I'm just damn mad.

She'd felt a sort of smug self-satisfaction when she'd watched Blake stalk across the hall, disrobing as he went. Seeing them together earlier at the party they gave for Greg and Sandy, she'd known Blake's resistance to Erin was hanging by a thread.

Glenna had deliberately left before they sank onto the big, new bed in a tangle of long arms and legs. Staying would have been too hard. Her love for Blake didn't allow her that kind of detachment, even if she could have stomached feeling like a voyeur.

She hoped Blake had at least given Erin pleasure before he broke her heart with some infernally honest admission of...of what? All she knew for a fact was that after Blake slammed out of the big master bedroom, Erin had lain there, the covers clutched tensely between her long, slender fingers while her shoulders trembled and tears poured down her cheeks.

And she'd seen Blake take refuge in the nursery, holding on to baby Jamie like the lifeline Glenna suspected he suddenly had become, emerging and giving Erin a halfhearted apology when the baby demanded succor at his mother's breast.

"Blake, what am I going to do with you?"

He'd hurt Erin. Said something to take away the joy Erin had found in his embrace. Glenna concentrated hard, needing to reconstruct what Blake had said.

Erin, I'm not over Glenna. I don't know if I ever will be. Every time I touch you — hell, every time I look at you and want you, I feel this awful guilt. I'm not being fair to you when I feel like this. Damn it to hell, I feel like I'm being unfaithful to her!

Glenna stomped her foot against the granite slabs that paved the hallway. *"How could you?"*

I know what I'd have done if you'd ever pulled a stunt like that on me! You'd better be glad you never brought another woman into our marriage bed, Blake Tanner!

I wouldn't have lain there with tears in my eyes and let you get by with telling me you loved someone else and then walking out. It wouldn't have made a damn bit of difference to me whether the woman were dead or alive! I'd... She had to think a minute, to come up with a punishment that fit the crime. *I'd have snatched up that big amethyst crystal I used to keep on the nightstand by the bed and cracked it over your dumb, unfeeling skull. Then...*

Glenna grinned at the thought of hard, brittle crystal fracturing over Blake's unsuspecting head. It felt exhilarating — almost as if she were alive again — to give a human emotion like jealousy and anger free rein, if only for a moment.

Could she go to Blake? Make him realize she was gone and he needed to let go of the past and live for now and tomorrow? Glenna shook her head. She could never reveal herself to him, no matter what. She'd decided that months ago, and nothing had happened to make her change her mind. Willing herself into Erin's presence, she materialized at the foot of the king-size bed.

What can I say to make her hurt less?

At a loss for words, Glenna stood and looked down on Erin, who had finally fallen asleep with tiny Jamie curled contentedly in her arms. She wouldn't wake Erin now.

Maybe she'd leave the task of smoothing Erin's battered feelings to Blake. He'd always been good at giving comfort, at least to her. Glenna couldn't help feeling that since Blake had been the one dishing out the pain, he was the only one who could truly ease it.

"I hope Blake's hurting as much as he hurt her tonight," Glenna whispered to the wind as she slowly faded into the limbo she couldn't escape, not until she righted the wrongs her well-meant actions had brought to the ones she loved.

Chapter Fifteen

∽

Blake pounded a fist into his pillow. He might as well get up, because tonight sleep was out of the question. Visions of a dark, sensual lover mingled in his head with those of a sweet Madonna nursing her baby. And a disturbingly fuzzy picture of Glenna tortured Blake throughout the night. He shouldn't have gone to bed at all, he told himself as he watched the sun rise through a long, narrow window that overlooked the stable.

Cursing Glenna and Erin and the whole damn situation, Blake stumbled out of bed and called Greg. He figured a long, hard ride would either wake him up or get him so damn exhausted he might be able to get some rest. Then he threw on jeans and a shirt before tugging on his boots and hurrying out to saddle the horses.

"You look like hell," Greg observed when they met outside the grassy paddock.

Blake managed a tired grin. "You're a great one to talk. Did one of your patients keep you up all night after you left the party?"

"No. Sandy did." Greg's expression darkened. "Is this horse tame?"

"Gentle as a kitten. I picked her out for Erin. Her name's Blaze."

"What brought on the invitation for an early morning ride?" Greg swung into the saddle and stroked the mare's neck.

"Impulse. And the realization that I wasn't going to get any sleep no matter how long I lay in bed." Not ready yet for serious discussion, Blake snapped the reins and took off on Renegade toward a wooded bridle path that wound around the back of his property.

The soft thud of metal-clad hooves against the moist clay of the trail and intermittent squawks of birds frightened at the equine invasion of territory long left to them reminded Blake of times long ago when he'd ridden this trail every morning before school. Times before Erin...before Glenna.

"Simpler times."

"What?" Greg asked.

Blake glanced over at Greg, realizing he had spoken out loud. "I was just thinking how much simpler life was when we were kids."

"As in?"

"Feelings. At the time, I never realized how easy I had it. My biggest worry was whether to spend the day riding, or studying, or lounging by the pool."

Greg let out a sigh. "Those were the days, all right."

"Dealing with one woman is hard enough. How do you manage, juggling not one but three and sometimes four or five?" Blake asked, recalling the tension that filled the air last night when Greg's daughter, mother and fiancée took civilized potshots at each other.

"I don't—at least not well enough." Greg shifted in the saddle before going on. "Sandy lets Shana snipe at her, and then lets me have it over my kid's nasty behavior. Shana whines to me about everything under the sun. And Mom gives me hell over them, Kay, Rhea and everything else she can think of. I guess I do a pretty decent job, letting their whining go in one ear and out the other."

Blake cleared his throat. "Well, if you can come up with ten thousand dollars cash, your worries with Rhea will be over. Her lawyer called me yesterday."

"Why didn't you say so earlier? Ten grand's just five months' worth of alimony."

Blake shrugged. "Your engagement party, remember. Somehow it didn't seem the proper place or time to bring up ex-wives and alimony."

"Why didn't someone drill that idea into my daughter's head?" Greg asked with a self-deprecating grin.

"Mom Sadie tried."

Greg looked surprised. "She did?"

"Yes. While you were at the buffet getting your mother some food, Shana took it on herself to tell Sandy how her mom's engagement rings, current and past, were so much bigger and better than Sandy's. Sadie shut her up before she could whip Sandy into a state of total fury."

"So that's what set Sandy off," Greg commented thoughtfully. "I wondered. Couldn't see much reason for the way she was screaming and ranting over the way I let my kid get away with murder."

"How did you settle it?"

"The usual way. Sweet words and hot sex. The thing that worries me is that I didn't really settle it at all. The only difference between this morning and last night is that for the moment Sandy at least believes I love her to pieces and can't keep my hands off her."

"But that's not enough for her?"

"It was, at the time. But Shana isn't going to turn into Little Miss Muffet, and Sandy's not about to give her an inch. Kay won't be back soon enough to keep the fur from flying, and Mom's getting too old to referee their fights."

Blake felt for Greg, who might as well have been on a medieval rack the way his emotions were being tugged in all directions by the three strong-minded women he loved. "How do you take it?" he asked as they reined in their horses in front of the stable and dismounted.

"One hour at a time. When I'm working, I just put it all out of my mind and concentrate on my patients. Hell, I know I should have picked some quiet, biddable woman without an independent thought in her head. But then if I had, she wouldn't give me the fire and lightning I've found with Sandy," Greg admitted with a grin.

Greg had himself pegged. Blake figured his friend must like having unrealistic demands placed on him. If he didn't, he wouldn't have taken up medicine at all, much less the sometimes heartbreaking subspecialty of high-risk OB. It was logical for him to thrive on demanding women as well.

"Unlike you, my friend, I like living in peace. I'll take my well-behaved boys and my lovely, tranquil wife, and leave the fireworks to you." Blake realized he'd referred to Erin and not Glenna when he spoke.

Erin had brought Blake a degree of peace when he most needed it, he realized while he silently rubbed down Renegade and put away the tack. Her calm and tranquil manner, the soft and soothing timbre of her distinctive West Texas drawl, the gentle sway of slender hips when she moved, all joined to create a restful aura in his home. An aura that was helping him heal.

"Blake?"

"Yeah, Greg?"

"Are you going to rub all the skin off that big black beast of yours?"

Blake looked at the currycomb in his hand. He *had* been going over the same spot on Renegade's muscled shoulder for a long time. Sheepishly he hung the grooming tool on a peg and joined Greg. "I was just thinking."

"Let's have some breakfast. Then I'll go tackle taming Shana while you sit back and enjoy…"

"If you and Sandy aren't doing anything tonight, come on over. Bring Shana, too. We can barbecue some steaks and play around in the pool."

Greg accepted his invitation almost too quickly, as if he were grasping at ways to keep a buffer between himself, Sandy and his daughter. As Blake walked back toward his house, he wondered if he, too, might be looking for excuses to delay facing up to how he had hurt Erin by venting his own grief and guilt.

* * * * *

"Did you enjoy your swim?" Erin asked Shana when she joined her and Timmy at a table beside the pool that afternoon.

"It was okay. Your pool is bigger than Dad's." She glanced over at the grill, where Blake and Greg were busy preparing the coals for steaks Erin had just brought from the kitchen. "You're a lot older than Sandy, aren't you?" Shana asked, her appraising gaze returning to Erin.

"Ten years. Sandy came to live with me after our parents died. She was just a few years older than you are now."

"You must have been awful to her. I bet that's why she's such a witch to me." Shana's nose wrinkled with apparent disgust.

Erin bit back a rude reply. "How do you figure my sister's being a witch?" Though she wouldn't say so, she figured Shana had it mixed up as to who was the witch in Greg's life.

"You wouldn't understand."

A car horn blared, and Shana bolted from her chair. "That's Marisa and her mom. We're going riding."

As she watched Shana grab her designer gym bag and sprint toward her friend's car, Erin shook her head. The spoiled young girl was gorgeous when she smiled. Pity she did it so seldom around her dad and Sandy.

"She's gone?" Sandy sounded relieved when she came outside, a carafe of wine in hand.

"Yes." The tension hung heavily in the air, but Erin didn't know how to relieve it. She almost wished Blake hadn't arranged this impromptu get-together, even though she'd liked the idea this morning as a possible diversion from her own tattered emotions.

"Well, sweetheart, you can breathe easy now," Greg told Sandy with false heartiness when he came over and joined them.

Sandy shrugged. "Maybe you can breathe easy, but I can't. You let her have her way again."

"Sorry, baby. I have a hard time telling my women no. Hey, Tim, how's it going?" he asked, playfully ruffling Timmy's hair. "Want to go swim?"

Timmy had already been in the water twice. Erin wasn't surprised when her son shook his head and told them he thought he'd go inside and practice Nintendo.

"Sandy?"

"What? No, Greg, I think I'll just sit with Erin and watch the sun go down."

Was there trouble in Sandy's paradise? Sensitized by her own raw feelings, Erin felt a subtle undercurrent of dissension between affable, easygoing Greg and her strong-minded young sister.

She had no time to find out what was going on, though. Before she could ask Sandy, Blake was there, not asking but insisting she help him check out the steaks.

"Something's going on between Sandy and Greg," she murmured just loudly enough for him to hear.

He nodded. "One word. Shana," he whispered as he held up a big T-bone steak at the end of a long-handled fork.

"What do you mean?"

"Greg's having one hell of a time trying to keep his little girl and Sandy from tearing him in two."

"I can't believe Sandy would try to turn Greg against his own child." Erin looked over at the telling scene of Greg doing determined laps in the pool while Sandy sat at a table, looking more than vaguely annoyed as she swirled her wine rhythmically around in a stemmed glass.

"It's not deliberate, at least not on Sandy's part, or at least that's the impression I get. Still, Greg is smarting over the knock-down-drag-out argument they had last night. Sandy thinks he lets Shana get away with anything short of murder."

"I don't blame her. It was all I could do last night to keep from grabbing Shana and shaking her silly." Erin frowned. Blake had been the one to step in and tell Shana to knock off her complaining. She didn't need to protect her sister from him. "You noticed how rude Shana was acting, too."

"I noticed. So did Greg. But underneath that laid-back attitude he shows the world, Greg's burying a soul brimming over with intensity. He never says much, but he's always felt guilty for not having done more to give his daughter a stable, two-parent family." Blake set the steak back onto the iced platter where it had been and replaced a domed, thermal lid to keep the meat chilled until they got ready to cook.

Erin couldn't help thinking that Blake himself carried around more than his own share of misplaced torment. "I know it's been hard on Sandy, too. She loves Greg so much. She wants to love Shana, but Shana wants no part of her."

Blake reached out and stroked her hand, as if to reassure her. Despite the way he left her last night, and the fact that he had avoided the talk he admitted they must have, Erin felt a jolt of sexual awareness at the casual contact. Reflexively, she jerked her hand away.

"You want no part of me now, either, do you?"

"You said we needed to talk, Blake. Last night wasn't the time or place for you. Now's not right, either. We need to entertain our guests, and looks as though it's just about time for us to start cooking those steaks."

As the evening wore on, Erin tried to make Sandy laugh. Blake teased Greg until he instigated a game of pool tag that forced both couples to touch and communicate, at least on a superficial level.

"Here, catch," Sandy cried, tossing the bright yellow beach ball at Erin. Blake leaped high, captured the prize and passed it neatly in Greg's direction before Erin managed to grab him from behind and pull him underwater.

"Oh, no, you don't!" Sputtering and laughing, Blake took off after Erin. Pretending terror, she squealed before taking a deep breath in preparation for her own dunking.

"You can do better than that, Blake," Greg called from the other end of the pool, and Blake took up the challenge by lifting Erin high in the air.

She braced herself to hit the water, but it didn't happen. Instead, he lowered her slowly, stopping when their gazes met and locking their mouths together in a hard, hungry kiss. When they came up for air, Erin burrowed her face into his chest. She knew her cheeks had to be beet-red, and she didn't want to seem like a crush-crazed teenager.

Blake didn't leave well enough alone. Laughing, he grabbed the top of her suit and dragged it down, exposing a nipple for him to nibble.

"Hey, you guys, that looks like fun," Greg yelled, scooping Sandy up and nibbling suggestively at her neck before grabbing her butt and grinding her belly into his crotch.

"How about it, Erin? Are we having fun?" Cupping her breast, Blake sucked the nipple into his mouth, sending shards of delicious, electric sensations all the way to her pussy.

Two—or four—could play these silly, arousing games. Erin lowered her hand into the water, found the waistband of Blake's swim trunks, and ran her fingers under the elastic until they grazed the swollen head of his cock.

"No fair," Greg yelled when Sandy got his suit off and tossed it onto the deck. "You're gonna pay now."

Sandy's suit soon followed, and though she wasn't about to look, Erin guessed from listening to the whimpers and moans that her sister and Greg had made up—at least for the moment.

"They're making love," Blake whispered against her puckered nipple. "Shall we?"

"Shhh." Group sex might be Sandy's thing, but it wasn't Erin's. "Behave yourself."

"Okay. But spread your legs. If I can't fuck you, at least I can make you feel real good."

He did. Before she could drag his fingers out of her pussy, she was whining and whimpering and wanting more…

More than he had to give. But he did make this sex game fun. By the time Greg and Sandy streaked across the deck to get their clothes, Erin was trembling with pleasure.

After finishing their childish game of one-upmanship, Greg and Blake seemed determined to keep up the playful banter as the sun went down. Erin wished she'd known Blake years ago, when he and Greg had been fun-loving college boys. Before failed relationships had molded Greg and tragedy touched Blake.

Erin didn't want to love Blake, but it was too late now for her to guard her heart. Not only did she love him, she liked him. Tonight he'd shown her a genuinely decent man who went out of his way to make good friends forget their woes.

By the time Sandy and Greg left, the physical attraction was crackling between them. There was nothing wrong with the chemistry between her and Blake, either.

Erin bade him a friendly, warm good night and went inside to tuck in Timmy and nurse baby Jamie. She hoped he'd come and join her, not to rehash the guilty feelings she was certain still plagued him, but to put out the sexual fire he'd stoked with nearness and goodwill.

* * * * *

"May I come in?"

Last night, Blake hadn't asked, but then Erin had invited him with blatant actions instead of words. Tonight he felt he was intruding into this space he'd designated as hers.

"Of course. Jamie's just about done nursing." Erin smiled down at the dark-haired baby who was nodding off to sleep at her breast.

Self-conscious, Blake took a seat on the edge of the bed. The sexual foreplay and suggestive conversation he'd initiated for the benefit of Greg and Sandy had backfired, because he wanted nothing more right now than to haul Jamie off to his crib and hurry back to take his fill of Erin.

"I promised we'd talk," he said when all he wanted to do was fuck her until he forgot all the reasons he shouldn't want her. Damn it, he felt like a total jerk. "I didn't mean to hurt you."

"I know. Here, put Jamie to bed and I'll slip into something more comfortable." She smiled when he cuddled the baby snugly against his chest.

If Blake didn't know better, he'd have thought Erin was out to seduce him. He doubted if that was going to happen, though, after the way he'd left her last night. Tucking a blanket around Jamie's plump, warm body, he checked the baby one more time before going back to Erin's room. This time he settled himself on a chair, out of temptation's way, and met her solemn gaze.

But was she solemn? Blake would swear he saw fire in those deep, blue eyes, strung-out need in the way she clasped her fingers against the quilted satin coverlet. He couldn't help noticing pale, narrow straps across her slender shoulders, or the top of a lacy nightgown that barely veiled her beautiful breasts.

Every day he was learning there was more to Erin than the calm, rational mother...big sister...friend. Last night, she'd shown him the sort of earthy sensuality he'd only dreamed about. Her fierce defense of Sandy proved she could fight tough and dirty if need be, for someone she loved.

If it weren't for the damn strangulating guilt he couldn't set aside, Blake could easily love this woman who was his wife. And he couldn't let that happen. It wouldn't be fair to Glenna. "I shouldn't have said what I did last night," he ventured gruffly. "I wanted you just as much as you wanted me. Probably more."

"I doubt that." Erin smiled, a slow, seductive grin that made his balls tighten, his cock swell.

"Let me apologize, Erin."

"Don't. I understand."

Blake shifted in the chair. "I'm glad you do, because I'm having a hard time understanding it myself."

"Look. We may be married, but we don't know each other all that well. Maybe the chemistry between us has something to do with—"

"Damn it, don't tell me I can barely keep my hands off you just because you had my baby. I've tried persuading myself that, and it won't wash. I want you because you're gorgeous and sexy and you're my wife, and wanting you is eating me alive.

"If I stay away from you, I hurt. And I feel just as guilty if I don't touch you as if I do, because I want you so damn much."

Blake watched Erin slip gracefully out of bed and cross the room to kneel at his feet. "Glenna wouldn't want you to go through life alone," she said, taking one of his hands and sandwiching it between her own in a gesture more comforting than arousing.

"How would you know what she would want? You hardly knew her. Can you possibly believe it wouldn't hurt her to know my cock is constantly throbbing for another woman just six months after she's been gone?" He rested his head on his chest, trying not to feel the gentle touch of Erin's fingers as she massaged his scalp.

"I know."

How could she sound so certain? She'd met Glenna just once, not long before she died. He, on the other hand, had known and loved Glenna most of his life…had known without a doubt that she loved him, too. Still he couldn't reach into Glenna's heart and be certain of how she'd feel today.

He'd almost found the words to express his doubt when Erin spoke. "Let's forget last night. We're hardly more than strangers in a lot of ways. Why don't we ignore the chemistry, get to know each other, and try to be friends?"

Her hands stilled, then withdrew. Slowly, she stood and moved to the chair at the other side of what seemed at the moment to be an insurmountable expanse of plate-glass wall. "All right, if that's what you want," he said, wondering how the hell he was supposed to forget how she turned him hard as stone and single-minded as a teenager hot on the heels of his first pussy.

"Is there anything we can do to help them cope with Shana?" she asked, abruptly changing the subject.

Blake forced a grin. "We could buy a one-way ticket for Miss Shana to join up with her mom and stepdad over in Athens or wherever they are," he said, only half kidding.

He liked the way Erin smiled, and the sassy look she gave him when she said, "Be serious."

"A muzzle?"

"Blake!"

He thought for a minute. "I could talk to Greg about the way he buys that child everything under the sun."

Now Erin laughed out loud. "This from the man who hardly ever comes back home without some new present for Jamie and Tim?"

"Yeah. Do I buy them too much stuff?"

"No," she finally said. "It would be too much if you didn't give them just as much of your time and attention, though."

"As far as I know, Greg has spent all the time the courts allow him with his daughter." He met Erin's gaze and instantly regretted their decision to turn down the heat on their relationship. "Hasn't he?"

"I guess so. Sandy's never said otherwise."

"Then maybe Shana's just reacting to the prospect of having a stepmother who's closer to her age than Greg's," Blake suggested, grasping at straws. Hell, what did he know about the care and feeding of a twelve-year-old girl?

"You may be right. I don't know. Sandy came to live with Bill and me when she was just sixteen, and she never gave me the kind of grief she's putting up with now."

Blake shrugged. "The girl may be just antsy about having any stepmother at all. Or Kay may have poisoned her mind about Greg, or Sandy, or both of them. I wouldn't put it past her." After all, the woman had a penchant for damning other people with innuendo veiled in a cloak of cultured civility. It would be a long time before he forgave or forgot the remarks Kay had made the day before Jamie's birth.

"Would Greg's ex-wife actually do something that mean?"

Erin obviously had never met Kay Halpern. Blake had witnessed the woman going for people's jugulars just for the fun of it. "I wouldn't put much past Kay if she was sufficiently provoked."

"Oh. Maybe I should let Sandy know what kind of influence Shana's been living with for all these years. It might make her go easier, be more understanding…"

"I'm sure she knows. There are damn few people close to Greg that he hasn't discussed Kay's antics with. When the two of them get together in the same room, I try to be sure there's a fire extinguisher on hand."

"They get together?"

Together was hardly the word Blake would choose to describe encounters between Greg and Kay. "Only to fight over alimony and child support, so far as I know. I'm surprised you didn't hear the fireworks when we had that meeting here, the afternoon before Jamie was born."

"I was otherwise occupied, I'm afraid. I didn't know you do divorces."

"I don't. And I didn't 'do' either of Greg's divorces. Kay and Rhea, his second wife, both took him to the cleaners. He asked me to attempt some damage control so he could afford to marry Sandy."

"I guess you were successful."

"Moderately. Kay's remarriage had more to do with the success than any skills I may have."

"I doubt that." He felt a surprising wave of contentment at her vote of confidence. "But we're not going to solve the world's problems, or Sandy's and Greg's, either, tonight. Don't you think it's time we got some sleep?"

Blake could think of several things he'd rather be doing than sleeping, though all of them involved making use of the big bed that suddenly seemed to fill the room. Beating down his sex drive, he tucked Erin into the king-size bed and brushed his lips briefly across hers.

Across the hall in his own lonely room, he kicked himself for not having crawled in bed with Erin. He could have lived with the guilt to get the pleasure.

Chapter Sixteen

ℰ

Peace was not in the cards for Greg. The minute they arrived at her apartment, Sandy laid into him again, this time over his giving in and lifting Shana's latest restriction to let her spend the night with a friend.

"She's just a little girl," he said in his most conciliatory tone.

Sandy stood up and put her hands firmly at her luscious hips. "Shana is a miserable spoiled brat. You're not entirely responsible for that, but you certainly do your share. Why did you say she could go riding and then spend the night tonight with Marisa?"

Greg shrugged his shoulders. "Would you believe so we could have some time alone?"

"Normally, I would, if you hadn't told your daughter just this morning that she'd be grounded for the rest of the weekend. Greg, you can't give in to her every little demand. Don't you know anything about being a parent?"

"You don't like Shana. That's what all this boils down to, doesn't it?" It bugged hell out of Greg when Sandy badmouthed his parenting skills. Probably because her complaints weren't altogether unfounded.

Sandy whirled around to face windows that looked out onto nothing but an empty street. "I'm trying really hard to like her because she's your daughter. But she's tearing us apart. Can't you see what Shana's doing?"

"She's my little girl, sweetheart."

"And she's determined to make my life miserable!"

Greg moved closer and tentatively touched Sandy's tense shoulders with both his hands. "You two got along all right before Shana came to stay with me."

"That was because all I did with her then was haul her wherever you told me to, which meant she considered me nothing but just another one of the hired help."

Greg stroked a pulsating vein at Sandy's throat. "Be reasonable, sweetheart. Shana's having to adjust to her mom being gone, and living with me for a while—us, after we get married next month. Try to see things as she does."

Sandy turned on him, her eyes flashing blue-green fire. "You mean, see you as a never-ending supplier of designer furniture and designer clothes that are never quite good enough for her royal little self? And myself as the combination maid, cook, chauffeur, and laundress, whose sole purpose on this earth is to cater to her every whim?"

"For God's sake, cut the kid some slack. It's not easy to grow up in a broken home. Besides, you don't know Shana's mother."

"What does your ex-wife have to do with your daughter's being a brat?"

Greg had to laugh. "Shana is her mother's daughter. Practically a carbon copy, personality-wise. It's as much my fault as Kay's, I suppose, since I never fought to be a bigger part of Shana's life after we divorced."

"Why?"

"Because at first I was too busy, trying to finish my residency and establish a practice. I let Kay get the divorce and worked like a dog to make enough money to pay her the alimony and support she demanded. I couldn't afford to take her back to court. But I've always seen Shana as often as the judge's decree allowed."

Sandy scowled. "And you've catered to her as if she were a precious little princess. You've never insisted that she behave, or followed through with punishing her when she decides to be unbearably rude. You've helped her mother create a monster, and damn it, Greg, you're still at it!"

"Please, sweetheart, getting mad isn't helping us solve anything." If she didn't calm down, she might walk out, and he couldn't stand that. Maybe if he seduced her...smoothly, quickly, he slid his arms around her waist and drew her tightly into his arms.

"Making love isn't going to solve anything, either," Sandy stammered, her voice muffled by the cloth of his shirt as she burrowed tighter against his chest.

"It won't?" He, for one, thought they needed to ease the tension, or rather convert its direction from anger to passion.

"No."

She sounded so sad, yet so certain. Greg sank onto a little sofa and pulled her onto his lap. "What do you want me to do?" He wiped away a tear that was making its way down her flushed cheek.

"I don't know. Greg, I need some time to think. Go home. I'll see you at work on Monday." Her expression resolute, Sandy got up, moved to the door, and stepped back so he could leave.

He was losing her. He felt her withdrawing bit by bit, and he didn't know what the hell he could do about it. On the way home, and later in a bed that felt cold and empty without her in it, Greg tried to hold on to his anger, if only to keep the fear in his gut at bay.

He didn't doubt Sandy loved him. Not at all. But it was becoming painfully clear that love alone wasn't going to be strong enough to weather the storms that hit every time Sandy had to endure one of Shana's snide attacks.

Somehow he had to reach his daughter, let her know he loved her but that he expected, no demanded, that she treat Sandy with the respect that was due her as his fiancée. How he'd manage this, he'd have to decide as he went along. That determined, Greg fell into a restless sleep.

In the morning after he visited his hospitalized patients, he picked up Shana from the sleepover that had set Sandy off.

"Shana, we need to have a little talk," he said sternly as they pulled into the driveway at his brand-new home.

* * * * *

"Shana's just a child," Erin pointed out reasonably to Sandy as she turned Jamie to nurse at her other breast.

Sandy shook her head with disgust. "She's a monster. And Greg won't do a damn thing about it."

"Why don't you talk to him?" She hated that she had no ready answers for her sister as to how to handle a recalcitrant preteen.

"I have. He just makes excuses for her, says she's the way she is because she comes from a broken home and all that psychobabble. Darn it all, our folks died when I wasn't a whole lot older than Shana, and I came to live with you and Bill. I had just lost my mom and dad, and on top of that, I had to leave all my friends back home. I was hurting a whole lot more than a kid whose biggest gripe is that her daddy won't buy her more than fifty pairs of jeans. But I didn't act that way. Did I?"

Erin smiled. Sandy hadn't been exactly a model teen, but then she had never had a mean bone in her body, either. "No. Not exactly. But it took a bit of adjustment for us, too, before you really accepted me as any kind of authority figure."

"Really?"

"Yes, really. And as I recall, you never really took much Bill told you as law, until I backed up his orders. Trying to be a parent to a girl just a few years younger than he was taxed his patience just about to the limit, lots of times." Erin recalled the stress that having responsibility for her sister had often placed on an already shaky marriage.

Sandy stood, her stance indignant. "I was never rude or mean or…"

"Yes, you were. Not often, but sometimes when you'd get really homesick, you got to be a real pain."

"Bill used to say I was jealous of Timmy," Sandy said quietly, as if she were trying to remember those times when she was more typical teenager than angel.

"Even before Timmy was born." Erin recalled the times when she'd been tugged from all directions, helpless to divide her loyalties adequately among her husband, her young sister, and her then-unborn son.

"Really?" Sandy looked stricken at the idea that she'd caused Erin any grief.

"Not all of that tension had to do with you." Erin couldn't let Sandy shoulder the blame for a situation long ago where she and Bill had been more at fault than the teenager whose life had been forever changed by their parents' untimely deaths.

Jamie had stopped nursing and gone to sleep, Erin noticed when she glanced down and watched the baby's dark eyelashes flutter closed against his soft, pink cheek. "Let me put him in his crib."

"What should I do?" Sandy asked bluntly once they'd moved out onto the patio to continue their visit in the warmth of a late September afternoon.

"What do you want to do?"

"I'm going to give Greg his ring back. I can't cope with his daughter."

Erin couldn't help it. She had to smile. "That's what Bill told me he'd have done if we hadn't already been married when you came to live with us."

Sandy's eyes widened. "That jerk!"

"And you're any less of one?"

"W-what do you mean?"

Erin couldn't tell if she was hurt or just plain angry. "Do you love Greg?"

Sandy's reply was instant and indignant. "Of course I do. I love Greg with all my heart. But I can't cope with Shana."

Six months, even three months ago, Erin had questioned the wisdom of a match between her sister and a man who, in addition to being fifteen years older and saddled with the emotional baggage of two failed relationships, was very obviously married to his work. Since then, though, she'd gotten to know and respect Greg, and she'd seen how he was changing his lifestyle to make Sandy, not medicine, the focal point of his life. Most of all, Greg had shown not just Erin, but everyone he came in contact with, that he loved her sister with the kind of love Erin had always wanted for herself.

Bill hadn't loved her that way, and neither did Blake. *Fool. Blake doesn't love you at all.* Quickly Erin shook off that sudden wave of self-pity and met Sandy's questioning gaze.

"What were you thinking?" Sandy asked.

"About you and Greg, and how sad it is that you love each other so much."

"What do you mean, it's sad?"

"That you're going to break up because you're such a coward you can't handle one kid who isn't even a teenager yet," Erin said soberly, intentionally baiting Sandy now.

"What do you mean, I'm a coward? I've tried everything I know how to do to make Shana like me."

Erin met her sister's accusing gaze. "Maybe you've been trying to make her like you, when you should be working at earning her respect."

"I don't think she respects anyone." Sandy sounded sad, defeated.

"Sadie."

"What about Greg's mother?"

"Shana respects her. Remember night before last, when just a word from Sadie shut her up like a clam?"

"Well, that's different. No kid would be out-and-out rude to her own grandmother."

"The way we grew up, Sandy, we wouldn't have dared be rude to anyone older than we were. But it's obvious that Shana hasn't learned that fine point of courtesy as yet. What do you think makes her toe the line for Sadie?"

"Is that a trick question?"

"Is it?" Erin watched Sandy's expression change from one of despair to one of tentative hope.

"Shana won't buck her grandmother's orders because she knows Sadie would chew her up and spit her out," Sandy finally replied.

"But you're so weak you can't put the pressure on one child? Is that what you're saying when you're threatening to walk out on a man you love to distraction?" After tossing that challenge, Erin waited, taking heart when Sandy's expression turned fierce.

"No. I'll bring the little princess around if I have to kill her to do it," Sandy declared through clenched teeth. "No twelve-year-old is going to get me down. She's not going to make me give up her daddy, either. By the time I'm done, that little wildcat will be as tame as that big, fat Persian cat that used to live across the road from us when we were kids."

* * * * *

Greg had stalled as long as he could. He went out on the patio, carrying a chilled bottle of raspberry seltzer for his daughter and an icy can of beer for himself. He should have grabbed the whole damn six-pack, he thought when he looked at Shana. God, how he hated that bored, pouty look she affected whenever he tried to get her into anything bordering on real conversation.

"Thank you," Shana muttered, stretching coltish legs out on the chaise as if she were a rock star and he the lackey charged with seeing to her needs.

Holding on to his temper by reminding himself that whatever Shana was, he was just as much at fault for it as Kay, Greg pulled up a chair and sat, close enough to touch the child he loved but did not understand. Before he spoke, he chose his words as carefully as if he were trying to cushion the blow of devastating news to one of his patients.

"What's wrong?" he finally asked.

"I hate you and that simple child you're going to marry. I hate this house and having to stay here when I could be having lots more fun at home. And I can't stand the way all of you treat me like I'm a baby." Shana accompanied her dramatic announcement with tears that came close to breaking Greg's heart.

"Maybe we treat you like a child because you act like one. Actually, you *are* still a child, princess."

"Whatever." Shana fixed her petulant gaze on some point on the other side of the pool.

Greg had to remind himself this child was the daughter he'd walked away from when he left her mother. "We need to discuss your manners, young lady," he said in the tone of voice that got nurses and interns cracking to follow his orders.

"My manners are just fine. Mother's made sure I know which fork to pick up and what to wear. Has little Sandy been whining again?"

Greg itched to drag her off that lounge chair and shake her until she begged for mercy. Damn it to hell, if Shana could get down and dirty, so could he. Clenching his fists to keep from smacking her, he riddled her with the dirtiest look he could come up with.

"We're not talking about my fiancée, we're talking about you. And from what I've seen in the week you've been with me, I'd say your mother has sadly neglected your education in basic human relations. She may let you get away with being rude and snide, Shana, but I've got news for you. I won't."

Shana tossed her head like a young, frisky filly. "Whatever."

"Remove that disgusting expression from your vocabulary." Sandy was right, his daughter could be impossible.

She sat up straight and stared him down. "Whatever," she repeated, and Greg sprang to his feet.

"You're grounded for a month," he shouted, feeling his blood pressure soar. "Forget riding lessons. Forget seeing your friends outside of school. And don't even think about going shopping. If you're lucky, I'll let you out of your room long enough to apologize to Sandy for the way you've been treating her."

"And what makes you think I will? I don't like her. All my friends think you must be a dirty old man, marrying a *shiksa* who's young enough to be your kid. You're both *disgusting*." She drew out that last word, emphasizing every syllable.

"That sounds like your mother talking, Shana. And it's a damn stupid statement, to boot. I'd have had to be pretty precocious to have fathered a baby when I was fourteen." When Greg realized how childish it was to take his own child's bait, he abandoned the sarcasm. "Besides, it's not your business."

"Whatever. Nothing's my business. But it screws up my life just the same. Mother didn't ask me before she decided to marry Pop Abe, who's got grandchildren older than me. You don't care that I can't stand Sandy. Do you have any idea how *humiliating* it is to admit I'm going to have a stepfather as old as Grandma Sadie and a stepmother that's not much older than me?"

That hurt, because at least the first of Shana's impassioned statements was true. He *hadn't* considered his daughter's feelings about his engagement to Sandy, any more than he'd consulted her several years ago before marrying Rhea. And he knew damn well Kay's only thoughts when she decided to become Mrs. Abe Goldman were of herself. Kay was that way.

Humiliating? Now that was a bit extreme. "There's nothing for you to be upset about, Shana. It's natural for men and women to want to share their lives with someone else. You know, honey, differences in age get less important when we get older. I love Sandy, and I'm sure your mother feels the same about Pop Abe. But we both love you."

Shana turned on him like a riled-up wildcat. He grabbed her wrists to keep her from pummeling his chest with furious fists. "Sure you do," she snarled. "Mother cares so much, she left to cruise around the world with him. And the only reason I'm here instead of stuck in some geeky boarding school is because she bribed you to take me!"

"What?"

"Don't try and say she didn't. Mother told me she let you out of supporting us to make you take care of me while she and Abe play kissy-face on some stupid world tour."

Greg wished Kay were around so he could strangle her. "I wanted you with me," The tears that hung in his little girl's dark eyes damn near killed him. He'd give anything to take away the pain she hid under her brittle, sullen exterior.

"Sandy wants you, too." That was true. At least it had been, at first.

"You wanted to quit giving us money so you could afford to marry her. Mother said so."

Greg reached out and stroked Shana's damp, flushed cheek. What could he do or say that would sweep away the bitterness Kay had instilled in his only child? "There's a lot of animosity between your mom and me," he said when she didn't immediately pull away. "That doesn't mean we don't both love you."

Shana shook her head and backed away. "You mean you didn't want the money?"

"The only thing I wanted was to be able to make a home for myself, and for you." Reading the disbelief in Shana's gaze, he went on. "To do that, I had to ask your mother to accept less alimony. She made that possible when she decided to get married again."

Tossing her dark hair over her shoulder, Shana sat back down, looking up at him with those dark, mistrustful eyes. "Why did you and Mother ever have me? Why couldn't I have parents like Marisa's? They're divorced, too, but they live just around the corner from each other. Her mom and stepfather even play cards once a week with her dad and stepmom. They're cool."

The swinging pathologists? He just bet they were playing cards when they got together. Greg closed his mouth before he burst his daughter's bubble. It wouldn't make Shana feel better to know Tom and Elaine and Mark and Cecilia had swapped off for years before making what hospital gossips insisted was a purely fanciful legal change of partners. Instead, he felt compelled to apologize for the way he and Kay had hurt Shana while attempting to injure each other.

"I'm sorry we're not cool, as you say. Your mom and I tried, but I guess neither of us tried hard enough to keep on loving each other. Before I left, we'd said and done too many mean, bitter things. There was no way we'd ever be friends. But Shana, we're both entitled to a little slice of happiness. My loving Sandy doesn't take away any of the love I feel for you, and I'm sure your mom doesn't love you less because she loves Mr. Goldman, too."

Greg could tell Shana wasn't buying into what he was saying. He watched the way her fingers tapped impatiently against the wicker arm of her chair. "He treated me just fine until he married Mother and they dumped me here with you."

"They deserve a little time to themselves, don't you think?"

"Six months?"

Privately, Greg thought Kay and her aging billionaire had gone overboard on their honeymoon plans, but it wouldn't do for him to say so. "It isn't really that long, when you think about it."

"Whatever. Do I get to stay here with prune-faced old Mrs. Watson while you take a trip to Tahiti or something?" Shana asked, her voice dripping sarcasm.

"No. I can't take that much time away from work. We'll just be taking a long weekend out at Possum Kingdom. You will be staying with Nana Sadie. Look, Shana. We've gotten off track here. I'm sorry you feel so put upon, but we were discussing your behavior."

"What do you want me to do? Lie and pretend I'm all happy because you're going to get married again? I'll never get to see you at all."

Greg offered up silent thanks to God that he had decided against a specialty in child psychiatry. He'd never understand kids, if his own daughter was typical. "What makes you say that?"

"Sandy doesn't like me any more than I like her. Once you're married, she'll make sure you don't have any time at all for me. Rhea did, and she was sweet as sugar to me when you were dating."

Greg thought he saw Shana's lower lip tremble, but he wasn't sure. "Rhea fooled me, too. You're here now, and you're staying until your mother gets home. We're going to be seeing a lot of each other, especially since you're acting like such a brat that I'll have to keep you on a tight leash."

"Oh, Daddy, you won't do that, will you?"

Now he had a feeling he was being conned. "I will, and there will be no wheedling your way out of your punishment."

"A whole *month*?" Shana's expression reflected horror along with a goodly dose of skepticism.

"Look, Shana. I'll make you a deal. We'll do this a week at the time. You apologize to Sandy and mean it. And you remember to treat her and everybody else you come in contact with respect and kindness. We'll talk about parole next Sunday."

Shana's mouth dropped open. "You're really going to marry her, aren't you?"

"Come hell or high water, princess. Give Sandy a chance. She's not your mom, but she'd like to be your friend."

They talked for a few more minutes before going inside. That night as Greg tried to get some sleep, he hoped to hell he had gotten through to the little girl who looked like him, but inside seemed to be almost a carbon copy of Kay. At least he felt fairly confident that his daughter wouldn't dare keep needling the woman he loved.

* * * * *

"How do you do it?" he asked Blake when they met the next morning to exercise the horses.

Blake hadn't the vaguest idea what Greg was talking about. "What?"

"Make your stepson crazy about you."

"My son. I've adopted Timmy. I guess he likes me because I like him and show it. He's a fantastic little kid. I wish I had half his courage." The cool, dry morning air was doing its job, and Blake was beginning to shake the cobwebs off his sluggish brain.

Greg sighed. "He is a brave little guy. How's his therapy coming?"

"Erin and I have to meet with his doctor next Monday. From what Michelle tells me, she's done about all she can do with physical therapy, until he goes through another operation."

"Who's his surgeon?"

Blake pulled up his mount and met Greg's gaze. "A guy named Dan Newman. Do you know him?"

"Yeah. He's good. Who's he working with?"

"What do you mean?"

Greg shifted in his saddle. "Newman's specialty is microsurgery on the peripheral nervous system. He'd get an orthopedic guy and maybe someone that does plastic and reconstructive surgery, too, to make up a surgery team for

Timmy. I think. Sandy described what happened to him. Damn rotten shame!"

Erin hadn't told *him* much. Not that he didn't know, in his head, most of what his little boy had gone through before he and his mother became Blake's responsibility. He'd talked with Michelle, and with Timmy himself. "Will Timmy be all right eventually?"

"I'm a women's doctor, my friend," Greg reminded Blake. "What's more, I've never looked at Timmy's legs from a medical standpoint, or studied his records. His therapist would know more than I about what your boy's future holds."

"I'm scared." Most things Blake could control. But not that. All he could do was stand by and offer comfort while Timmy did all the suffering. "I don't want him to hurt anymore" He'd give anything he had if he could only make his child whole and strong.

"No one does, my friend. You know, they say that kids make the best patients, because they forget the pain and get on with their lives. Maybe that's true in the sense that they can cope better with physical discomfort than adults. But it damn sure is a pile of shit when it comes to psychological pain."

"Erin's done nothing but love Timmy."

"I wasn't thinking about your boy. My mind was on the emotional wreck Kay and I have managed to make of Shana."

"Shana? She's got more confidence in herself than most grown women I know."

Greg shook his head. "She puts on a good show. But deep down, she's a frightened little kid who doesn't think she means much to either Kay or me."

Blake doubted that "frightened" fit Shana Halpern nearly as well as "spiteful" and "spoiled rotten" — terms he recalled hearing Sandy use with every other breath last night to describe the behavior of her soon-to-be stepdaughter. But he hesitated saying that to Greg, no matter how good friends they were. "You and Sandy are going to have a time with her."

"If Sandy doesn't decide I've got too much baggage and call the whole thing off."

"From what she told Erin, I gathered that Sandy has no intention of letting you slither away. If I were you, though, I'd warn Miss Shana to be on her best behavior. Your fiancée has decided that no twelve-year-old's a match for her." Blake noted the relieved expression on Greg's face as they walked the horses back to the stable.

After Greg left, Blake showered and headed to his office. Before he surrendered his little boy to more suffering that he couldn't prevent, he wanted to do something really special, something Timmy would remember for years to come.

Between appointments that morning, Blake considered and discarded a dozen or more attractions he had heard friends say their children loved. Disney World...Six Flags...the Grand Canyon. Timmy wouldn't be able to run and ride and do all the things that made these places fun.

Then it came to him. They'd go to Possum Kingdom, to his cabin on the lake where he hadn't been for years. They could do as much or as little as they wanted to, and he and Erin could get to know each other while spending uninterrupted, quiet time with the boys.

"Erin?" he asked when he recognized her soft voice on the phone. "We're going on a little trip. Can you and the boys be ready to leave early Thursday morning?"

Chapter Seventeen

🙝

Portable crib…stroller…disposable diapers…changes of clothes for three days and nights, vitamins, lotion and baby powder… and plenty of clean linens for Jamie's bed. Erin wondered if all this stuff would fit in the trunk of Blake's car. Then she grinned. She had nearly forgotten what a production it could be to prepare for a trip with children.

Blake loaded everything, even Timmy's folded wheelchair, and they were on their way. Timmy and Jamie went to sleep in the backseat almost as soon as the car started moving, while Erin sipped her coffee and admired the confident, competent way Blake handled the big car in morning traffic.

She wanted to reach over and stroke his hard, muscled thigh through his faded jeans. The material looked soft, touchable, much more so than the suits he favored. Casual suited him. It was all Erin could do to keep her hands off broad shoulders encased in a soft, old Longhorns sweatshirt—and to drag her gaze away from his rugged, handsome profile.

"What kind of car do you want?" he asked as they passed a full-size sport utility vehicle full of preschoolers.

"Car? You have three of them already." In addition to the Mercedes sedan Blake was driving, she'd seen a late-model pickup truck and an older station wagon in the garage behind the house. Miguel used the wagon to take her shopping and to the pediatrician's office, and she guessed Blake kept the truck for hauling feed and lawn supplies. "Besides, I appreciate the thought, but I haven't driven for a long time."

"It's not something one forgets."

"I'm sure you're right."

"Are you afraid to drive?" Blake's voice hinted at his apparent concern.

"I don't think so. Not any more. For a while after the accident, even the idea of getting into a car put me into a cold sweat. But I got over that pretty quickly. If there had been any way, I'd have bought a car about the time I had to start taking Timmy to therapy almost every day."

Blake didn't reply for a few minutes as he concentrated on pulling off the interstate onto the state highway that went to Possum Kingdom. "You'll need some wheels to get back and forth from the hospital."

Erin could have done without the reminder about Timmy's impending surgery, but she had to concede that Blake had a valid point. She couldn't depend on him to take her everywhere. "Can't I use the station wagon? It seems wasteful to buy another car when there's a perfectly good one in your garage."

"The wagon's five years old. Besides, Mary needs something to go grocery shopping in. And the truck won't do for you. It's a stick shift, not to mention there's no room to put the kids. Come on, Erin, most women would be thrilled to death at the prospect of getting a new car." Blake's his teasing tone made Erin smile.

"All right. Never let it be said that I wasn't like most women." Better to give in than to spoil the day with a meaningless argument.

As they drew farther from Dallas, Erin watched the scenery, mentally comparing fall in North-central Texas with the West Texas ranch where she and Sandy had grown up. Trees had been scarce there, with an occasional scrub oak, mesquite, or cactus punctuating an otherwise bare, dusty horizon.

Here, she reveled in a riot of color. Dark evergreens and deciduous trees whose leaves were turning shades of scarlet, gold and orange, nestled in valleys with reddish-looking rivers running through them. The colors repeated themselves in patches on the hillsides, contrasting with pale, golden beige sandstone and red earth. She could hardly wait to get to Possum Kingdom, where she could enjoy the beauty of the countryside up close.

"Pretty scenery, isn't it?" Blake asked as he turned onto a secondary road and slowed down to maneuver around a poorly banked curve.

Erin nodded. "I've never been out here in the fall before." She recalled her summer camping trip here with Bill the year before Timmy's birth and wondering if Blake had brought Glenna to Possum Kingdom during the lazy days of Indian summer.

"Mommy?" Timmy sounded sleepy. "I think Jamie's waking up."

Twisting sideways in the bucket seat, Erin turned around to check on the boys. Jamie's eyelids were twitching, an almost sure sign that his naptime was nearly over, and Timmy looked as uncomfortable as Erin knew he must be after an hour and a half of sleeping sitting up. "Blake, we'll need to stop soon so I can feed Jamie."

"Hang in there, boys," he said, grinning. "The turnoff's right up here."

"You're taking a shortcut?"

Blake shook his head. "The cabin is just a mile or so down this road. It's on the southern end of the lake."

"Oh." Erin had assumed they would be staying at the lodge in the state park, some miles farther down the two-lane highway. When she saw the big, rustic-looking old house with its porches all around, her heart nearly stopped. "This is beautiful," she murmured, her gaze darting from the house to a sturdy rock and wooden dock nestled among trees and shrubs decked out in breathtaking fall colors.

"I thought you might like it here." He chuckled as he stopped at the side of the house. "My great-grandfather built it, as sort of a semi-retirement cottage. Come on, let's get the kids and gear inside so we can enjoy just doing nothing."

Blake looked happier and more relaxed than Erin had ever seen him. She wished she knew if he'd brought Glenna here. Of course he did. They were married for...

"Fourteen years. We came here a few times, but not too often. You know, I wasn't much of an outdoor girl. Forget me and enjoy yourself."

Forget Glenna? How could she, when she never knew whether the ghost was lurking about? Erin looked around. It was Glenna's voice, as clear as day.

"I'm going to float away for now, Erin. Enjoy!"

Erin laughed at herself. She had thought of Glenna and abracadabra! There she was, out of sight but answering questions Erin had asked only in her mind. Today, the antics of Glenna's ghost struck her as funny. Maybe that was because she was here in this magical place and wasn't willing to let anything stand in the way of having a perfect family weekend with the man who was both Glenna's husband and her own.

"What's so funny?" Blake asked as they made another trip to the car for the last of their gear.

Erin visually searched the area one more time. "Nothing. I'm just so happy to be out here in this gorgeous place with nothing to do except take care of you and the boys for three whole days."

"Here, if you can grab these, we can start having fun." Blake handed her Jamie's diaper bags before wrestling the porta-crib from the trunk and setting it on the ground. Dazed, Erin watched the play of muscles in his neck when he lifted the nursery equipment and headed for the house.

"Mommy, Daddy! Aren't you gonna bring Jamie in?" Timmy called from his vantage point on the porch.

Erin looked at Blake, and he stared back. She saw his grin turn into a full-fledged belly laugh just about the time tears came rolling down her own cheeks. Finally. For a few short minutes she and Blake had managed to go without thinking of the tiny boy whose existence was the only reason they were a family now.

* * * * *

"They're both plain tired out," Erin said later, after they'd taken Timmy and Jamie on a long but leisurely trek through the woods.

Blake nodded as he laid Timmy on his bed and began to remove the little boy's clothes. "Can you hand me his pajamas?" he asked Erin, hoping their walk hadn't been too much for her.

"Here. Timmy, do you want something to eat?" she asked, leaning over to smooth a stray lock of hair from the boy's forehead.

"No. I'm stuffed. Night-night, Mommy. Daddy."

Blake had sort of figured the two peanut butter and jelly sandwiches and assorted candy bars that Timmy had scarfed down during their hike would take the edge off his appetite tonight, but what the hell. This weekend was for Timmy. It would take a long time for him to recover from his upcoming surgery, too long for them to be able to promise a return trip before the weather turned too cold.

Digging back into memories of long, long ago, Blake wove a story about when Possum Kingdom was a wild and wooly no-man's land where outlaws hid from the Texas Rangers. He had no idea if the yarn were true, but he had loved it when his grandpa used to tell the tale to him.

"Tell me another story, Daddy," Timmy begged, but Blake could see he was fighting sleep.

He leaned down and kissed the little boy's wind-burned cheek. "Tomorrow, sport. Go to sleep now."

Quietly he got up and doused the light. Why was it he felt a sense of peace here that eluded him at home? He shelved the question, not willing to risk spoiling the good, simple feeling of contentment by analyzing the reasons.

He found Erin putting Jamie into the little crib. She fairly glowed when she gazed down at their sleeping baby.

"Join me by the fire?"

Erin looked up and met his gaze. "I'd like that." Her tone reminded Blake of milk and honey and soft, naked woman, but he quashed that thought from his mind. He'd promised her time...time for them to get to know each other...and for friendship to grow.

She seemed tense, curled up at one corner of the U-shaped gray leather sofa in front of a fireplace where he'd laid a modest fire. Her brow was creased, as if with worry, and he detected a tightness in her shoulders beneath the soft, dark red robe that covered her from neck to toes.

"Are you worried about Timmy?"

Erin looked up at him. "Yes," she said, bringing her bare feet up close to her hips and hugging her knees with both slender arms. "I'm glad you thought of bringing us here. Timmy hasn't had many chances to enjoy the out-of-doors the way he did today, with you carrying him on the trail.'"

"I enjoyed it. I thought I'd take him fishing tomorrow. Would you like a drink?" It would do her good to relax, set aside her worries for a while.

She smiled. "A beer would taste good."

Blake brought two frosty cans from the bar refrigerator and handed her one.

"Thanks."

"You're welcome." Blake deliberately sat at the opposite end of the sofa. He wanted to talk, but if he got close to Erin, his unruly cock was likely to overrule his brain. "What was Timmy like before he got hurt?"

"Like any bright, curious four-year-old. He's always been a basically happy child." She paused, as if she were sorting out thoughts inside her head. "He's quieter now. I think it's more than him just being older now and not being able to get around like he did before."

"How did you stand it? Having Timmy hurt and losing your husband at the same time?" Erin had never talked much about her marriage, and Blake wondered if a part of her was still grieving.

"I didn't have a choice, Blake. Bill was dead. Nothing was going to bring him back. And all I could do for Timmy was be there for him . . ." Erin's voice trailed off and she looked out the windows toward a starry sky.

"Tell me about it. I'd gladly go through what's in store for Timmy if I could. All I've done lately is wonder if there's anything, no matter how insignificant, that I can do to make it easier for him."

When Erin met his gaze, Blake felt as though she were looking all the way to his soul. "All we can do is love him. He'll have the surgery, and he'll be able to walk again or he won't. We'll be there for him, either way."

She'd gone through hell, might very well suffer a lot more. At best, she'd suffer each and every one of her son's pains and disappointments as he moved slowly toward recovery. At worst, she might find all his suffering was for naught and Timmy would never again be whole and strong.

Blake slid closer took her hand. "I'll be there for him, too." Unlike the vow he'd made when they married, he meant this one from the heart.

"I know." She brought his hand up and brushed it against her lips, then rested her head against his shoulder. "Timmy's lucky to have you."

She looked beautiful, with her dark hair shimmering like satin in the firelight. Blake couldn't resist tangling his fingers in the sleek, silky strands. "Tell me about Timmy's mom." Feeling mellow, he leaned against the couch pillows and cradled Erin against his chest.

"There's nothing special to tell. I grew up on a little ranch about halfway between Midland and San Angelo. Until I was nine, there were just Mom and Dad and me. Then Sandy was born. In high school, I edited the school paper for me and went out for cheerleader to please my mom. I graduated and got a scholarship to SMU. Four years later I had a degree in journalism and a brand-new husband."

"Did you ever work?"

Erin chuckled. "Outside the house? No. I fantasized about writing all kinds of compelling feature articles and selling them to magazines and newspapers. Even wrote a few pieces, but they didn't sell. Bill wanted me at home because we had to do fair amount of business entertaining. After he died, I tried writing again, hoping I could make a little money to help out with Timmy's medical bills. Again, no luck, or maybe just no talent."

"I doubt that." Blake liked the tenacity that had kept her trying, apparently not embittered by rejection. Did she still dream about a home-based career? "You could write now, you know."

Erin smiled up at him when he stroked the soft, soft skin at the back of her neck. "I've thought about it. Now I have time, even with both boys. Have I thanked you for hiring Theresa? It really wasn't necessary, but I appreciate her help."

"She needed a job, and Mary's not as young as she used to be. I don't want you tied to the house and kids twenty-four hours a day. I didn't marry you to be a nanny." But he had, at first. That was exactly what he'd envisioned the day they said their vows.

"Anyway, thanks. Would you like some coffee before we go to bed?"

Bed? As in together? Blake's cock twitched at the prospect. "Not unless you do. Isn't it about time for Jamie to have his midnight snack?" Desire slammed into him when he pictured her wet and warm and welcoming him into her gorgeous body.

She drew him like a moth to a flame, and there wasn't a thing he could do to make himself stop wanting her. Pushing week-old promises and old, tearing memories from his mind, he pulled her closer and sampled the sweet temptation of her mouth.

When he realized that if he didn't stop now, he never would, Blake ended the kiss and cradled Erin's head gently against his shoulder. "You go on and get ready for bed, before you get me so hot that I forget my good intentions. I'll check on Timmy and change Jamie before I bring him in to you."

As he watched her go, his cock ached. But they'd agreed to wait…not give in again to the compelling mutual chemistry until they developed real emotional ties.

* * * * *

"This place will be perfect for Sandy and Greg's honeymoon," Erin murmured, her gaze on Jamie who was nursing contentedly at her breast.

"Uh-huh."

Blake seemed to have lost his usual articulate way of speaking. For fifteen minutes he'd sat beside the bed in an old oak rocking chair, staring at Jamie and her as if trying to memorize their features. Every time she tried to start a conversation, he gave some monosyllabic reply, as if he'd rather she wouldn't intrude on his private thoughts.

"Blake, what's wrong?"

"Nothing."

Not one to give up when they had been communicating so nicely earlier, Erin tried another tack. "I told you all about me. Now it's your turn."

He met her gaze, and she saw sadness as well as smoldering desire. When he spoke, his voice was raspy, as if he were dragging the words from somewhere deep inside his soul.

"We're here together because fate took…Glenna…away. But you know that. One day she was here, and the next she was dead, shot down by that psycho…" He paused, apparently reliving that nightmare. "You've been through hell, too. Maybe more than I. We've both been handed a lot to deal with, but in one way fate hasn't treated us as badly as it could have."

Hope sprang to life, but Erin beat it down, unwilling to risk disappointment if she misunderstood what Blake was trying to say. When he didn't elaborate, she asked, "What do you mean?"

He seemed at a loss for words. "We got together because of *him*." Blake nodded toward their sleepy baby. "And because of me losing...*her*. But it could be worse, much worse. You love that little guy, and so do I. I've got two boys now that have given me more joy in living than I ever thought I'd have again."

He paused, his dark blue gaze locked with hers. "We've got a whole lot more going for us than some couples do. I like you and I believe you like me, too. Besides, we can't ignore this...chemistry. Damn it, Erin, I can't get around you without my cock going wild. Wanting you is driving me fucking insane."

She'd hoped for more but expected less. Blake still couldn't bear to hear Glenna's name. Erin doubted if he would for a long time, if ever. But he'd admit liking and wanting her. That was something.

She smiled. "Are you saying we're lucky not to be stuck in a marriage of convenience where neither of us can stand to look at the other?"

"Yeah. I can look at you a long time without getting tired of the view. Is our son asleep?"

She nodded.

With infinite care, Blake lifted Jamie and anchored the baby firmly against his muscular shoulder.

"Good night, sweetie," she whispered to the sleeping infant, and to the man she was coming to love far, far more than she'd loved Bill.

"May I come back?"

She tried to say no, but her heart screamed yes. Loving him could, almost certainly would, hurt. So would denying them the sexual pleasure they both wanted.

Maybe he was right. Fate could have dealt each of them a rougher hand than it had. She'd play the game and bet the next card falling would bring not a royal flush, but the love they'd lost in other games, other times.

Erin nodded and smiled. And counted the minutes while he was gone.

Chapter Eighteen

જી

When Blake came back, Erin's pussy clenched with anticipation. Hair tousled, cheeks freshly shaved, he reminded her of a sexy ad, standing in the doorway barefoot and wearing nothing but tight unbuttoned jeans.

He was already hard, his big cock straining against the faded denim. The expression in eyes almost black with passion reminded her of a predatory male animal on the prowl. "I intend to spend the night in here," he said, challenge in his words and his stance.

Erin wasn't about to say no. Every pore in her body ached for him and the fire inside her burned too hard to be put out with one fast fuck. She laid back the covers and held out her arms. "Come here, lover."

For a long time he stood and looked at her. "You come here."

Breathless, she slid off the bed and took three steps, stopping when she was close enough to reach out and stroke the hard, lightly furred expanse of his chest.

Slowly, he pushed his jeans down his legs and stepped out of them. He held her with a hot, needy gaze. She heard rather than felt the teeth of her robe's zipper whisper, sensed his long, nimble fingers tugging at the tab, felt her skin prickle as a soft breeze caressed her naked skin. She moved closer, close enough that she heard his heart beating and saw his pulse in the muscular column of his neck.

"We've got all night, honey." He caught her seeking hands and brought them gently to his lips. When he sucked one finger into his mouth her nipples puckered and her pussy grew wet. This wasn't the impetuous lover who'd taken her in a frenzy of desperate lust then come back to satisfy her needs. Tonight Blake seemed intent on weaving an erotic fantasy, slowly arousing himself and her and…

"Touch me," she begged as he sucked first one finger, then another, bathing each with his hot, slick tongue. The cool air might as well have been a blazing furnace. She burned from the tips of her fingers to her toes. To her pussy that had already soaked her thighs, her aching breasts. "Please touch me."

"Patience is a virtue." He voiced restraint but released her hands and slid his inside her open velvet robe. The warm coarseness of his callused palms sweetly abraded her skin. "Are you hot?"

She wasn't just hot. She was smoldering from the inside out. That was how he made her feel. And she wanted more. She wanted him to lay her on that bed and fuck with her until she fell apart in a conflagration of sensual delight. "You make me burn," she whispered, her hands burrowing into his soft chest hair in search of taut masculine nipples.

"Not yet." Again, he took his hands off her to halt her exploration. "Let's do this slow and easy."

When she stilled her hands, he released them and began caressing her shoulders. This time, though, he slid his hands under the robe, down her arms, slipping the smooth, soft velvet away until she felt the robe puddle around her feet. The night breeze caressed her naked flesh, cooling her skin despite her arousal.

He must have seen her shiver and thought it was from cold air, because he pulled her close and wrapped her in his arms. Though he didn't hold her tightly, the heat of his pulsing erection throbbed against her stomach, made her want…

She couldn't help arching her hips and brushing his hard cock with a sinuous rhythm. Taunting. Teasing. Wanting that hot, hard flesh in her, filling her aching pussy. His fast, shallow breathing hinted that his control was slipping, too.

"Shower time." He punctuated his words by lifting her as if she weighed no more than Timmy and striding in fluid, efficient movements to the adjoining bathroom. Setting her down in the large white-tiled shower stall, he turned on the water and joined her there.

His jutting cock was rock-hard, so hard he had to be in pain. She knew her pussy was hurting, weeping hot wet tears for want of him. But he seemed in no great hurry. With not a little resentment she watched him adjust the twin showerheads and sigh as pulsing warm water prickled his big, gorgeous body.

Turning, he grasped her at the waist and positioned her in front of him so the water pounded at her breasts and belly. She gasped at the contrast of sensations when he caressed her with soapy-smooth, callus-roughened hands. Her nipples tightened and beaded at his touch. Her stomach muscles flinched in response to the water's sting, then relaxed as he slid his hands over the sensitive skin of her mound, shielding it from the tingling spray.

Weak from wanting him, Erin turned to face him and leaned back, welcoming the smooth, impersonal coolness of the tile against her back. Her head still spun, even more so when he stopped and lathered his big hands again. When he knelt before her, she had to move her legs apart to keep from falling in a heap of quivering limbs and frustrated need.

Rivulets of water streamed from his thick, sable hair, down his chiseled cheeks. His hands branded her with fire as they moved up her calves...her thighs. All the time he showed no concern for the swollen, sopping core of her that fairly screamed for his touch.

As if she were a helpless baby, he bathed her. Damn it, he had to know what he was doing to her, couldn't help knowing he had her trapped where she couldn't reach out and play with his velvety balls, suck the irresistible plum-like head of his magnificent cock.

As soon as he paused with this fiendishly slow seduction, she'd go down on her knees, take his big, throbbing cock in her hands and lick away the drop of lubrication she knew she'd find at its tip. Then she'd slide her hands lower, roll his hot balls between her palms. She'd flick his hard, pulsing erection with her tongue. She'd return the sensual torment he was inflicting on her, in spades.

Through a haze of half joy, half pain, she felt him reach between her legs and wash her. She opened her stance, silently willing him to use his hand, his mouth—anything to ease the ache in her pussy. But he didn't touch her, not the way she wanted him to. Instead he reached for the lower showerhead, pulled it off its stand, and directed its needlelike flow to rinse off the soap.

"Blake, please." Her pussy spasmed, her abdominal muscles cramped painfully. If he didn't fuck her soon, she'd die.

"Soon, honey."

He replaced the showerhead. With a maddening lack of haste, he turned to her, using his hands to caress her inner thighs and spread them farther apart. She held her breath, waiting— knowing when he took both hands and opened her to his gaze that he'd only begun his sensual assault.

His breath was hot, searing her like a brand when he finally rested his clean-shaven cheek against her mound. His tongue snaked out, wrapping itself around the tiny nub of her clit, already so hard and throbbing she thought she might scream.

"Fuck me now. Please."

He only sucked harder at her clit, then spread her legs wider and inserted first one then two fingers in her dripping pussy.

He muttered something, but it blended in her haze of sexual excitement. She was coming. Damn it, she didn't want it this way. But she couldn't... "Oh, God yesss," she hissed when he sucked her harder, slid another finger inside her and found her G-spot. She'd never felt so wanted...so needed. She shook with the force of wave after wave of breathtaking pleasure.

Her fingers tangled in wet strands of his hair as she slumped against the shower tiles. Shudders of ecstasy wracked her body from head to toe. Before she could catch her breath, he started all over again, licking and finger-fucking and building up the pressure all over again. "Stop. You're killing me. Ohhhh Blake. Don't. Don't stop." When he'd driven her to another screaming orgasm, she collapsed, only to be lifted in his strong arms, supported against his rock-hard body as he turned off the pulsing jets.

He hadn't come, was still hard as stone. His hot cock probed her flesh, pressed insistently against her butt cheeks through the big bath sheet he'd wrapped around her wrung-out body. It beckoned, aroused her again, made her turn to face him and weigh him in her hands before he scooped her up again and carried her to bed.

Now it was her turn now to feed her fantasies on his helpless flesh. "Sit on the edge of the bed, now." Her boldness shocked her because she'd never done anything so blatant before.

If he hadn't just made her his helpless prisoner, Erin doubted she'd have found the courage to go down on her knees, spread his legs, and nuzzle the unyielding hardness of his belly. Her tongue swirled around his navel, sampling the textures of firm, smooth skin and fine, silky body hair. He smelled like the soap he'd used to tease her.

With the tip of her tongue, she circled the blunt, swollen head of his cock, felt and saw it grow even larger with each caress. Could she go down on him? Would it please him as much as he'd just pleasured her?

"Ohmigod, you're killing me. Take me in your mouth, honey. Suck me dry."

The creamy lubricant that oozed from the dimpled slit in his cock felt like rich cream, and his velvety skin there tasted good. Slightly salty and a lot sexy. Erin took him in her mouth and sucked him, using one hand to caress his balls while she wrapped the other around the base of his huge cock.

"Yeah. Like that." He put his hand over hers. "Squeeze me harder. Please."

Taking a deep breath, she relaxed and took more of his cock, swallowing reflexively and sucking him deep down her throat. His coarse pubic hair tickled her lips. The strange texture made her draw back a little, but then he flexed his hips and made her swallow him again.

She'd never before been so hot…so eager to taste his come, feel his cock jerking in her mouth. He came in quick bursts. She wished they'd go on for hours, feeding the climax that was building deep in her belly. The pressure built in her pussy as his cock caressed her throat while she squeezed his balls.

"Stop. For God's sake, stop."

She wouldn't. She wanted him to come with her mouth, wanted to pay him back for the exquisite pleasure he'd given her. Suddenly, though, he lay back, lifting her onto the bed and twisting her around until she straddled his face.

He rolled her nipples between his thumbs and forefingers, tugged them and squeezed them while she kept on sucking his cock. Then he moved his head between her legs and plunged his tongue deep into her wet, aching pussy.

When she worked her mouth up and down his cock, he tongue-fucked her harder. God, but he turned her bones to jelly, her clit to a rigid, sensitive little nub. The sudden tightening of his balls in her hand hinted he wouldn't be able to withstand much more.

"No. Damn it, I've got to feel your wet, hot cunt around my cock." He lifted her shoulders, and with total efficiency of motion, he positioned her face down on the bed, raising her hips and plunging deep inside her needy pussy in a single powerful thrust.

He didn't move inside her right away but tugged her nipples gently and rolled them between his thumbs and forefingers while she milked him with internal muscles that seemed to have a mind of their own. She didn't think she could get any hotter until she felt his hot breath and velvety tongue on the nape of her neck.

When he moved inside her, the pressure inside her built with every thrust of his hips, each feathery touch of his fingers on her nipples and each love-bite. She felt a part of him, and she wanted more.

Bracing herself, she met his next wild plunge with one of her own. Her breasts cried for their loss when he moved his hands and lifted her buttocks higher off the bed, but her body soared when he began to stroke her clit with nimble fingers while he sank his huge, hot cock harder and deeper in her pussy with every stroke.

More of her hot juices spilled, wetting his fingers and her clit. When her pussy began to spasm, she ground her hips into his, taking him deeper. Taking all of him. Before the incredible sensations overcame her, Erin heard Blake shout and felt his cock begin to jerk and spurt out his come.

He didn't leave her as he'd done before but rolled to his side, taking her with him and keeping their bodies joined. He still filled her, as sated as he must have been, and her own long-neglected pussy muscles gripped his half-hard cock as if they never wanted to let him go.

* * * * *

Blake woke to the sound of the baby's plaintive wail. For a minute, he was disoriented. Then he realized it was Erin's warm, pliant body next to him. He wasn't alone.

They'd spent the night together, explored every inch of each other's bodies, sucked and fucked and come more times than he'd have thought possible. He reached out and touched her face, so relaxed and peaceful as she slept. Then he slipped out of bed and stretched tired muscles he'd severely taxed the night before.

He pulled on his jeans, noting his cock seemed raring to repeat the fuckfest. Hell, it should have been wrung out and hung up to dry. He grinned. He might be thirty-eight and feeling every muscle in his body, but he could still wake up with a hard-on like he'd sported as a horny sixteen-year-old.

Humming a sprightly tune, he looked in on Timmy before answering Jamie's escalating demands. "You're a real screamer, aren't you?" he asked the baby while he cleaned him up. "You've got to take it easy on your mom this morning, son. I'm afraid she didn't get much sleep last night."

When he brought Jamie to Erin, he shed his jeans and joined them in bed. The old demon, guilt, washed over him, but he fought it down. Glenna was dead, he was alive.

Erin deserved his respect and his passion if not his love. And he deserved the pleasure he'd found with the mother of his children. His guilty feelings banished for the moment, he adjusted the pillows behind his head, then reached out for Erin and settled her against his chest.

"Does that feel good?" he asked as he watched Jamie suckle greedily at her full, pale breast.

"Not as good as it does when you do it, but it makes me feel useful to know Jamie needs me as much as I need him."

"Lucky baby." Blake stroked her breast lightly, his finger close to his son's busy little mouth. When Jamie grasped his finger and tugged at it with surprising strength, he decided life was good. "Did you nurse Timmy?"

"Only for a month or so. It bothered Bill—he thought enlightened mothers fed their babies formula from disposable bottles."

"It turns me on to watch you feed my child." The fact that his cock was hardening again beneath the concealing blanket made him wonder momentarily if he were some form of pervert. "You know, I never saw a baby nursing before. Never expected to. But I like it."

Erin shifted Jamie to her other breast. She seemed as unconcerned by her nudity as he had been with his own, until that day not long ago when she'd brought his dormant hormones to a resounding state of alert.

"You're the sexiest woman I've ever known." And she was. Gently, he reached down and stroked her velvety soft mons and labia.

"You make me feel sexy," she said, reaching under the covers to tangle her fingers in the thick hair at his groin before tracing the length of his cock gently with her palm.

Blake wasn't used to such honest, easy sexuality. He wasn't accustomed to his woman telling him straight out without guile that she liked his body and what it could do for her. But damn! She made him want not only to give and get sexual relief, but to experience every nuance of erotic pleasure he'd ever experienced or heard about.

"I'll give you about an hour to stop that," he growled as he bent and suckled at the breast his son had almost emptied.

She squirmed, opening her legs wider. God, how hot and smooth she felt. Her clit was swollen and hard as stone. Her finger scorched his flesh when she stroked the very tip of his cock, coaxing out a pearl of lubrication to ease the gentle friction that was beginning to drive him insane.

"Jamie's gone to sleep," she told him, her voice languid as she kept up the circular motion around his cock head that was threatening to make him come.

"Good." He raised his lips from her breast and licked away the drops of milk that lingered there.

She acted as if she never wanted to let him go. "Just a minute," he told her, tossing back the covers and dragging a soft quilt off the bed. Quickly, he folded it into fourths and set it on the floor. "Give me the baby," he said, and when she did, he settled Jamie on the makeshift bed. "We should have about an hour before Timmy wakes up."

Erin settled her gaze on his cock and balls. "You're magnificent, you know."

"So are you." He raked her with his gaze, from the top of her tousled head to narrow feet with their neatly painted toenails. But it was her pussy that beckoned him. She lay there naked, without see-through nighties or erotic toys. Raw desire glowed in expressive eyes that reminded him of a calm, still sea. Desire for him.

He bent and swirled his tongue down her body, savoring the tremor he felt when he laved her mound. Playfully he flicked at that impudent little nub of flesh that demanded his attention before nipping at her firm, slender thighs and swollen labia.

"Blake." She tugged and pulled at his leg until he gave in and straddled her face. At first she teased him by breathing gently on his balls while he readied her cunt with his fingers. Then she took him fully into her mouth, and it was his turn to shudder.

Her tongue teased and tormented him, and her fingers stroked and kneaded his ass, pulling his cock deeper into her throat. His nostrils full of the smell of her and him and sex, he buried his face between her legs and devoured her honey. He sent his tongue deep inside her again and again, then drove three fingers into her and rode her hard while his teeth caught her clit for his tongue to flail.

When her mouth went slack on him and she gasped for breath, he reversed positions and draped her legs over his shoulders. Mindful that the night's activities might have left her sore, he entered her slowly, an inch at a time, until his balls rested tightly against her wet, satiny skin. Deliberately he ignored her begging and withdrew, taking time to sheath himself before joining their bodies again.

He watched her writhe, silently asking for more, apparently wanting all he had to give her. But he wanted more, too. Rhythmically he slid in and out, delving deeper each time until he felt the tip of her womb with his cock. He looked at her, found her beautiful face damp with sweat and slack with passion. Her eyes, half shut, focused unashamed on his cock as it reamed her creamy cunt.

He looked at them, too, torturing himself by fucking her slow, savoring the erotic picture of the act he'd only known before by touch and feel. Oh, shit. He was going to come and there wasn't a thing he could do to delay it. Desperately he worked his fingers on her nipples to bring her with him.

"Blake! God, Blake, don't stop. Please don't stop."

"I won't. I can't." His breath came in short, shallow bursts as she bucked and convulsed against him. He let go and let her climax carry him over. A long time later, he got up to take care of his sons.

* * * * *

Erin hummed as she slipped into jeans and a bright plaid western-style shirt for the day. She felt like pinching herself. Before last night, she'd have laughed if anyone had told her it was possible to make love so many times in just one night.

But Blake had been insatiable and so had she. Even this morning. An hour later, she was still feeling aftershocks of pleasure from their last wild lovemaking.

"I want us to make this a real marriage." Erin savored Blake's parting words, uttered a few minutes earlier when he left her to get the boys ready for a boat trip around Possum Kingdom Lake. Still, she reminded herself, he'd never mentioned love.

But he wanted her. And she had no doubts about his love for Jamie and Tim. Maybe, in time, she could love away the emptiness inside him and he'd come to love her, too.

"Do I smell coffee?" she asked a few minutes later when she joined Blake and Timmy in the big, old-fashioned kitchen.

Blake grinned. "It's instant. I hope you don't mind."

"Not at all." She dumped a spoonful of crystals into a mug and filled it with the water Blake had boiled on the stove. "Don't tell me you made breakfast, too."

"Daddy made pancakes in the microwave." Timmy grinned when Erin sat beside him.

"Better eat up, sport. We've got a big day ahead of us." Blake pulled another package of pancakes out of the freezer. "Want some?"

"Sure. Where's Jamie?"

"Taking another nap. I cleaned him up again, so all we have to do when we finish here is collect him and go on down to the dock."

Later, when they munched sandwiches and chips in a secluded cove surrounded by trees and bushes in all their autumn glory, Erin watched Blake teach Timmy how to bait a hook and cast his line. Neither of them caught a fish, but then they didn't have to. Just being together this way seemed enough to put them all in a wonderful, relaxed mood.

On the way back to Dallas the next day, though, her sense of well-being began to slip away. Erin worried about Timmy, and she sensed his upcoming surgery was on Blake's mind, too. If that weren't enough, she'd taken on much of the planning for Sandy's wedding, a wedding that might not happen if those two couldn't reconcile their differences over the care and handling of Greg's willful daughter.

At least she and Blake were of like minds when it came to handling the problems that loomed immediately in their future.

* * * * *

He hated hospitals.

Late the following Friday afternoon, Blake paced a small anteroom off the operating suites at Children's Medical Center. Impatient, he checked his watch again, wondering when the hell this Doctor Newman would finish up in surgery. This place where helpless children suffered and died got to Blake even worse than hospitals where most of the patients were adults.

"Sorry to keep you waiting, Mr. Tanner," Doctor Newman said briskly a few minutes later when he greeted Blake. "Come on in here."

Blake glanced around the sparsely furnished cubicle that did nothing to inspire confidence in its occupant's stature, before taking a seat in the single, scarred oak armchair. "Thanks for making time to see me," he said politely, his gaze coming to rest on a wall full of diplomas displayed in mismatched frames.

"You said you had more questions about your son's coming operation," Newman said, his tone expectant.

"Yes. What are you going to do, exactly, and what results do you expect?"

The surgeon rifled through an untidy stack of papers on his desk and came up with the folder he apparently was looking for. "This will be Timmy's fourth operation," he said. "I've gone over all this with Mrs. Tanner."

"I'd appreciate your running through the details again with me. For my own peace of mind." Blake reminded himself that Greg had given this guy a vote of confidence.

Newman started at the beginning, when Timmy had nearly died, and continued to chronicle in graphic detail each operation and therapy regimen Timmy had endured over the past three and a half years. Blake shuddered.

"Basically, I'm going to go in and do more nerve grafts in his left leg. The orthopedic team will graft more bone and replace some of the hardware in his right ankle, if they find the leg is viable. If not, they'll amputate it just above the site where we initially reattached the severed right ankle and foot. We'll do the procedures on both legs simultaneously, to reduce the time under anesthesia. The operations will be long, but they aren't particularly risky in terms of life and death."

Newman's explanation made Blake shudder. "How many more operations will Timmy have to endure before he's as good as he's going to get?"

Blake watched the expression in Newman's deep brown eyes. The doubt he saw there increased his apprehension. "I asked you a question."

"I'm hopeful that this surgery will be the last on Tim's left leg."

"How about the other one?"

"That depends on what the orthopedists decide. If they believe the leg can be saved, long-term, they'll have to go in periodically until Tim is grown, or until they change their minds. He'll need more nerve grafts as well. On the other hand, if they amputate, that should be the last surgery Timmy will need."

What a choice! "I didn't know his leg was that badly damaged," he ground out, knowing he sounded like a blithering idiot.

Newman shrugged. "Timmy's legs were both nearly severed in the accident. But the right foot and ankle were crushed as well. From just below the knee to the toes, that leg is a hodgepodge of hardware. No nerves or muscle to speak of. In my opinion, Tim will never be able to use it fully."

"You recommend...amputation?" The word stuck on Blake's tongue.

"Yes. If they go that route, Tim could be mobile in just a few months with an intelligent prosthesis. If not, he will be wheelchair bound at least most of the time, with a nonfunctional natural leg that will require frequent surgical lengthening. That decision, though, won't be entirely mine. The orthopedic surgeons are deferring judgment until they open up the ankle and take another look."

Feeling poleaxed, Blake bid Newman farewell and drove home, wondering how in hell Erin had lived with Timmy's uncertain future and constant pain for all this time. How did she manage the brave face she always showed her son?

Hell, he didn't even know what he should be hoping for. If Timmy were consulted, would he opt for losing part of himself to gain faster and surer mobility and freedom from pain? As he pulled into the curving driveway, Blake let out his frustration in several virulent blasphemies and Anglo-Saxon oaths he hadn't uttered since the day Glenna died.

Once inside, he put on a smile and went looking for Erin. If anyone needed distraction, she must. He intended to let her know he was and that he would be beside her, no matter what.

"What's that?" he asked when he found her at the table in the sitting room where they'd celebrated Jamie's one-month birthday, a jumble of boxes and papers strewn over the tabletop. Apparently she'd found her own way of keeping her mind off Timmy's surgery.

Erin returned his smile. "These are a bunch of old family pictures. Sandy's going to wear our mother's wedding gown, so Greg asked if I could find a picture for him to give the florist. He's a thoughtful man, wanting to surprise Sandy with a bouquet that looks like Mom's did."

"Uh-huh." Blake pulled out a chair and sat down. "May I help?" He needed to concentrate on something, anything except the worries his visit with Timmy's doctor had fed more than alleviated.

"Here, you can look through this box." She used a rag to dust off a tattered shoe box before dumping its contents on the table.

Blake sorted through snapshots of Erin and Sandy at various stages, and of the pleasant-looking couple who must have been their parents. Realization of the other loss Erin had suffered hit him when he found the formal photo of a smiling bride and groom. "I think I found it. Here, take a look." The faded image showed a dark, rugged-looking groom in an ill-fitting black tux, and a delicate looking bride wearing a simple white gown that emphasized her tiny waist and full breasts.

"Did you wear her dress, too?" Suddenly Blake wondered what Bill had looked like, whether Erin sometimes thought of him when they were making love. An emotion very much like jealousy threatened to erupt, but he fought it down.

She laughed. "I'd never have fit into it. I'm at least five or six inches taller than Mom was. Besides, the dress is velvet, and I got married in the summertime."

Both times. But Blake doubted she thought of the sad little ceremony they'd had as a wedding. He hadn't thought of it as one at the time, but each day he was feeling more like her husband, wanting more of Erin than he'd imagined he ever would.

Obviously looking for something specific, she rooted through the pictures he'd found. "Look, Blake, here's Mom's bouquet. The flowers aren't orchids. They're poinsettias."

Blake looked at the photo, apparently taken at a reception where the bouquet formed a centerpiece on a lace-covered tablecloth. Sprigs of holly decorated a tiered cake and candlesticks that held skinny, red candles. "They must have had a Christmas wedding."

"Christmas Eve. Daddy used to call Mom his little Christmas rose. Someday I'll get all these pictures arranged in albums. Here, help me put them back in the boxes for now. But leave that picture out. I'll take it to Greg."

Blake sat there, staring at the picture. "Erin, this is really pretty, but…"

"You don't like it." She sounded hurt.

He chose his words carefully. "It's beautiful. Except, what color dresses are Sandy's attendants going to be wearing?"

"Royal blue."

Blake breathed a sigh of relief. "Then if I were you, I'd tell Greg to have the florist use white poinsettias. Otherwise the color scheme will be remind people of the Stars and Stripes."

Erin laughed, a joyous sound that lifted his spirits. "You're right. Unless there's some kind of big flower that's blue?"

"None I can think of. Why couldn't they reverse the colors?"

"You mean, use white poinsettias — or orchids? And tiny blue flowers around them?"

"Yeah. That would work. Be sure and tell Greg, though, or he's likely to have the florist make up a bouquet exactly like the one your mother had." Blake had no doubt that Greg would, if he thought it would please Sandy. He could just imagine what Mom Sadie would say if he did. "Are they coming over tonight?"

"No. Sandy called. She and Greg want us to come to his place for dinner. Do you mind?"

"Should I?"

"Sandy's making dinner, she said, and I'm afraid cooking isn't among her finer talents." Erin shrugged.

"We survived my efforts in the kitchen out at Possum Kingdom. I'm sure your sister's masterpiece won't kill us." He stood, then bent to brush his lips across Erin's cheek. "Should I go change?"

Erin's gaze settled for a minute on his crotch, and he wished for a minute that they could forget about eating and spend the evening in bed. "You can if you want to, but Sandy doesn't do fancy. I'm going to wear what I have on."

Erin had on a soft, chic jumpsuit they'd found at Saks earlier in the week while doing the shopping he'd hoped would distract them after they'd met jointly with Timmy's surgical team. He loved the way the soft, off-white wool hugged her body and made her look sexy as hell, yet still elegant and ladylike. "Are you wearing that teddy I picked out, too?" he asked, fighting down the urge to strip it off her and see for himself.

When she nodded, he got a whiff of that perfume that turned him six ways from Sunday. "Be good and I'll show you later," she whispered. "If you're going to change, you'd better hurry. We're supposed to be there at eight. I'll go check on Jamie."

* * * * *

"Erin looked happy tonight," Sandy said to Greg later, after their guests had left.

"Yes, she did. So do you." He pulled her against him and nibbled gently at on her earlobe.

"I'm glad we asked her to plan our wedding. If she weren't so busy, all she'd be doing is worrying about Timmy. Greg, stop it. Shana's upstairs."

He turned her around and dropped a kiss on her cute little nose. "And it's Ms. Watson's night off, so I can't even go home with you tonight. Full-time fatherhood has its drawbacks. I wish to hell I didn't have to wait four more weeks before we can stroll upstairs to bed in front of God and everyone."

She looked up at him, happiness shining in her eyes. "Behave, darling." She patted his shoulder like she might pet a friendly but troublesome mutt. "At least one of us has to act like an adult instead of a horny teenager. Besides, we still have some addresses to copy down for the calligrapher."

Greg let out an exaggerated moan. "Okay." He stuffed his hand in his pants pocket and felt the picture Erin had slipped to him earlier. He made a mental note to drop it by the florist's tomorrow, between hospital rounds and office hours.

"Why don't we just write out the damn invitations ourselves?" he asked as he finished copying what seemed like the thousandth name from his mom's dog-eared address book onto a white index card.

"Just because."

"Because, why?"

"Because you write like a doctor," Sandy said, a saucy grin on her face.

Greg shook his head. "You're making me print. If the calligrapher can read the cards, certainly the mailman could read the addresses if I printed them on envelopes."

Sandy tossed her head back and laughed out loud. "Quit griping and let's get this done. Don't you want our invitations to be pretty? And uniform-looking?"

Greg couldn't see the point of fussing over putting names on envelopes that everyone would toss in the trash. But he really didn't mind, since Sandy had quit making noises about canceling their plans. The past week, since he'd grounded Shana, had been peaceful.

Sandy and his daughter must have come to some kind of truce this afternoon. He wasn't sure he wanted to know exactly what went on, but he'd noticed during dinner that the two managed to tolerate each other's company without bloodshed.

"Get busy! I've filled out twice as many cards as you." Sandy picked up her cards and set them on top of his much smaller stack.

"Okay." He had to know, but he hated to risk opening up barely closed wounds. "Did you ask Shana if she'd like to be a bridesmaid?" he asked, reaching out and taking Sandy's hand.

"I asked. She said no. But she did agree to come to the wedding."

Why couldn't his kid be a little angel like Timmy? "Her not coming was never an option. I'll talk to her again." Damn it, why couldn't his daughter give in and wish them well?

"Greg, don't. You'll just back her into a corner, and she'll have to rebel. Let it go. I promised I'd take her shopping for a really special dress, one she can wear to the wedding and maybe later to a dance at school."

"Are you okay with that?"

"Yes. Shana and I are starting to come to an understanding…but we're nowhere close to being friends. Probably won't be for a long time yet. It's too much for us to expect her to set aside all her fear and hostility at once."

He took Sandy's hand and toyed with the sparkling diamond he'd thought for a while she'd be tossing back in his face. "I'm sorry, sweetheart." Damn it, Greg would give anything not to be coming to her with the baggage of two broken marriages and a troubled, sullen child.

"You haven't done anything to be sorry for." Setting the cards into a neat stack, she got up and moved behind him, her talented fingers kneading the tense muscles of his neck and shoulders. "I love you and you love me, and don't you ever forget it." She bent and dropped a series of wet, arousing kisses between his collar and his hairline.

"I won't. Don't you ever forget it either." Greg leaned back and let her magic fingers lull away the tension. "By the way, your dinner was great," he murmured, knowing how hard she'd worked to fix that practically inedible meal.

"You don't have to lie." Sandy stopped her sensual massaging and faced him, hands on hips. "I know I can't cook worth beans. But I'll learn. Maybe your mother…"

"Honey, I don't care if you burn water trying to make coffee. We'll just get Mrs. Watson to fix some stuff and leave it for us to warm up on her days off. Or maybe I'll have to make a standing date to take you out two days a week. Would you like that?"

Sandy pouted, but Greg saw the sparkle in her eyes. "I want to be a good wife. A good mother."

"You will be. You're already the best thing that ever happened to me. The best office manager I've ever had. The best lover. And in four weeks, you're going to be the best little wife in Texas."

"Really?"

Greg stood and took her in his arms, cupping her breasts and grinding his cock against her flat abdomen. "Really. Now you'd better get your gorgeous little tush out of here before I decide to hell with protecting my kid from the facts of life and drag you off to bed. Hell, I'm ready to try out that new couch in the living room. What do you say?"

"I say we'd better wait. What if Shana decides to come downstairs for a snack?"

He held up his hands and groaned. "You're right, damn it. Go on, get out of here while I still can let you go."

"Good night, darling." She stood on tiptoe and gave him a long, hard kiss. "I made sure to book you a free lunch hour tomorrow. What say we try out one of your examining rooms?"

Chapter Nineteen

ᴇᴑ

"Who was that?" Blake pulled his head out from under a pillow and stared at the digital clock on the nightstand in Erin's room. "It's just seven o'clock."

"Sandy."

"What did she want? To be sure we'd survived getting our stomachs pumped?" he grumbled.

"Blake! For all you know, I can't cook either." Erin agreed with his assessment of the charred casserole they'd choked down earlier, but she needed to defend her sister.

"At least you don't try to cook."

Erin laughed. "Actually, I'm a pretty good cook. Mom taught me. I guess I neglected Sandy's education, though."

"What are you going to do today?" Blake rolled to the edge of the bed and dragged himself upright.

Stretching, Erin tried to shake the cobwebs out of her fuzzy brain. "I thought I'd spend the morning with Timmy and Jamie. The caterer's coming over at noon so we can go over the menu. How about you?"

"I'll be in court this morning. If you'd like, I can have Sharon reschedule some appointments and spend the afternoon with you and the kids."

"You don't need to. I appreciate the extra time you've been making for us lately, but there's no reason for you to disrupt your routine at work."

"Yeah, honey. There is."

Actually, Erin didn't know how she'd have survived since the doctors had scheduled Timmy's surgery, if she hadn't had Blake practically glued to her side. Whether they rode the horses, took care of details for Greg and Sandy's wedding, or just sat inside and watched old movies when the weather turned rainy and cool, Blake had been there for her. At night, she loved the way he held her for hours after they made slow, hot love.

It bothered her that Blake slept so fitfully when he shared her bed in the room where he'd lived with Glenna for so long. It obviously held memories he hadn't been able to sweep away by having the room stripped down to bare walls. Still he lay beside her each night, holding her long after she went to sleep. Realizing how being there for her taxed Blake's endurance, Erin appreciated his kindness all the more.

Chapter Twenty

Glenna's Ghost

෨

It had been a long time since Glenna had visited Blake's office.

Since she'd popped in on Erin when they first arrived at Possum Kingdom, Glenna had pretty much sat back and watched Erin and Blake's relationship develop. Even though she drew the line at checking out how they were progressing in a physical way, she concluded from the way Erin glowed that they were getting on just fine in her bedroom, where Blake had been spending most of his nights.

She had no doubt, either, that Erin was deeply in love with Blake. How could she not be? Her Blake was nothing if not lovable.

Blake was the one she worried about. It hurt to see his beautiful eyes still cloud with grief sometimes when he was deep in thought. And it bothered her that he could want Erin as much as he obviously did but still withhold his heart.

I'm going to give it back to him.

And that was why she was here, to jar him into realizing what he had now was so much more than what he'd lost—so much more than *her*. Clutching a paper bag in her hand, she crossed the room and stopped in front of Blake's cluttered desk.

Seeing the empty spot on his credenza hurt. Every time she'd come in here when she was alive, Glenna had begged him to let her swap that picture of her in her wedding gown for a newer, less formal shot. But he'd been adamant about that particular portrait, so it had stayed.

Maybe he'd finally started to get on with his life and put it away. Then she remembered. When she'd looked in on him here just days after her funeral, seeing him suffering and wanting baby Jamie's life destroyed, the picture had already been gone, along with everything in the master suite at home that had apparently reminded him too much of her.

"Just as well." Glenna set a brand-new, brushed silver frame in the place where Blake used to keep her wedding portrait. *"These go better in here, anyway."*

She took a moment to stare at the enlargement. It was her favorite of some photos Blake had captured of his new family at Possum Kingdom. Erin, Timmy and Jamie lay stretched out on a blanket under a tree, looking happy but tired out from a long day's play. This was the kind of family Blake deserved—the kind she hadn't been able to give him.

It had been quite a task to levitate the negatives from Blake's study, materialize in a photo shop she'd never frequented as a living being, and get this shot blown up and framed. But it had been worth the effort. She perched on the windowsill next to a couch in the corner of the office, made herself invisible, and settled down to catch Blake's reaction.

Chapter Twenty-One

ઐ

Blake hadn't slept worth a damn, but he shrugged off his fatigue and put on a cheerful face for Timmy and Erin as he drove them to the hospital. He felt bad about leaving them there alone, but the case he was defending was at a crucial point, and he could hardly delegate the final arguments to one of his young associates. He had to be in court at eleven, and in his office for a while before that to review some new notes his clerk had made.

Thoughts of Timmy and the ordeal he faced tomorrow distracted him as he drove to his office, but he managed to shelve those worries in a corner of his mind when he opened his office door. His client deserved his full attention.

Then he saw the photo.

"What the hell?"

"Is something wrong?"

It took a minute for Blake to realize he'd yelled out loud, and that Sharon was standing beside him, looking at him as if he'd lost his mind. Still, he couldn't tear his gaze from the picture.

"Did you put that there?"

Sharon shook her head. "Nice shot, but no. I never saw it before."

"I have. At least, I think I have. I took a picture like that one, last weekend out at Possum Kingdom. But I didn't have it enlarged or framed, and I didn't bring it here."

"Maybe Mrs. Tanner…"

"She hasn't been here."

"Do you want me to put it away?" Sharon asked, her tone relaying a bit of exasperation as well as a lot of confusion.

"No." As the shock of seeing Erin and the children smiling back at him from the spot where he'd kept Glenna's wedding portrait wore off, Blake realized he liked having an image of his new family here where everyone could see them. "It's all right. Maybe Erin had it framed and delivered. Would you ask Jared to bring in the research he did last night?"

"Right away." Blake didn't blame Sharon for hurrying out. He wouldn't want to be around somebody he'd just figured out might be insane. He turned back to the photo, picking up the frame and looking closely at the picture, when he got a strange feeling that the thing was nothing but a figment of his imagination. It was real, though, as real as the one he'd locked into his credenza's bottom drawer the day after Glenna's funeral.

He didn't know what compelled him to waste time like this on a day when he had to appear in court. Before he began reviewing the additional precedents Jared had found in some old, obscure cases, Blake fumbled in his top desk drawer for the key to the credenza, opened it, and took one longing look at the image of his first, lost bride.

Despite the late start and the nagging question about where that picture had come from, Blake wrapped up his summation at three and heard the judge's ruling before four o'clock. Usually a victory as big as this one gave him an adrenaline rush. Today, his only feeling was relief that the case was finished and he'd be able to stand by his son. And ask Erin about that blasted picture.

Blake strode into Timmy's hospital room minutes before five, loosening his tie as he went. "How's our boy?" He hoped Tim and Erin wouldn't see straight through his false heartiness.

"Timmy's fine. But you look tired." Erin looked up from the novel she'd been reading.

"I'm not, really."

"How was your day?" she asked.

"Good. The judge ruled in our favor. XCon offered a compromise settlement, and my client agreed." Suddenly he noticed the empty bed. "Where is Timmy?" Trying hard to relax, he shed his suit coat and settled into the other lounge chair.

"He's having an MRI. It shouldn't take much longer."

Just then, an orderly opened the door and wheeled Timmy in on a child-size gurney. "Daddy!" he said, his eyes bright as they settled on Blake.

"Hey, sport."

Blake stood and helped the orderly move Timmy into bed. For an hour or so, they talked before Timmy nodded off to sleep. Erin had put on a happy face, but Blake felt her fear, and that fueled his own apprehension. In the car as they drove home, and later when he held her, he tried to shake off the sense of foreboding that had begun last week and escalated today.

He wanted to share his fear with Erin, and he wanted to ask her about that picture that had appeared as if by magic in his office, but he couldn't find the words. All he could do was hold her, be there for Timmy, and hope for…he wasn't sure just what he prayed tomorrow would bring.

* * * * *

"He's going to be all right."

Erin wished she felt as confident as Blake sounded. "Blake, I'm sorry. I've never been such a basket case before, not even the first time they operated on Timmy. I don't know what's gotten into me," she told him as she choked back tears.

Timmy had been in the operating room for hours. Here in the VIP lounge a cherry-smocked attendant offered freshly brewed coffee and a selection of fragrant home-baked sweet rolls with annoying regularity. The VIP treatment didn't help. Erin fretted as much as she had through others of Timmy's operations in the big, spartan main surgery waiting room where the only refreshments came from quirky vending machines.

Nervous, she paced across the room and looked out from a wide expanse of windows onto neatly manicured grounds. The glass reflected her image, so different now when she was wearing a fine light wool coat dress and matching burgundy heels than it had been those times when she'd waited in that other place in tired old jeans and a faded sweater.

She looked at Blake. He'd been only a source of funds for Timmy's last surgery. Now Timmy called him Daddy, and she looked to him for strength and comfort. She was glad he'd come. Nothing seemed to faze him. He pulled back a lever and settled into a recliner, coffee and rolls at his fingertips on a nearby table. Then he met her gaze, and she saw the stark fear in his eyes.

"Timmy will come through this just fine," she murmured, echoing Blake's earlier words as she knelt beside the chair and sandwiched his hand between her trembling palms.

He nodded. "Sit down, Erin. Try to relax."

She sank onto the sofa and tried to smile. "It's been nearly four hours," she said as she glanced at the stylized clock on the opposite wall.

"Doctor Newman warned us this would take time."

"What will happen to Tim if this doesn't work?" Erin pictured her little boy as he was last night, excited and certain that soon he would be able to run and play like other kids.

"We'll just have to help him cope, I guess. Show him there's more that he can do than there is that he can't."

"Of course." What Blake said made sense. Still, it broke Erin's heart to think of Timmy having to watch his baby brother grow and develop, learn to walk and run—while Timmy was confined to a wheelchair.

"Everybody has disabilities, honey. They just don't all show. There are plenty of things Timmy can excel at, even if he can't use his legs."

"Blake, do you know something I don't?" Had Timmy's doctors talked to him alone, told him something they hadn't said to her?

He met her questioning gaze. "I know Timmy's not likely ever to be an Olympic runner. I believe that's what Dan Newman said when I tried to pin him down. Erin, my work demands that I be able to sense when I'm hearing the unvarnished truth and when I'm being snowed. We were getting a snow job when we met with Timmy's treatment team. I went to Newman later and made him give it to me straight."

"Straight? And all he said was that Timmy would never be in the Olympics?"

"That's all he would predict outright. They don't know whether all this surgery is going to work. They don't know if Tim's legs are going to grow properly. Hell, they don't even know whether they'll have to take his right leg off."

Though she'd heard the same warnings repeatedly since Timmy's accident, Erin panicked when she heard them now. But then she looked at Blake and saw him hurting, too. "And you've known this for..."

"Four days." His tone was bleak as he got up from his chair and joined her on the sofa, putting his arm around her.

He'd known for four days what she'd lived with for years. Four days he'd spent trying to keep her spirits up. She leaned against his muscular chest, soaked in his strength. At that moment when they shared their fear, she loved him even more than before. And she felt his love for Timmy spilling over and encompassing her. They sat there for a long time, sharing what strength they could in silence while they waited helplessly for news.

"Mr. Tanner? Mrs. Tanner?"

Erin jumped at the sound of a woman's voice.

"Yes?" Blake said, that one word reflecting all the tension she felt in his warm, hard body.

"I ordered you some lunch," the woman said, indicating a small table draped with white linen and centered with an incongruously cheery bouquet of orange and gold chrysanthemums.

Erin made herself smile. But when she stood, she wondered if her shaky legs would hold her. Blake must have seen her tremble, because he put his arm firmly around her waist and led her to the table.

"Eat, honey. You need to keep up your strength."

Looking at the sandwich and garnishes on her plate, she doubted she could swallow a bite. But Blake was right. She had to keep going, not only for Timmy but for baby Jamie and for him. When she looked at him, she tried to smile, before picking up a triangle of the large sandwich and taking a bite.

"That's my girl."

Only when he saw that she was eating did he dig into the food on his own plate. Erin remembered those other times, when she'd sat alone in that other waiting room, surrounded by so many other worried parents, and her heart filled with gratitude and love because now Blake was here for her.

Those feelings carried her through until, as the sun was setting in a blustery late autumn sky, an exhausted Doctor Newman came to tell them Timmy's surgery was done.

"His left leg should be nearly good as new," Newman told them as he sank onto a chair that faced the sofa where Blake and Erin had settled down to wait.

"And," Blake prompted.

Erin's muscles tensed. They'd warned her when Tim had his first surgery that, even if the leg survived, it might never work again. Every time Tim had gone to surgery, the operative permits she'd signed had included…

"We did all we could. We took the leg off just above where we'd reattached it."

We took the leg off. The doctor's words rang in Erin's ears as blackness overcame her.

*   *   *   *   *

Blake felt as if someone had slammed him into a brick wall. He gasped for breath. It took moments for him to realize he was cradling Erin's unconscious body tightly against his chest, and that Doctor Newman appeared to be waiting for something.

"Do you want me to call someone?"

Blake looked down at his unconscious wife. "Greg Halpern."

Newman picked up a phone from the table beside him and punched out four numbers. Blake listened to him tell someone to get Doctor Halpern as he felt Erin begin to stir.

Newman set the phone down and met Blake's gaze. "I know it's a shock, but the news I brought was good, no matter how it sounded. Your son will be able to walk, even run. Soon. He'll be minimally disabled."

Blake shot the surgeon a disbelieving look. He couldn't get the words out, but apparently his horror showed.

"Better to get around almost normally with a prosthesis than to sit in a chair all your life with a leg that won't grow and won't work," Newman said with a tired-sounding sigh.

"How the hell would you know?"

Newman kicked the table leg hard with his left foot. Blake's mind registered a hollow, metallic sound immediately, but it took a moment for the significance to set in. "You?"

The surgeon nodded. "Bone cancer. I was nine years old and damn lucky they got it before it spread," he explained before Blake could voice a question. "I was up on a prosthesis in three months, and out of therapy in six months. Kids bounce back faster than adults."

Blake tried to remember if there was anything about the way this man moved that should have tipped him off. He couldn't. Maybe he was losing the keen power of observation that made him a good attorney. "I couldn't tell," he admitted, more to himself than to the doctor.

"Most people can't."

Erin stirred again, and Blake watched her dark lashes flicker against pale, smooth skin. "Blake?" Her voice made the barest whisper of a sound in the still, quiet room.

"I'm here, honey."

Her eyelids fluttered, then opened. "I—I'm sorry. Doctor Newman, is Timmy..."

"He's in recovery. Because the operations took so long, it's going to take him a while to wake up. But he came through the surgery fine."

Blake met Erin's newly determined gaze and sensed she was going to demand all the details Newman had just provided him. He wished she wouldn't. He'd rather tell her himself in the familiar surroundings of home, where he could emphasize the positive and offer the comfort of his body.

Greg strode in, Sandy at his heels. Blake had never been so glad to see his friend. Erin let her sister hug her and share her tears while Greg digested Newman's detailed medical explanation—information Blake himself was in no state of mind to grasp.

"You all can stay here as long as you want," Newman said, drawing Blake's attention from Erin and Sandy who were quietly weeping in a corner of the pleasant room. "I'm going to check on Timmy."

"How can he be so damn matter-of-fact?" Blake asked Greg when Newman had left. "And so technical? The man's a walking, talking robot." He knew he wasn't being fair. Newman had a human streak, and he'd shown it by revealing his own disability to ease Blake's mind.

Greg shook his head. "He knows shit happens and life goes on. I guess he found that out young. If he didn't, a few years working in his particular surgical specialty probably taught him pretty fast. Timmy's going to get along okay, even if losing his leg won't be quite as easy for him to accept as Newman thinks it will."

"I knew the guy was a quack."

"Blake, he's not. Dan Newman and his trauma team are as good as you'll find anywhere in the world. Trust me."

Blake looked over at Erin. "How…"

"How can you make Erin stop hurting?" Her heartrending sobs had stopped, and she was wiping at her tear-streaked cheeks with a Kleenex.

"Just love her."

Blake met his friend's solemn gaze. "Love?"

"Don't you?"

Did he? Of course he didn't. He loved Glenna and Glenna alone, since before he could remember and until eternity. Before he could blurt out the negative reply, he checked himself. "I love Timmy," he replied. "I like and respect Erin."

"Well, I hope that's enough. Come on, Sandy and I are going to take you two home. There's nothing any of us can do here tonight."

* * * * *

"Are you okay?"

Blake's question startled Erin and made her jerk involuntarily. She couldn't help smiling when Jamie yelped his protest at the interruption of his late evening snack. "I will be. How about you?"

"I think I'll make it, too. Did our little guy miss his mommy today?"

"Some. I think I missed him more. It's not too bad to skip nursing him once, but three times…"

"I should have had Theresa bring him to the hospital."

"A hospital's no place for a baby. I'll be fine when he finishes nursing." Deftly, she turned Jamie and offered him her other aching breast.

It seemed to Erin that Blake was skirting around the subject of Timmy until he finally blurted out, "What in hell can I say to him?"

"Tell him how he'll be able to get out of that chair now and walk. Let him know how great you think it is that he'll be able to go to school like other kids." Erin had been preparing herself for this for years, but Blake had only four days to digest the reality that Timmy's physical abilities would always be compromised.

"I'm going to be there for his therapy, while he's in the hospital at least. It will be too hard on you."

"Thank you," she said simply, holding those other words, words of love and sharing, deeply in her heart.

Blake glanced at Jamie. "Is he done?"

"Yes. He's sleeping now."

"I'll put him to bed." He got up and took the baby from Erin.

"Come back?" She needed him to hold and comfort her, but she thought from noticing his haggard expression that he might even need her more.

"Sure."

Through the night, she lent him her warmth, waking when harsh dreams wracked his mind and body and holding him as she often held Timmy. With every gentle touch, each soothing motion of her hands across muscles tense with churning emotions, Erin silently gave Blake the love she hoped someday he might consciously accept.

She hoped she, Blake, and all the family and friends who cared for Timmy would help him accept what fate had decreed for him.

Chapter Twenty-Two
Glenna's Ghost

ॐ

You're so little, so helpless. What you need is a guardian angel, but I guess you'll just have to make do with a ghost. A ghost who loves you as much as she loves those sweet babies she wasn't able to nurture in her body until they were ready to nurture in her arms.

Glenna leaned against the icy windowpane and watched over Timmy as he slept, seeing but not seen. She fought back an urge to stroke his face, smooth back an errant strand of hair that curled damply against his pale forehead.

Her gaze wandered to Timmy's legs, one heavily bandaged from thigh to toe, the other wrapped like a mummy to its blunted end a few inches below his knee. Then, as the sun was coming up, she noticed his little body twitch and focused on his dark eyelashes that fluttered against baby-soft cheeks. It was all Glenna could do to stay back, let Doctor Newman get up from the bedside chair where he'd spent the night and perch on the edge of the narrow mattress.

He's going to tell him what they did. Glenna wanted to scream out, *No!* Timmy would need his mom and dad to help him face this. She was furious yet powerless to still the doctor's voice.

"We had to take your right leg off, Tim," she heard him say in a tone that was so matter-of-fact, she wished she could make her presence known and slug him. But she couldn't. All she could do was will Timmy to feel a caring presence, to reach out for Blake and Erin's love that would see him through.

"Why?"

The way Tim murmured just one word expressed all the horror Glenna knew he had to be feeling now. And the look on his face told the same tale when he raised his head and stared, as if not believing, at the empty space on the bed where his lower leg and foot should have been.

I wish I could hold you, sweetheart, erase that look of terror from those innocent eyes. Where are Erin and Blake? What are they thinking? They should have been the ones to tell you your life is going to be changed forever.

Newman's explanation was simple enough that Glenna imagined Timmy could understand. "Hey, there," the doctor said gruffly when he apparently saw the tears running down Timmy's cheeks. "You'll be running and playing soon. No more wheelchairs — or crutches."

Glenna felt like balling up a fist and letting this callous jerk have it! Who was he to tell Timmy he'd be grateful that he no longer had half of one of his legs? She dragged her gaze away from the little boy's anguished face and focused on the doctor.

What was he doing? She watched him swivel toward Timmy and roll up the left leg of his baggy surgical scrubs. And then she knew.

"Look, Tim," he said, unfastening a leather brace that cradled his knee and extended halfway up his thigh. "I've had this since I wasn't much older than you. I'll bet you didn't know."

Timmy shook his head, his wide-eyed gaze fixed on hands that worked the prosthesis off and set it aside, then peeled off a white sock and held up the leg so Tim could see.

"Will I look like that?"

Newman grinned. "Well, you won't quite look this neat, since you already had a fearsome bunch of scars, pal. But the length and shape's going to be pretty much like this."

"And I'll get a leg like this one?" Timmy gave the prosthesis a visual once-over.

Newman replied as he pulled the sock back over the stump of his leg. "Eventually. Until you quit growing, yours won't be exactly like this, because they'll have to make yours so they can adjust it as you grow. If you got a leg like this one now, you'd have to get a new one three or four times a year until you're grown."

"How do you put it on?"

"Like this." He showed Timmy how the stump had to fit in the socket of the prosthesis just so, and explained how it stayed on by itself. "You may not need a brace. I wear one because my knee bothers me when I have to stand in one place a long time, like I did yesterday."

Newman answered every question Timmy put forth, from how long it would take his legs to heal, to whether he'd be able to wear his new leg in the pool. Soon, Timmy was chuckling with the doctor over what Glenna figured had to be a private joke.

Erin and Blake came in then, windblown and looking as if neither of them had slept a wink. Glenna saw Blake look at Newman, and watched the doctor nod his head. Blake clutched Erin's hand, and they moved together to the other side of Timmy's bed.

"Mommy! Daddy! Look. Doctor Newman fixed up this leg just like he said he would. And he cut the bad one off so I can get a new leg and run and play."

Glenna saw that Tim was giving Erin and Blake what he considered fantastic news—but her heart went out to Erin, who obviously was fighting a new wave of tears. And Blake. He looked as ravaged as he had that day when she'd gone to his office and witnessed what she'd done to him by dying.

Timmy didn't need her now, and there was nothing she could do that would ease Erin or Blake. Silently Glenna floated away, leaving them all to cope with life's realities while she lingered in this spaceless limbo. Each day the promise of heaven beckoned her, while those she had loved compelled her to stay and help them find their way.

Chapter Twenty-Three

ဆ

The following afternoon, Sandy gasped when Greg told her they were stopping by the hospital on the way to her apartment. "Go see Timmy? Greg, I can't. He's going to know, the minute he sees my face."

Greg looked up from the chart he had just finished annotating and met Sandy's anxious gaze. "He's going to know, love, with or without seeing your face. Newman was going to tell him as soon as he woke up last night. Come on, cheer up. Tim's going to be better off in the long run."

"Without his leg?"

They'd been over this before, last night and again this morning. Greg didn't envy Blake having to be strong for Erin, knowing his friend was damn near as upset as Sandy over the amputation.

Patiently, Greg went over the reasons for the radical surgery again. "Sweetheart, Timmy will be walking soon."

Sandy sniffed. "Still…"

"I know. It's not fair. But he'll be okay if we all let him know we love him. Come on, let's go."

For the first time since they'd been together, Greg realized just how young she was—not only in years, but in life experience. Though she could cope, just barely, with his difficult daughter whose failings were invisible to the naked eye, the realization that Timmy would have to live life as an amputee seemed more than she could handle. He'd help her get through this, somehow.

Instead of herding her toward a sad confrontation she was nowhere near ready for, he sat down and held her as if she were no older than Timmy. "Cry, love. Let it out. I know you're hurting. I am, too."

Two hours later than he'd intended, he and Sandy finally met Blake outside the door to Timmy's room.

"Don't go in if you're going to cry," Blake warned them, his gaze on Sandy's tear-stained cheeks. Greg gave her hand a squeeze.

"I won't. Is Erin with Timmy?" Tiny tremors still ran through her body, but Greg noted the determined set of her shoulders and the smile on her lips.

Blake nodded. "I brought her back a few minutes ago."

"Don't you want to go in?"

Greg doubted the hospital would enforce its two-visitors-at-a-time rule, but he figured to cut his friend some slack. "Go on, sweetheart. Blake and I will visit out here for a while." He watched her take a deep breath before opening the heavy door. Then he took a good look at Blake.

"Come on, we can duck in the docs' lounge down the hall. You look dead on your feet."

Blake sighed. "I feel worse. Erin and Sandy must come from tough stock. How they can smile and act like nothing's wrong is beyond me. I lasted about five minutes. Knew I'd break down if I didn't get the hell away."

"You're talking about your wife who fainted dead away yesterday afternoon? And Sandy? She's been practically hysterical. I just spent hours trying to make her believe Timmy's losing a leg wouldn't keep him from living a happy, productive life."

"Try persuading me."

"Intellectually, you know. It's just taking your emotions awhile to listen to your head."

Blake smiled when he met Greg's gaze. "Did they teach you that in med school?"

"No. It's just something I've picked up, observing folks reacting to the 'good news, bad news' *schtick*.

Blake looked puzzled.

"'Your baby's fine, but there can't be any more.' Or, 'Your wife's alive, but I couldn't save the baby.' Don't know how many times I've had to tell those things to anxious husbands. It takes a while for them to figure out the good news outweighs the bad. It's got to be tougher when it's a little kid that can't be fixed just as good as new. But the idea's the same."

Blake nodded. "I know."

"Does Timmy?"

"Yes. Erin and I came back this morning, right after Doctor Newman told him."

Greg didn't envy his colleague that job. "And?"

"Newman said Timmy cried a little at first, but by the time we got here, he was asking when he could get his new leg."

"When can he?"

"Supposedly he'll be walking soon, and running by the time school starts next fall."

"That sounds right. I don't know a lot about rehab therapy, but when Sandy told me about Timmy's injury, I did a bit of reading. Below-knee amputees, especially kids, usually get fitted right away for artificial limbs and start using them as soon as the swelling goes down." The sooner Blake realized Timmy would be up walking quickly, the sooner he'd stop agonizing over the boy's tragic but not fatal loss. "Sounds as though Timmy's taking it pretty well."

"I guess so. He's drugged up with painkillers, and both legs are bandaged up like a mummy's. Come on, let's go see him. Timmy's the bravest little kid I've ever seen."

As Blake opened the door, Greg glanced at his watch. Fifteen minutes since Sandy had squared her shoulders and stepped inside. He'd imagined her determined cheeriness would have worn off by now, but when she looked up at him, she gave him a genuine, brilliant smile.

"Can we stay a while longer?" she asked.

"Sure. Mrs. Watson's with Shana, and I'm not on call." When Greg glanced at Erin, he saw she was about as strung out as Blake. "Hey, Timmy. How's it going?" he asked, ruffling the boy's light hair.

"Okay. I'm sleepy. Did you know I'm gonna get a new foot?"

"I heard."

"Wanna see?"

"Later, okay?" Shooting a reassuring glance toward Sandy first, Greg glanced at Erin. Blake had his hands on her shoulders, and both of them looked like they were about to drop. "Why don't you let Mommy and Daddy go home and get some rest now, Tim? Sandy and I will stay until you go to sleep."

"Okay. Mommy, give Jamie a hug for me. And bring my Game Gear tomorrow, and my box of games. Daddy, you know where they are." Timmy hugged Erin first, then fiercely held onto Blake's neck when he bent to say good night.

"Can I show you now?" Tim asked. Greg nodded, concerned for Sandy but determined not to upset Timmy by declining to look at the surgeons' handiwork.

He rested his hands at Sandy's slender waist while Timmy lifted the top sheet. "See? The doctors cut off my old leg 'cause they couldn't make it work. Doctor Newman says I'm gonna get a new one so I can walk again, just as soon as my other leg gets well."

"That's great, Timmy," Sandy exclaimed, bending over and giving the bandaged limbs Tim seemed so proud of a close look. Greg pretended to examine the bandaged stump before pulling up the covers and encouraging the little boy to sleep.

When he and Sandy walked out together, Greg realized he had yet another reason to love her. She'd just proved that instead of a strong-willed girl, she was on the way to becoming a strong, caring woman. His woman, he thought with pride as he took her in his arms that night at her apartment and gave her all his love.

* * * * *

Blake gave Erin his passion, comforted her when she woke in a cold sweat, and treated her like she was a fragile mannequin. When she thought of what he gave in those terms, she got quietly furious. The sleepless night she'd just endured had done a number on her composure.

She couldn't fault Blake's sweet, thoughtful lovemaking or the way he'd held her when she finally broke down and sobbed for her son's loss. He'd even brought Jamie and held them both while the baby nursed and she sobbed. Blake gave her satisfying sex and caring concern, but he withheld the one thing Erin needed to take her through these sad, trying times.

"Damn it, I want more than you have to give. You love Timmy, why can't you love me, too?"

No one heard her, for Blake had gotten up again once he thought she was asleep and tiptoed across the hall as he did most every night. Tomorrow Timmy would come home. And Sandy's wedding was just three days away.

"He does. He just doesn't know it yet."

Erin looked around, searching for the source of Glenna's now-familiar voice. Shivering when a sudden gust of cold air brushed her sleep-warmed skin, she turned toward the patio. The ghost perched on a chair beside the door. "You startled me."

"Sorry. I've been lurking around these last few days, seeing how you and Blake handle worrying about your precious little boy. You've gotten along just fine on your own, but this morning it seemed as though you need a friend."

Erin's cheeks warmed at Glenna's reminder that she was always around, hearing and seeing but not always being seen or heard. Had she watched when Blake held her? Heard them making hot, passionate love?

"Don't worry. I may be a pest, but I'm not a voyeur. He is a wonderful lover, though, isn't he? Glenna paused, as though enjoying her own stored memories. *You don't need to answer—I can see it in your eyes. You love him. I knew you would."*

It never ceased to amaze Erin that Glenna expected the marriage that came about because of her own untimely death and Jamie's imminent arrival to become a love match. "Yes, I love him." Ironically, one of the reasons she loved Blake was the fierce loyalty he'd inspired in Glenna—a loyalty that survived beyond the grave.

"Tell him. He's hurting now, more than you know, and not just for your little boy. Haven't you noticed how hard he's been trying to keep your spirits up?"

"I know. Blake's a good man. And he loves Timmy as much as if he were his birth father. That's only one of the reasons why I've fallen in love with him." Erin met Glenna's ethereal gaze and smiled. "But you're wrong. He doesn't love me. He can't. He still loves you."

Glenna stomped her foot. The gesture, a silent one, gave Erin an eerie feeling even though she had to smile.

"He'll love you. He knows I'm never coming back. You tell him. Do it tonight. By the way, something tells me Timmy's going to get along just fine."

"I'm going now. These visits take a lot out of me, and I've got a feeling you two are going to put me through a lot more before you settle down. I have to see you in a loving marriage with Blake before I can find peace."

Glenna's image was fading, but Erin still felt her presence. "I'll try." Blinking back tears, she tried hard to believe the ghost's predictions.

* * * * *

Timmy certainly had Blake's love. He'd spent their son's first day home, learning to change Timmy's bandages, talking with Michelle and the prosthetist, and encouraging Timmy to do the painful therapy the doctors had prescribed.

He'd given Erin a chance to finalize the plans for Sandy's wedding and keep her mind off Timmy's loss. She couldn't think of anything, other than a declaration of love, that he could have done to please her more. Glenna's words floated in her head as she halfway listened to Blake and Timmy bantering, and later while she and Blake walked across the patio to their suite.

Glenna's advice resonated in Erin's head. Tell him you love him "I will," she said, realizing when she said it that Blake would probably think she'd lost her mind.

Blake shot her a peculiar look but didn't pursue the subject. "Thanks for the picture," he told her, giving her hand a squeeze.

"What picture?"

"The one of you and the boys that I took out at Possum Kingdom."

"You should be thanking yourself. You took them." She'd pouted at the time because no one had been around to hold the camera and get at least one shot of all of them together.

"But you or someone had to have taken the one where you were sitting on the blanket with the boys, and had it enlarged and framed. It turned up in my office the day before Timmy's surgery."

"Really? I'd like to take the credit, Blake, but it wasn't me."

"I did it. But you can't tell him!"

Glenna! Erin heard her, plain as day. This was too much, the ghost playing with Blake's mind. She was going to give Glenna a serious scolding, next time the ghost turned up.

Blake sounded doubtful when he said, "Well, it certainly was strange. It wasn't there the night before. I'm sure of it. Sharon got to work about a half-hour before I did, and she said no one went into my office then. I'd meant to ask you about it before, but with the surgery and all, it slipped my mind."

"That's understandable." Erin was hardly able to contain her annoyance with Glenna. "Did you like the picture?"

"Yeah. You're a beautiful woman and we've got two good-looking kids. I'm damn proud of the way Tim's holding up, aren't you?" He opened the patio door to the bedroom and they went inside.

"Yes, I am. You know, you're a lot of the reason he's accepting this so well. Thank you."

He didn't respond except to whisper in a husky voice, "It's been a long day, honey. Let's shower together. We can get to bed faster that way."

Erin thought of the shower they'd shared at Possum Kingdom. Her heart beat faster and her cheeks got hot. "That sounds like a good idea," she murmured as her hands went to the fasteners on her jacket.

She'd felt his passion, experienced his skill at making love before, but tonight, she sensed more as he loved her with infinite tenderness and care. A tiny voice inside her head whispered that what he was feeling might be compassion, but she pushed that warning aside and let herself believe that he was finally expressing love for *her*.

Tonight she held nothing back, let nothing mar the pure pleasure she felt in touching him, caressing his strong, stubbled jaw, stroking the strong column of his throat. She loved the way his flat coppery nipples responded when she ran her fingers over their tips, the ripple of his abdominal muscles when she splayed her hand across them and used one finger to explore his navel.

His kisses drugged her, first cajoling, then demanding her surrender. Unconditional surrender she eagerly gave to his mouth…his hands…his huge, hard cock that filled her with its searing heat.

He touched her everywhere, whispering raw, needy words of sex when he thrust in her, over and over until she was nothing but a quivering mass of sensation. His words became throaty growls, growls gave way to moans as he trembled above her. Her pleasure undulated, grew and spread, fed his own, when she lost control.

Unable to hold back longer, they exploded together, their triumphant shouts mingling, merging in one fiery climax. Blake had touched her body before, but tonight he'd touched her heart. She finally trusted that she had reached and touched the part of him he'd guarded with a vengeance for so long.

As they lay together in the darkness, half-asleep, their arms and legs entwined, savoring the quiet aftermath of what had been the most profound experience of her life, Erin found the courage to gamble with her heart. "I love you, Blake," she said softly, and she waited for his reaction.

He stirred. She held her breath, wondering if he had heard her. Then, he turned and locked her in his arms, and burrowed his face into the crook of her shoulder. "Oh, Glenna. I love you, too," he murmured so softly Erin could barely hear him.

She felt him breathing softly against her neck and knew he had fallen back to sleep. Loving him the way she did, she couldn't disturb him, so she lay there in the dark and held him, tasting the salt of her own tears as the world she had let herself dream of shattered along with her broken heart.

Chapter Twenty-Four

Glenna's Ghost

ഔ

"I never thought I'd say it or even think it, but my darling Blake, you're a goddamn first-class asshole!"

Glenna had known tonight would be crucial in Blake and Erin's marriage, so she had forced aside that lingering jealousy and lurked in the shadows of their darkened room, listening and looking only enough to see that Blake was making love, not simply gaining release from pent-up sexual desire as Erin had hinted he did.

I was right. They belong together. The sparks they make could wake the dead!

Yes, she was dead but she wasn't gone. And she wasn't about to go until her stubborn ox of a husband put her to rest and admitted that he loved Erin as much as he ever loved her.

No! Blake would have to admit he loved Erin more. The jerk came alive in every nerve in his gorgeous body the minute he looked at Erin, while sometimes Glenna had found it necessary to resort to elaborate seduction and erotic toys to get him in the mood.

An hour ago he'd been hard as stone before they'd touched, before either of them had shed a lick of clothes. He'd worshiped every inch of Erin's long, lithe body with his hands and mouth before taking care of his own very obvious need. He wouldn't have bothered if all he'd wanted was to relieve his damn male lust.

He'd been the perfect lover, and Erin had risked giving him the words of love she wasn't sure he was ready to hear. And what had he done?

Glenna laughed, with disdain, not glee. *"The stupid, unfeeling asshole had to call her by my name!"*

Glenna watched him now, sleeping on Erin's shoulder without a care in the world while Erin sobbed quietly. Damn, she wished she had the power to conk him in the head. The guy might have graduated fourth in his class at law school, but he didn't have a lick of brains.

"What do I have to do to knock some common sense into your thick skull? Damn it all!" She slammed an ineffectual fist onto the sleek glass tabletop. *"I know you love her, Blake. What do I have to do to make you realize it?"*

Weary of the one-sided conflict with the man she'd once loved more than life, Glenna tried to think of tricks she could pull to make Blake see the light.

She'd have to get some rest tonight, because if she weren't mistaken, she'd have to deal with an irate Erin in the morning. Still muttering curses at Blake for his unfeeling *faux pas*, Glenna faded away, still hearing Erin sobbing as if her heart were broken.

Chapter Twenty-Five

ಬಿ

It had been all Erin could do to hold her tongue while Blake whistled his way from bed to his dressing room, and then down the hall toward breakfast. When she was sure he was out of earshot, she leapt out of bed and jerked on a disreputable looking pair of sweats.

Last night, she had hurt. This morning the pain had turned to anger. No, not anger but plain, unvarnished fury. She might have agreed to be a stand-in mother for his baby, but she damn sure never consented to be a stand-in bedmate for his meddlesome dead wife! Fuming, Erin stomped into her dressing room and started opening drawers.

If Timmy didn't love Blake so, she would take him and Jamie, leave this place and never come back. She'd have to content herself with moving back to the other wing where she'd lived before the farce of a wedding. Who cared if everybody in Dallas found out she and Blake had a marriage-in-name-only?

Where was Glenna's interfering ghost? Erin wanted to give *her* a piece of her mind, too! None of this would have happened if the woman had stayed wherever it was that ghosts stayed and left Erin alone.

Grabbing an empty pillowcase, Erin emptied a drawer of her lingerie chest into it and opened the next drawer. She repeated the process until the pillowcase was bulging at its seams.

"He didn't mean it, Erin."

Erin refused to look and see whether Glenna had decided to appear in person. If she saw her, she'd want to strangle her. She wasn't sure it was possible to wreak physical havoc on a ghost, though. Then she realized the implication of the ghost's words and looked up to meet that familiar, glowing gaze. "You didn't mean to eavesdrop, either, did you?"

"Well…"

Erin had never heard Glenna hesitate before. "What's the matter? Do you actually have the decency to be embarrassed, admitting you invaded my privacy and watched us having sex?"

"You're not leaving. You can't."

Erin widened her stance and set both hands on her hips. "No, I'm not leaving. You saw to it that I couldn't. Not when my son is so attached to Blake. But I damn well am moving out of this room, and there's nothing you can do to stop me."

Whirling around, she opened another drawer and began emptying it into another pillowcase. When she filled it, she turned to set it by the first one she'd stuffed with undies, only to notice the bag was gone.

While Erin gawked, the second bag floated out of her hands as if by magic, and clothes settled once more in the drawers she'd just emptied. "What are you doing?"

Glenna grinned down at her from her perch on top of a tall, skinny chest of drawers. *"Saving you from yourself. You don't want to do this."*

"Why not? How would you like feeling like an overpaid nanny who earns her keep by filling in for Blake's *real* wife in bed each night?" Erin opened another drawer and began to empty it. "How would you like having the man you love call you by someone else's name?"

"The guy's a real ass, isn't he?"

While Erin gawked at Glenna, hardly believing the ghost would say a word against her husband, Glenna managed to get the latest sack of clothes she had filled replaced in the drawer from whence it came. "Leave me alone. Haven't you done enough to me?" She watched Glenna float down from her perch to keep her from getting to more clothes she intended to pack.

"Don't you move out of here. If you're really that mad at Blake, make him go back to sleeping on that daybed in his study where he hid out for God knows how many months."

That was the first halfway sensible suggestion Erin had heard come out of Glenna's mouth. Still, she balked. "It's not far enough away."

"What will Timmy think?"

Erin choked back a bitter retort. She knew as well as Glenna that it would distress her boy to think she and his new, wonderful daddy weren't getting along. Timmy already had more than enough for a seven-year-old to cope with. "You know how to deal low blows," she muttered, but she reached around the ghost and closed the only drawer that still gaped open.

"I'll do whatever it takes to see you all happy together," Glenna said, her voice still strong though her image was beginning to fade.

"You stay here," Erin ordered, not ready to let the ghost escape without her having her say. "I've listened to you for long enough. Now it's your turn to hear what I have to say."

Glenna smiled. *"Hurry. I'll stick around as long as I can."*

"Okay. First, don't you go planting pictures or playing mind games with us anymore. Second, keep your nose out of what's going on between me and Blake. You didn't make me love him—I managed that all by myself. Finally, get it through your head that you can't make him love me."

Glenna's lower lip trembled, and Erin saw regret in the ghost's benign expression. Suddenly she felt guilty. "Look. I'm not blaming you. I'm glad you've let me get to know you, even if it had to be this way." Erin gestured toward the golden aura that gave the ghost an otherworldly look. "But you can't push me and Blake around like we're a couple of puppets. Life doesn't work that way."

"I know," Glenna said softly as Erin watched her fade away.

* * * * *

"It's almost time for us to get ready for the rehearsal," Blake said jovially as he strode into the suite early that afternoon.

"I know."

"Need help with any last-minute details for tomorrow?" He paused to drop a quick kiss on Erin's inviting lips. The chill he'd heard in her voice suddenly intensified when she pulled away. "What's wrong?"

"Nothing. If you consider calling the woman you're sleeping with by someone else's name nothing, that is." Erin's tone fairly dripped venom.

"What?" His good mood disintegrated in the face of her anger.

"Do the words, 'I love you too, Glenna,' ring a bell?"

Blake hesitated. Of course those words rang bells. He *did* love Glenna. "I've never confused you with Glenna when we make love." He cursed himself silently for the way his cock hardened just thinking about fucking Erin.

"Maybe you didn't say it consciously. Whether you remember or not, though, you said it. And it hurt. I can't sleep with you, wondering when you might next mistake me for *her*."

Shit. He must have talked in his sleep. He certainly couldn't remember uttering those damning words. He'd never have been so boorish as to whisper words of love to one woman while he was with another, even if he was thinking them.

When he searched recent memory, Blake realized that when he was having sex with Erin, Glenna never crossed his mind. And that revelation produced not the tearing guilt he would have expected but a gentle sense of sadness.

The last thing he wanted to do was move back into that lonely daybed to toss and turn and try in vain to sleep. Now, though, was not the time to argue. He sensed that Erin's tight, controlled expression masked fury best kept contained until this wedding was over and their time was once again their own.

"If that's what you want. For now. I'm sorry for whatever I said that hurt you." He laid a hand gently on her shoulder, and although she trembled, she didn't pull away.

She met his gaze with sad, dark eyes. "I know. If you'll excuse me, I'm going to spend some time with Timmy."

Blake watched her cross the patio to Tim's room. Women! He'd never understand them, not if he lived to be a hundred. Erin knew he loved Glenna. He'd been nothing but honest when he'd argued that they should marry. He'd reiterated the same feelings when he told Erin he wanted her in his bed. These past few weeks had been trying, but he'd found peace as well as sexual release in his wife's arms. He liked her more each day, and wanted her with an intensity he'd never experienced before.

Apparently he'd vowed his love for Glenna in his sleep, and that got Erin incensed. Rightly so. He'd straighten out this problem as soon as things settled down. Right now he tried to focus on Sandy and Greg's wedding and his duties as surrogate father of the bride.

* * * * *

Erin's heart ached with envy at the obvious love that flowed between Sandy and Greg at their casual rehearsal dinner. Seeing them so happy made her yearn for an honest, loving relationship of her own. She tried to be happy for them when Blake stood to greet the members of the wedding and their escorts.

She'd never seen Sandy look so excited. And Greg beamed with pride as they made the rounds of all the tables, meeting his bride's young attendants and introducing Sandy to friends and his flamboyant family members who'd flown in from all over the world.

To the understated accompaniment of soft instrumental music, young college friends of Sandy's mingled with Greg's far-flung family members and older, more sophisticated colleagues. Somehow in denim and khaki and without trappings that broadcast personal taste or finances, the group integrated to celebrate.

The differences were there, of course. Facets of light caught the huge diamond one of Greg's Houston cousins had on a beautifully manicured finger. The sleek blonde's ruby-red denim jumpsuit bore the unmistakable mark of a famous designer. Self-consciously, Erin touched the collar of her own denim dress and toyed with its trim of turquoises and silver conchos as she waved at Katy, Sandy's childhood pal and maid of honor, who had on faded Levis and a western shirt.

Sandy laughed at something Katy said and gave Greg a quick, hard hug before they moved to the next table. Even without their matching shirts, no one would have failed to tag them as the bride and groom. They exchanged a few words with Shana, who'd apparently decided to join in the fun instead of causing havoc.

"Erin?"

"What?" Why did he have to look so good he made her mouth water, when his heart belonged to someone else?

"We should mingle."

Mingling was the last thing on Erin's mind. She'd rather have vicariously shared her sister's happiness than played Blake's contented wife. "In a minute," she said, taking a deep breath and an analytic look around the room.

Sandy's attendants and their escorts laughed and chatted among themselves. Erin shrugged off their exuberance as the province of the very young, and turned to their older guests. Greg's cousin with the apparent penchant for precious jewels had her arm draped around her blond, patrician-looking husband, who smiled at her with what looked to Erin like puppy-dog devotion. Feeling like a voyeur, she looked away, turning her attention to another couple at that table.

They, too, looked like lovers. Damn it, surely she wasn't the only person in this wedding party who lacked for love. Her gaze settled on Greg's best man, the youngest of his Houston cousins

Jake Green. Darkly handsome like Greg, but taller, broader and more deeply tanned, he smiled at something Sandy said, then turned to the model-slender beauty next to him. Erin noticed his brooding expression and realized he, too, seemed to be feeling left out of all the love and goodwill that abounded tonight.

"I'm ready now." She didn't want her mood to put a damper on the festivities, though her heart wasn't in the bright smile she kept firmly pasted on her face. Having Blake so close, feeling the warmth of his body against her when they stopped to greet their guests made her want him in spite of her anger. She felt a sense of kindred spirits when Blake introduced her to the brooding best man and his gorgeous wife.

Animosity stirred beneath their brittle veneer of conviviality, and her own self-pity fell aside in a burst of sympathy for the tense couple. Alice, the blonde, spoke just enough to keep from appearing rude, while Greg's cousin Jake struck up a conversation with Blake about some oil rights problem. Erin assumed Blake was handling some litigation about the problem, but she thought it odd for Jake to have brought up business tonight.

"Greg's cousin has a serious problem on his hands," Blake said as they strolled back to their own table.

"The one you two were talking about?"

"No. The one he brought to the wedding."

It surprised Erin that Blake had noticed the undertones of marital dissension. "His wife?" She needed to make certain they were on the same wavelength.

"Yeah. Jake and Alice were barely speaking to each other."

"How well do you know them?"

Blake paused for a moment. "I've known Jake since I've known Greg. Close to twenty years. Of course, Jake was just a kid back then."

"And you weren't?"

"At the time I thought I was pretty grown up, compared to Jake. Greg and I were freshmen at UT, and Jake couldn't have been more than eight or nine years old. He spent a weekend with us, and we took him to a Longhorns football game. He and Greg have always been close—neither of them has brothers—so our paths crossed regularly while he was growing up. For the past few years, my firm has handled his family-owned oil company's legal matters."

"What makes you think something's wrong?"

"Jake doesn't talk business when he's having fun. And he doesn't ordinarily ignore Alice. I'm surprised you couldn't feel the tension between them."

"I felt it. We'd better circulate some more." It stung Erin to realize Blake could easily interpret others' feelings but seemed oblivious to hers.

Later, when the party was over and she crawled into a bed that suddenly felt too big and empty without Blake, Erin let down her defenses and cried.

* * * * *

Blake sat on the daybed across the hall, wondering when and how he'd uttered the damning words that got him tossed out of his wife's bed. All he remembered was feeling sated and totally relaxed last night, lying on his side with Erin curled comfortably against him. And the lovemaking.

He sighed. He still couldn't believe the chemistry that made him want Erin more each time than he had the last. Hell, he had trouble accepting that his cock, throbbing against his zipper now after less than twenty-four hours' denial, was the same one that had placidly waited out long periods of celibacy in years gone by.

His breathing turned ragged. The walls felt like they were closing in. He had to get the hell out of here. Bolting off the daybed, he started to go to Erin, then stopped. He had to honor the damn agreement she'd insisted on earlier. Frustrated, he jerked around and headed outside.

A burst of cold air greeted him, but he welcomed the discomfort. By the time he reached the stable, the throbbing in his balls had simmered down to a dull ache, but the turmoil in his mind raged on. Absentmindedly, he went to Renegade's stall and stroked his glossy black neck.

He loved Glenna. For years she'd been his friend...wife ...lover. Leaning against the cool, smooth stall door that still smelled of fresh paint, Blake closed his eyes. He saw Glenna's smiling face the way it had been the day he'd brought her home as his bride. She'd been so *alive*, so thrilled at the prospect of putting her mark on their home.

Renegade bumped his head against Blake's hand, reminding him he was still there, wanting attention. And that for years he'd forgone his animals because they'd frightened Glenna almost to the point of hysteria. *"I'm not the kind of wife you need,"* she'd said when they'd watched the van pulling out of the drive with his four horses and Beau. God, how he'd missed that mixed-breed mutt once he was gone.

"She was wrong. She gave me everything I needed."

Renegade's ears pricked, as if the colt understood his words. Suddenly another picture filled Blake's mind. As crystal clear as day, he saw Erin, riding beside him and laughing as she'd done one day last week. He'd wanted to reach over, drag her off her mare, and fuck with her in the shade of a venerable oak tree near the bridle path.

Who was he kidding? His cock was always in overdrive around Erin. He always craved her hot, honest sexual response. But he'd had trouble keeping his hands off Glenna. Hadn't he? Funny, that wasn't what he remembered most...

Sure, he'd wanted her. They'd been sixteen, friends who'd suddenly discovered the rush of sexual attraction. God, they'd been a couple of green virgins until that awkward, quick encounter in the back of the Bronco he'd gotten for his birthday. Glenna's teasing that they'd practice 'til they got it right had saved him from complete humiliation when he'd shot his load the minute he rammed his cock inside her.

They had gotten it right. His technique had improved, and Glenna had seemed to delight in learning new, titillating tricks to turn him on. Hell, he couldn't fault their sex life, but he'd never been obsessed with fucking her night and day, the way he was with Erin. Blake waited for the gut-wrenching shame and guilt he expected, but it flickered then floated away on a gust of cold, crisp air that suddenly roared through the stable.

Instead, memories assailed him, of his smiling playmate …his best friend and confidant…his lover and the soul mate with whom he had expected to share the rest of his life. Glenna had been his promise of love and family, his anchor against his own nearly rootless beginnings. They'd clung together, the boy from new Texas money and the girl who sprang from old Dallas aristocracy. Glenna had been the breath of fresh, pure optimism he'd needed.

Remembering didn't hurt as much as he'd feared. Each spring she'd found some new horizon for them to explore, giving him joy and laughter and a bit of her zest for life. And when the leaves began to turn in the fall, she'd been there with the promise of a new, more brilliant season than the one just passed.

Glenna had made him see lush, verdant beauty in tropical forests and stark majesty in deserts and snow-capped mountains. While he'd trekked through those forests, explored the deserts and climbed the mountains, she'd gifted him with appreciating them for themselves instead of seeing mere obstacles put there for him to conquer. She'd been an observer, his Glenna, and he saw now he'd molded his life to mesh with hers.

Blake stroked Renegade's velvety nose. It wasn't just the animals she'd feared. When he'd climbed mountains, she'd cheered from the valley below. She'd hunkered down under a beach umbrella and read, refusing to watch him surf the wild waves off Maui. And she'd tamed him. Usually by his own volition because he wanted to be with her, but not always. When he recalled how she'd put her dainty foot down when he'd wanted to ride a bronc at an amateur rodeo in Wyoming, he had to smile. She'd controlled him well, using no more ammo than his love.

He'd loved Glenna, would always cherish the memories they'd made together. They'd shared their seasons, some triumphant, others not. But now it was time to let her go. In his grief, he'd let what had been healthy love mutate to almost obsessive worship. As he headed back toward the house, he saw things in a different light.

He'd married Erin to give Glenna's son a mother. She'd married him so she could keep Jamie and get help for Tim. Fate had brought them together. But he'd be damned if he didn't love Erin now with an intensity he'd never felt for Glenna.

It wasn't only the mind-boggling sex or the way she loved to ride and fish and hike in the woods. Blake loved her fierce way of caring, her strength and protectiveness over those she loved. He loved seeing her face light up with joy at his smallest considerate gesture.

"Goodbye, Glenna," he whispered, saying farewell to the muted warmth of spring and fall with their soft promises. Back inside now, Blake began preparing to seduce the woman he knew now was his destiny.

For Erin was his future, his reality. Loving Glenna had prepared him for this vivid woman, who gave him the heat of the fieriest summer days, the frost of the coldest winter nights. He'd felt Erin's love when he hadn't been ready to accept it. And, like a blind, dumb fool, he'd damn near thrown it away.

As he made hurried phone calls to formalize his plans, Blake vowed he'd do whatever it took to earn Erin's love.

Chapter Twenty-Six

Glenna's Ghost

ဆ

Finally, Blake, you've seen the light. I hope your talents for persuasion don't let you down — and that you don't put your big foot back in your mouth by telling Erin all about your stroll down memory lane.

Oh, don't get me wrong, darling. You had to look back before you could see your future. I wish you hadn't, in a way, because you won't remember me as kindly.

But maybe you will. You loved me, faults and all, and I believe we made each other happy. Maybe someday, somewhere, we'll meet again. It will be kind of sad if we do, because what you're going to have with Erin is going to make what we had pale by comparison.

From her perch on an oak limb outside Blake's window, she saw him flipping through an address book, making calls. She grinned. Her determined, methodical Blake would follow through and make Erin forgive—and forget—his tardy realization that their falling in love had been destined from the start. At least, Glenna hoped she and Blake hadn't already made such a tangled mess that Erin would never open up her heart again.

No matter. If she balks, I'll be there.

And as Glenna faded slowly away into the pink of dawn's first light, she let out a huge sigh of relief that rustled the old oak tree's branches like a sudden gust of wind.

Chapter Twenty-Seven

ဆ

What a gorgeous day for a wedding!

The sun had come up bright in a cold, cloudless sky this Sunday in late November, and Erin was glad. Sandy and Greg would have a beautiful wedding day. According to a saying her mother had repeated the day Erin had married Bill, good weather for a wedding bode well for a good marriage.

A chilly breeze caught the fur in her collar, and the soft strands tickled Erin's chin as she got out of the car. Everything was set for Sandy's wedding, just as Blake had assured her it would be. Still, she'd needed to drive over to The Manse and see for herself that nothing had been forgotten.

His car was here, so he'd finished whatever it was that had taken him away most of the day. Where, she had no idea. While he had no obligation to keep her informed about his comings and goings, she'd expected him to have the common courtesy to stay around today in case she needed help with something before the wedding. After all, it was Sunday and he ordinarily stuck to her and the kids like glue.

She and Blake were going to have to have a talk. Erin's moods swung like a pendulum between fury and hurt, and she had no intention of spending much more time in this limbo of emotion. Closing the door to her rooms a bit harder than was necessary, she slid off her jacket and kicked off shoes in favor of fuzzy slippers Theresa must have set by the door.

"Erin?"

Blake stood in the doorway to her room, looking hesitant about his welcome. Well he should. She tried hard to tell herself she didn't want his strong, gentle arms around her now. "Where were you?"

"I had to go downtown. Look, Erin, something's come up and I'm going to have to fly to Jackson Hole tonight after the reception."

She hoped her expression didn't reflect the disappointment that slammed into her. "Really?"

"Yes. Something came up with a client. I hate to spring this on you at the last minute like this, but you're coming, too. He's bringing his wife, and she'll need someone to keep her company while we conduct our business."

"But what about Timmy? And Jamie?"

"Mary and Theresa can handle them. And Michelle has agreed to live in while we're gone. It will only be for a few days."

Erin didn't know what to do. She should be here for Timmy and the baby. But a small voice urged her to go, to try once more, away from this house and all its memories, to make their marriage work. Responsibility finally won out over desire. "I can't."

"Think about it, at least. I already had Theresa pack your bags."

Hours later, as she dressed for the wedding, Erin still hadn't decided about the impromptu trip. She had talked to Michelle, who'd suggested Timmy might do better with his first lessons in using his new prosthesis if his doting parents weren't around.

But she'd risked her heart and gotten it battered. Why should she do it again, just to please her husband whose heart belonged to someone else?

"I wouldn't go if I were you!"

Erin set down a tube of concealer and looked around for the ghost who hovered near the ceiling in a corner of the dressing room. "I thought I told you to mind your own business."

"I couldn't help but hear him. He's got one awful nerve, asking you to do him a favor after what he said to you."

"Why should you care?"

"I've decided I want his love all for myself. I can wait for him to join me, out there somewhere."

Suddenly Erin wanted to scratch Glenna's eyes out. "You can't have him. You're not even alive. In fact, all I think you are is an apparition sent from hell to make me pay for planning to give away my baby."

"I gave you your chance. You failed."

"We'll see about that. I'm going to go with Blake, and there's not a thing you can do to stop me!" With that, Erin stepped out of the dressing room and waited for the damn ghost to disappear.

Chapter Twenty-Eight

Glenna's Ghost

ဆ

Glenna hovered just outside the house and chuckled, delighted with the success of her desperate ploy. She should have tried reverse psychology before.

The parting look Erin had shot her way could have frozen ice cubes on a July day in Dallas. That was good. She'd begun to wonder whether Erin had a temper.

Blake needed a strong woman as well as one who loved him, to drag him into the future she, Glenna, hadn't been meant to share. Erin was that woman, and she'd know it as soon as Blake managed to convince her of *his* love. Glenna chuckled. She'd give anything to see him eat the words he used to get Erin to marry him.

But she had to leave Erin to Blake now. She'd done all she could, even tricked Erin into making this trip she'd lay odds had nothing to do with any of Blake's clients.

Blake would do all right. Glenna hoped he'd remember he wasn't in a courtroom, though. Erin needed to hear him talking from his heart. Satisfied for the moment, she floated away to haunt the beautiful Victorian mansion where in less than two hours, her friend Greg would marry Erin's pretty young sister. That, she didn't intend to miss.

Chapter Twenty-Nine

⮂

Feeling decadent in an ebony mink jacket Blake had pulled from a huge Saks box and draped across her shoulders moments earlier, Erin watched him stash their bags in the trunk with trepidation. And excitement.

He'd raked her with his gaze when he came into her room, making her feel as if her royal blue, floor-length velvet sheath covered no more of her than the sheerest of negligees. Then, his touch as gentle as the breeze, he'd wrapped her in the soft, dense fur.

"You'll need this in Wyoming. Are you ready?"

"For the wedding? Yes." Erin doubted she was ready for three nights alone with Blake in some undoubtedly romantic ski lodge in Jackson Hole.

"They were lucky to get The Manse on such short notice." His comment broke an uneasy silence as they drove along streets where, like Blake's, large homes generally sat well back away from the view of passers-by.

"They'd had a cancellation for tonight."

"Change of plans?"

Erin smiled. "The other couple's parents decided to hold the wedding at a temple, instead."

"That was good for Sandy and Greg." He pulled into a discreetly marked drive and stopped the car at the front of the hundred-year-old mansion an enterprising young couple had renovated into an upscale wedding chapel. "Here we are." He got out of the car and tossed the keys to the uniformed attendant who had just opened Erin's door.

Sandy had fallen in love with the old-world charm of this place, and Erin was glad. While Blake's home could easily have accommodated the wedding, she'd hesitated to suggest that after he told her he wasn't ready for mass gaiety there. While Blake handed his topcoat and her jacket to a butler, she peeked into the ballroom.

Blake rested his hands at her waist. "I told you Caitlyn's would take care of everything."

"And they have. Oh, Blake, look! The florist managed to find blue columbines. Sandy will be thrilled." She leaned down to sniff one of the small topiaries that topped each snowy-white covered round table, pleased at the effect of fragrant herbs and pert, blue wildflowers that the florist had tucked in among miniature gardenias and pastel roses.

"They look like little replicas of those." He strode over and inspected four giant arrangements that marked off the corners of a raised, polished dance floor, then settled his gaze on her as she came to join him. "Erin, you look beautiful tonight."

"Thank you."

He took her left hand and lifted it to his lips. "I should have bought you diamonds." For a moment, he traced the swirly design on her wedding band with one finger, a half-smile on his lips. What was going through his mind behind that enigmatic smile?

Sandy's attendants had her well in hand, Caitlyn's had the food ready and all the candles lit. A photographer and video crew waited to capture the wedding on film. Erin had nothing to do but wait until one of Greg's cousins—Scott—came to escort her to her seat.

Did Blake think she was going to bolt and run away? He'd never hovered before, but tonight he was sticking to her like glue. Restless, she circulated among the nooks and crannies off the big ballroom. Blake followed. She felt his pulse, his body heat warmed her, and the subtle cologne he wore kept reminding her he was there.

"Blake. Good to see you," Scott said when he joined them by the door. "Erin, are you ready to get this show going?"

"Is it time?" She smiled at Scott, then turned to Blake.

"Just about. They're signing the marriage contract now. May I?" He extended his arm.

The melodious sounds of an organ wafted softly through a ballroom lit by thousands of tiny white gaslights in three magnificent chandeliers. Scott seated her at a table larger than the rest.

Mom would have loved this! Erin swept that sad thought away. Today was a day for joy, not fretting about what should have been. Shana was heading toward the table on the arm of Greg's best man.

"Take care, little Shana," Jake said in a teasing tone as he held her chair.

"Little Shana?" Erin couldn't believe the incongruous nickname.

"Jake's sister is Big Shana. She couldn't come because she and her husband live in Kuwait," Shana said matter-of-factly. "I wouldn't let anybody but Jake call me 'little,' though."

Erin just realized she hadn't seen Jake's wife tonight. As she was about to ask Shana about that, the piped-in stereo music stopped and a live combo began to play a lilting, romantic piece. The guests quieted down, and Judge Adkins took his place in the center of the raised dance floor.

Erin watched the attendants, young women who'd spent many hours around the kitchen table at her house when Sandy was in high school. Tonight they looked like Victorian ladies in their sapphire velvet gowns. A tuxedoed groomsman escorted each bridesmaid. Katy came last, wearing a gown identical to the others except for its lighter blue color, on the arm of Greg's cousin Jake. Erin smiled. Everything, from the gowns to nosegay bouquets that featured the same flowers in the table decorations, had turned out just the way Sandy planned.

Greg followed Jake and Katy, escorted by his mother and uncle. Erin sighed. He looked ecstatic. The music faded, then rose again. Tears came to Erin's eyes when Sandy appeared, looking radiant in their mom's simple velvet gown and the pearl-encrusted tiara with its floor-length veil of gossamer silk illusion. Her flowers were perfect, blue columbines and tiny rosemary sprigs surrounding several perfect, white poinsettias.

But Blake took Erin's breath away. Suddenly she couldn't wait for the nights she and Blake were about to have together, business trip or no.

"We have gathered here tonight to share Sandy and Greg's joy as they celebrate their marriage."

Erin listened as the judge repeated the words he'd said not long ago when she'd married Blake. *Same words. Oh-so-different people and feelings!* She forced down her envy and concentrated on the ceremony.

"Who gives this woman in marriage?"

Blake turned and Erin met his gaze. "Her sister — my wife — and I do," he said quietly as he placed Sandy's hand in Greg's and stepped down to join her at the table. He reached out and took her hand while the judge explained that the bride and groom would make their vows in their own words.

"Sandy, I'll love you for the rest of my life. I'll do everything I can to keep you happy and secure, and to keep harm and sadness away. I'll be there for you always, no matter what, to take care of you or let you try your wings, whatever you need. I promise to be faithful and provide for you and any children we may have. By provide, I don't just mean material things, honey, I'll provide quality time for you as well."

"I think the traditional words say it all, Greg. I promise to love, honor and cherish you, to be faithful, in sickness and health, for richer or poorer, for better or worse, as long as we both live. I love you."

Tears rolled down Erin's cheeks. Dabbing a hanky at the corners of her eyes, she watched Sandy and Greg exchange the matching wedding bands they'd chosen together. Her gaze shifted to Blake's ringless left hand, and she nearly started to cry again. Fortunately Judge Adkins' words drew her attention back to the bridal party.

"By the power vested in me by the great State of Texas, I pronounce you husband and wife. You may kiss the bride."

As Greg and Sandy embraced, Erin's eyes filled with tears. Those vows, spoken so sincerely and with so much love, made her ache for what she wanted so much to have with Blake. She met his gaze, and he gave her hand a gentle squeeze.

* * * * *

"You did a great job with the wedding," Blake said later as they flew toward Jackson Hole in the otherwise empty first-class section of a commercial jet.

Sandy's wedding had been beautiful, down to the last detail. "Surprising Sandy with that video must have been Greg's idea," she murmured, glad he'd thought of doing the picture montage that featured highlights of their lives both separately and together.

"Uh-huh. They did one for his cousin Shana's wedding a few years back, and she liked it so well, Greg decided he'd put together one for Sandy."

"Speaking of Shana, she acted like an angel tonight." The girl had sat at the table next to her uncle Jake, and she'd actually behaved as if she were happy about the marriage.

"Greg thought so, too. He said he figured Jake had given her a talking to this afternoon. They spent most of the day together. Apparently she idolizes him."

Erin frowned. "Where was Jake's wife?" Her sympathy had gone out tonight to Greg's handsome cousin, whose jovial smile never quite reached dark, empty eyes.

"She went back to Houston this morning. Jake asked me tonight to recommend a good divorce lawyer. Said their marriage was over."

"I'm sorry. They were a beautiful couple." Erin paused. "Do they have children?"

"No. Jake wanted them, though."

"She couldn't..."

"Wouldn't. Last month she had an abortion that she just told him about after the rehearsal last night, during a whopper of an argument."

Any sympathy Erin might have felt for Jake's coldly beautiful wife dissipated instantly. But tears welled up in her eyes for the misery Jake had masked so well except for that haunted look in his eyes.

"Erin?"

"What? Oh, sorry, I was just thinking."

Blake cleared his throat. "Were you thinking of the time I asked you to do that to Jamie?"

"Of course not." She gave his forearm a reassuring squeeze. "I was thinking of how hard it must have been for Jake to act the charming, happy best man tonight."

He rubbed a callused thumb over her palm. "Yeah. You're right. The wedding's over. Sandy and Greg are out at Possum Kingdom, and the guests have all gone home. We'll be landing in a few minutes, and there's something I've got to tell you."

The muscles in Erin's neck grew tense. "What?"

"There's no client. No meeting. I tricked you into coming with me so I'd have a chance to court you, somewhere where there aren't any memories to haunt us. Honey, I want us to fall in love."

He wants us to fall in love? Doesn't he know I love him already? "Blake, I—I..."

"I know I've hurt you, but I'm asking for this time to convince you what we've got is worth building on. Please give us a chance."

Erin wanted to shout, but all she could manage was a tight smile and a heartfelt sigh.

"We don't have to sleep together until you're ready. Hell, we already know we're dynamite in bed. All I'm asking is that we spend this time alone together, do some of the fun things most couples do before they say 'I do'."

If Blake hadn't been watching, she'd have pinched herself. "All right."

For the rest of the night and the following day, Erin let Blake pamper and cosset her. She felt like Cinderella in fur-lined boots instead of glass slippers, with her fantasy prince in his Scandinavian knit sweater and snug, sexy ski pants. He made her feel young and carefree as she hadn't felt in years. The heady combination of this fairyland of pristine, powdery snow—and a laughing, teasing Blake—lifted years of worry from her shoulders and let her enjoy the moment.

What moments they were! If she lived to be a hundred, Erin knew she'd never forget the exhilaration of speeding down a snowy hill on a two-man sled, secure in Blake's arms. Their impromptu snowball fight left her panting from exertion, while Blake was scarcely winded even when he picked her up and tossed her into a snowdrift. She could hardly wait for the moonlight sleigh ride he'd promised.

* * * * *

That night the moon shone bright against newly fallen snow, and Blake pulled Erin closer under the cover of a woven wool blanket. Sleigh bells jingled against the horses' harnesses. Not able to resist the sweet temptation of her lips when she smiled, he bent and kissed her. "Having fun?"

"Oh, yes." When she looked at him with sparkling eyes, he realized again how much he loved her.

Seeing the brightly lit lodge up ahead, Blake reined in the matched pair of grays. "Hungry?"

"Are you?"

She had to know what he was hungry for. "Uh-huh. Let's go eat."

He hardly tasted the prime rib. And Erin barely touched her salmon steak. "Would you like to go dancing?" He glanced across the dining room toward the muted sounds of soft, romantic music.

"I'd rather spend time just with you."

"Upstairs?"

She nodded, but he saw wariness in her beautiful blue eyes. That was all right. If she'd listen, he'd give her the words he hoped she still could echo from her heart. "Let's go, then." He scribbled his name and suite number on the bill and hustled her upstairs.

The staff had done well. Candles, flowers and a blazing fire in the fireplace created the scene exactly as Blake had envisioned. Erin bent and sniffed appreciatively at a creamy gardenia in the mixed bouquet on the table.

She rubbed her cheek against his shoulder. "You didn't have to do all this."

He nudged her down onto the sofa where he'd slept last night before conscientiously sitting down a respectable distance away. "I told Glenna goodbye, Erin. I'll always remember her with love, just as I'm sure you'll remember Bill. But I've put her in the past. She's gone. I'm alive, and I want to do more than go through the motions of living."

"What are you trying to say?"

"That I'm ready to love again. That I'm ready to love you, if you're willing."

"Do you mean..." Her voice trailed off, but she stared at him with what he wanted to believe was plain and simple sexual need.

"That, too." He chuckled. "Let me make love to you, Erin."

She felt as if they were making love, not simply satisfying the compelling chemistry that had first brought them together like this. He kissed her so gently, so carefully, she might have been made of glass. Then he scooped her up in his arms and carried her to the king-sized bed.

With a total lack of haste, he undressed them both, before lifting her onto the bed and staring down at her as if she were a priceless work of art. For the first time in her life, Erin felt truly beautiful, because she was seeing herself mirrored in his soft, adoring gaze.

Then he touched her, not like an impatient lover but like a man in love. The feather-light strokes of his fingers against the wind-sensitized skin of her cheeks produced tiny sparks of arousal that enticed rather than inflamed, and brought a warm glow that spread lazily throughout her body.

"I love the way you respond to me," he murmured as he bent and traced the line of her jaw with gentle love bites.

"Mmmm." With his slightest touch, with just a wanting glance, he could make her wet and ready. Set her to tingling in her most erogenous places.

The bed shifted when he stretched out on his side beside her, his head supported on one hand while he used the other to stroke softly around the undercurve of one taut, aching breast.

His tongue snaked out and circled a nipple, arousing her nearly to a fever pitch. She couldn't help draping one leg across his muscular thigh and rocking her lower body rhythmically against his rock-hard cock.

Finally he stopped his delicious torture. Raising his head, he took her lips in a soft, open-mouthed kiss, bathing her lips and teeth with his tongue.

She moved her hips harder against him; coaxing him to fuck her; but without breaking their kiss, he stayed her with a callused hand that pushed her back against the satin sheets. Then that hand began playing havoc with her senses, too, as it drifted over her abdomen and lower.

She squirmed beneath his light, teasing touch as he dipped into her belly button with one finger, then traced across her mound. When he finally touched her clit, she was already aching, all it took to make her shudder and beg for more was a flick of his fingers.

He plunged his tongue deep within her mouth, then withdrew and positioned his big body between her legs. She opened fully to him, expecting him to fill the emptiness inside her. But he didn't.

Sliding down farther on the bed, he bent his head and swirled his tongue across her belly. His warm breath tickled her as he made his way downward. Every swipe of his tongue on her mound, her labia, her clit...even the sensitive flesh of her inner thighs, drove her crazy with need. And when he opened his mouth over her clit and kissed her there, the delicious suction coaxed out climax after climax. She felt limp, drained, yet strangely unsatisfied. Wanted to feel his cock stretching her pussy, filling the void in her body and her life.

"Blake. Please." She tried to drag him upward by pulling at his broad, muscular shoulders.

He was letting her position him the way she wanted, she knew when it suddenly became ridiculously easy to make him stop his erotic play. But when she tried to make him enter her by pulling at his narrow hips, he balked, his hard cock poised inside her sopping labia, just outside her needy pussy. He raised his upper body, holding himself steady with his powerful arms.

"Let me say this first." His voice was raspy, breathless sounding. "Erin, I love you. I think I've loved you since long before we ever did this."

She felt the tears come— but they were tears of joy, this time. "I love you, too, Blake." No one else's name intruded now, she thought before she felt him plunge inside her and drive them both quickly to oblivion.

* * * * *

On their last day in Jackson Hole, Blake watched Erin precede him down the bunny slope. Like him, she welcomed challenges, embraced new activities. He loved that about her. Come to think of it, there wasn't anything about his wife that he didn't love. From now on he intended to tell her every chance he got. Tonight he'd planned a special evening he hoped Erin would always remember, one that celebrated this magical place…and the white-hot love that had blossomed between them and grew stronger every day.

"Come on. Let's try the snowmobiles," he urged her later after they'd come in off the slopes and warmed up with mugs of mulled red wine.

"Can we ride on one, together? My legs feel like jelly from the skiing we did this morning."

"I know you, honey. What you want is some touchy-feely. Right?"

"Always."

"Then let's go."

Like carefree kids, they blazed a trail up the mountain on a snowmobile, stopping often to share the majestic beauty of snow-capped evergreens and the occasional winter-coated deer or elk. Everything seemed bright and new to Blake. While he'd set himself free from his crippling grief, Erin had shown him how to live again.

When they got back to the lodge at dusk, he stopped her at the door to their suite and scooped her up in his arms. "I think I forgot something the day we got married," he told her with a smile.

"You'd have had a time of it, trying to do this then."

She was right, not only because she was just about ready to deliver their son. But Blake was a different person now. "Come on, honey, indulge me." Fumbling with the old-fashioned brass key, he opened the door and stepped inside.

"I wanted us to have a special evening, all to ourselves," he told her as he set her down in front of the fireplace.

"Oh."

She sounded stunned and thrilled all at the same time, and her eyes widened when she saw the dozen candles that lit a small buffet and the round table for two, set with fine china, sparkling crystal and sterling silver.

"Shall we get comfortable?" He shrugged out of his insulated nylon jacket, then helped her take hers off. "Our dinner will be arriving shortly."

She met his gaze with smiling eyes. "How comfortable?"

"That's up to you, love."

"I like having your finer parts easily accessible," she said, licking her lips and leering at the bulge in his ski pants. "How about robes?"

"Fine with me. Want a quick shower?"

"Together?"

That suggestion sounded good, too good since making love wasn't part of his immediate plan. "Well, maybe we should dine as we are and save that shower for later. But hold the thought."

"All right. Would you like some wine?" She headed for the silver bucket on the bar, but he reached out to stop her.

"Let's wait."

They talked for a few minutes, and Blake began to wonder if he'd ever get a minute to himself. He needed to get into one of his bags without attracting Erin's attention. When she finally excused herself to freshen up, he practically dived for his luggage, then rushed over and tucked his gift into the wine bucket just as he heard a discreet knock at the door. Their dinner had arrived, and not a moment too soon.

"Aren't we going to have some of that wine?" Erin glanced toward the silver bucket on the buffet, apparently curious because they'd finished eating and he hadn't broken open the bottle.

"It's champagne. I thought we'd save it for dessert." Blake got up and removed their dinner plates, setting them on the buffet before taking the plate filled with little cream puffs and éclairs to their table.

"Those look fantastic."

Blake didn't get nervous. He *never* got flustered. But he was all that and more tonight. "I'll take these and fill them while I'm up," he muttered, snatching up the saucer champagne glasses and turning back to the buffet. Resolutely he set them down and worked the cork out of the chilled bottle of *Dom Pérignon*, making sure he stood so his body blocked Erin's view.

"Do you need help?"

"No thanks. I've just about got it." A sudden loud pop confirmed his words.

But her innocent question had nearly made him drop his surprise noisily into one of the glasses. Catching himself, he managed to salvage the moment and finish pouring the bubbly wine without incident. His heart raced as he brought the glasses to the table and set one down in front of Erin.

Then he sat and looked deliberately into her dark, sparkling eyes. "I've been thinking the last few days. About you. Me. Us. About how we're married but we aren't, not really. Most of all, I've been realizing how much I love you now, and how happy it makes me that you love me, too.

"I want us to say our vows again, this time with feeling." Needing desperately to touch her, he took her hand and brought it to his lips.

"Erin, will you marry me? For all the right reasons this time?"

Her initial shock showed, but within seconds she was looking at him, a breathtaking, lovely smile on her face. "Yes, Blake. Oh, yes." With one hand she reached out and caressed his cheek.

"Then I think it's time for us to drink a toast," he said smoothly, raising his glass. "To us."

How long was it going to take her to notice the ring? Her movement was ballet in slow motion, fueling his impatience as she lifted the glass off the table and brought it up in a graceful arc.

Seconds ticked off in his brain.

Then she let out a piercing scream. "Oh, my God! Blake, you didn't. Yes, you did!"

Grinning, he helped her fish the diamond solitaire out of her glass and slipped it on her finger, in front of the wedding band that had sealed a business deal.

"How did you get this? When?"

"Sunday, before the wedding. I persuaded a client who's a diamond wholesaler to open up his showroom and help me pick it out."

"It's beautiful. I love it. I love you. But you didn't have to do this." Erin could keep protesting all night, but Blake saw by her reaction that his giving her that chunk of prehistoric carbon had made her happy.

He watched as she moved her hand at different angles, observing how the three-carat round stone glowed, reflecting light from the fire and the candles. And he, too, was caught up in the magic of its sparkling message.

"Do you really want us to have another wedding?" Erin asked later, as they lay in bed, content and sated.

"Yes. I want to commit myself to you and mean it."

"Me, too." She stroked his hand, and he felt the love in her touch.

I won't wear a ring. He had meant that when he took off the wedding band Glenna had given him. But now the words rang harsh in his mind. Did Erin remember that conversation, too? If she did, he imagined his grief-inspired words still caused her pain.

Lifting her hand to his lips, he looked into her eyes. "This time I'd like to wear your ring. Will you get me one?"

* * * * *

After they got home, she did that and much more. How she managed to keep from floating in a haze of pure euphoria, she didn't know. But she'd kept functioning somehow.

Erin held the etched gold band and read the inscription. "From Erin, with all my love," it said simply but from her heart. The courier had just delivered it, and she could hardly wait five more days to put it on Blake's finger.

Funny how love made problems seem less significant. Timmy's mastery of crutches improved each time she saw him, and she trusted they'd soon go the way of his wheelchair as he healed and became accustomed to using Buddy, as he'd whimsically named his new prosthesis.

"Would you like the baby now?"

She turned and smiled at Theresa. "Yes." She'd feed Jamie, and then she and Sandy were heading to Saks to find the perfect dress to wear when she and Blake renewed their vows.

Later, as she searched through designer gowns, Erin remembered another day, another store, where she'd been looking for a dress to wear for what had almost been a cruel farce. Glenna's ghost had brought a light, cheery bit of humor to what could have been a somber experience. Where had Glenna been hiding lately, anyhow?

A simple ivory sheath of soft, silk crepe caught her eye. "I'll try that one on," she told the saleslady, recalling how Sandy and the ghost had coaxed and cajoled to get her to buy her other wedding dress. Moments later, Erin and Sandy left the store, mission accomplished.

On their wedding day, Erin thought again about Glenna's ghost—and felt a little guilty for having run her off. Not about loving Glenna's widower, though. Nothing could dull the joy Erin found in his love. But she'd *liked* Glenna, and she had a feeling that without the ghost's downright pushy interference, she and Blake might have floundered around for years before they found happiness together.

"What are you thinking about?" Blake asked when he joined Erin in the garden room.

He'd think she'd lost her mind if she told the truth, or even if she mentioned ever having seen and talked with Glenna's ghost. Erin was certain of that, so she merely smiled. "Tonight."

He grinned. "Me too."

She'd been right the day they'd met. When Blake was happy, he could break hearts with that ruggedly handsome face. He certainly had captured hers.

"This is for you," he told her, setting a narrow velvet box on her lap before joining her on the sofa.

He isn't much into buying baubles.

Glenna had said something like that at the store. Well, she must have been wrong, Erin thought smugly, noting the solitaire on her hand as she picked up the box that could hardly contain anything *but* a piece of jewelry.

"Aren't you going to open it?"

"Oh. Yes." She snapped open the lid and gasped. It was a sapphire as big as a marble, as dark as Blake's mesmerizing eyes. A sunburst of sparkling diamonds surrounded it, reflecting its brilliant color in their twinkling facets. Set in gold, the pendant hung suspended on a finely worked chain. "The sapphire reminds me of your eyes," she murmured when she found her voice.

"It reminded me of yours. Will you wear it tonight, for me?"

Erin nodded and moved into his arms. For a long time, he held her, until it was time for them to dress and greet their guests.

Chapter Thirty

ಐ

"If I keep officiating at weddings, I'm going to have the ceremony memorized," Judge Adkins commented good-naturedly as Blake ushered him into the formal living room.

"That's good." He and Erin had opted for tradition, instead of rewording the promises they would give each other. Uncharacteristically nervous, he straightened his bow tie and adjusted the cuffs of his tux shirt.

He'd greeted the fifteen or so people he and Erin had invited to share their joy, cuddled Jamie before handing him over to Theresa, and introduced Timmy to the friends who had come. Now he was getting impatient to see his beautiful bride.

Suddenly Erin appeared, a vision in creamy silk that gently skimmed curves of the body he could hardly wait to explore again in minute detail. Every time she moved, the long slit skirt swayed and gave him a glimpse of shapely calf and thigh. He liked the way she was wearing her hair, too, artfully tousled and loose against her bare, tanned shoulders.

She had on the pendant he'd given her, nestled just above the upper curve of her breasts. The fragrance of *La Mer l'Été* and a scent of the roses she carried mingled to assail his senses.

Looking radiant, like a woman in love, Erin took his breath away. He reached out and took her hand, drew her closer until he felt her warmth against his side. In a small, sane corner of his mind, he realized Greg and Sandy had come to stand beside them.

The words were familiar. He—like Greg, yet for different reasons, he thought with just a twinge of regret—had repeated them not once but twice before. They seemed new and fresh tonight, like his love for this strong, beautiful woman who miraculously loved him, too.

"Erin, with this ring I marry you and pledge my faithful love," he said, holding her gaze as he slipped a new, wide band on her slender finger.

The judge's voice intruded on Blake's thoughts. "Erin, repeat after me…" The judge's instructions faded. All he could see was Erin.

"Blake, with this ring I marry you and pledge my faithful love." She spoke softly, her tone low and melodious. Her wedding band felt solid, right on his finger.

Judge Adkins cleared his throat. "You may kiss your bride."

Gently, Blake took his wife in his arms and gave her a tender kiss. Then, they turned back to the judge.

"These rings you have exchanged have no beginning and no end. May your commitment to each other be the same. My friends, it is with the greatest pleasure that I introduce you to Mr. and Mrs. Blake Tanner."

His arm possessively wrapped around Erin's slender waist, Blake turned them to face their guests. Suddenly, a bright, golden aura nearly blinded him. He stared, unable to tear his gaze away, and slowly he was able to make out the image as it crystallized from the gold dust. *Glenna.*

Erin squeezed his hand, hard. Did she see this, too? Or had the Scotch whisky he'd had just one shot of earlier gotten to him?

"Mr. and Mrs. Blake Tanner. Has a nice sound, doesn't it?"

Blake didn't believe it. He stole a glance at Erin. For some reason he didn't understand, he was sure she could see and hear this ghostly apparition, too. But she seemed unflustered, unaffected.

He wanted to interrogate this—this *ghost*—the way he'd ream a witness in the courtroom. But he couldn't. Judge Adkins and everyone else in the room would know he'd taken leave of his senses and haul him off to the funny farm if he started talking to someone or something that wasn't there.

"Don't mind me, darling. I just came to say goodbye. I've accomplished what I wanted for you two — a real, happy marriage filled with love. You're going to get along just fine without me, now."

Blake watched the specter of his beloved wife's face turn soft and dreamy as it faded into the golden aura that shone around her. He had to strain to hear her parting words.

"Now I can go. It seems I've discovered three adorable little girls who belong to me, and it's time for me to start being their mother."

Nonplused, Blake watched the surrealistic presence of his dead wife slowly fade away. Then he turned to Erin. "Did I just see what I thought I saw?"

She smiled and gave him a quick hug. "Uh-huh. And you know what, my love? She's been around here the entire time."

"You've seen her before?"

"Seen her, and talked with her. I've listened to her advice. I've even argued with her."

Blake leaned closer and whispered in Erin's ear. "About what?"

"You. You've had at least two women who love you to distraction, Mr. Tanner," she replied, pretending to nuzzle at his neck. "I've had a feeling she was gone for good, but I'm glad she came to tell us goodbye. Aren't you?"

Erin shot him an impish grin. He couldn't help returning it. Soon, those grins dissolved in gales of laughter. Was it hysteria or relief? He wrapped his arms around his wife and held her for a long time.

"Is it all right — that she came?" Erin asked quietly.

He hesitated. "Yeah. It's okay now." Not getting to tell Glenna goodbye before she died had been a bitter reality for him to swallow.

Now, even if Glenna's ghost had been a product of his and Erin's imaginations, she'd given him the gift of closure, the freedom to love Erin with all his heart.

And he did. Erin was his greatest miracle of all.

~ About the Author ~

ഇ

First published in 1996, Ann Jacobs has sold more than thirty-five books and novellas. A CPA and former hospital financial manager, she now writes full-time except, of course, for the hours she devotes to being a wife and mother to seven kids. A transplanted midwesterner, she's lived in west-central Florida all her adult life.

Ann loves writing Romantica - to her, it's the perfect blend of sex, sensuality, and happily-ever-after commitment between one man and one woman.

Ann welcomes mail from readers. You can write to her c/o Ellora's Cave Publishing at 1056 Home Avenue, Akron OH 44310-3502.

Why an electronic book?

We live in the Information Age—an exciting time in the history of human civilization in which technology rules supreme and continues to progress in leaps and bounds every minute of every hour of every day. For a multitude of reasons, more and more avid literary fans are opting to purchase e-books instead of paperbacks. The question to those not yet initiated to the world of electronic reading is simply: *why?*

1. *Price.* An electronic title at Ellora's Cave Publishing and Cerridwen Press runs anywhere from 40-75% less than the cover price of the <u>exact same title</u> in paperback format. Why? Cold mathematics. It is less expensive to publish an e-book than it is to publish a paperback, so the savings are passed along to the consumer.

2. *Space.* Running out of room to house your paperback books? That is one worry you will never have with electronic novels. For a low one-time cost, you can purchase a handheld computer designed specifically for e-reading purposes. Many e-readers are larger than the average handheld, giving you plenty of screen room. Better yet, hundreds of titles can be stored within your new library—a single microchip. (Please note that Ellora's Cave and Cerridwen Press does not endorse any specific brands. You can check our website at www.ellorascave.com or

www.cerridwenpress.com for customer recommendations we make available to new consumers.)

3. *Mobility.* Because your new library now consists of only a microchip, your entire cache of books can be taken with you wherever you go.

4. *Personal preferences are accounted for.* Are the words you are currently reading too small? Too large? Too...**ANNOYING**? Paperback books cannot be modified according to personal preferences, but e-books can.

5. *Instant gratification.* Is it the middle of the night and all the bookstores are closed? Are you tired of waiting days—sometimes weeks—for online and offline bookstores to ship the novels you bought? Ellora's Cave Publishing sells instantaneous downloads 24 hours a day, 7 days a week, 365 days a year. Our e-book delivery system is 100% automated, meaning your order is filled as soon as you pay for it.

Those are a few of the top reasons why electronic novels are displacing paperbacks for many an avid reader. As always, Ellora's Cave and Cerridwen Press welcomes your questions and comments. We invite you to email us at service@ellorascave.com, service@cerridwenpress.com or write to us directly at: 1056 Home Ave. Akron OH 44310-3502.

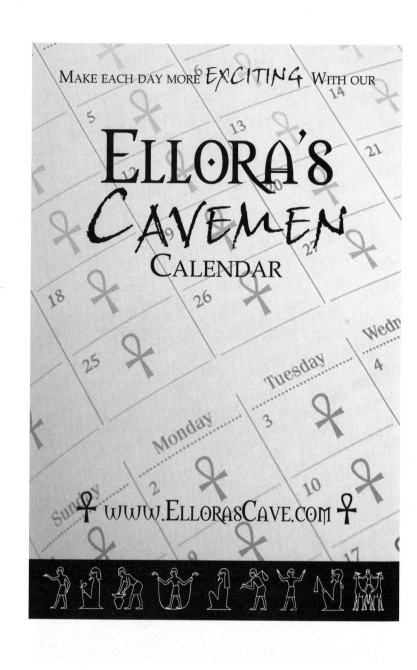

THE
☥ ELLORA'S CAVE ☥
LIBRARY

Stay up to date with Ellora's Cave Titles in
Print with our Quarterly Catalog.

TO RECIEVE A CATALOG,
SEND AN EMAIL WITH YOUR NAME
AND MAILING ADDRESS TO:

CATALOG@ELLORASCAVE.COM

OR SEND A LETTER OR POSTCARD
WITH YOUR MAILING ADDRESS TO:

CATALOG REQUEST
c/o ELLORA'S CAVE PUBLISHING, INC.
1056 HOME AVENUE
AKRON, OHIO 44310-3502

Discover for yourself why readers can't get enough of the multiple award-winning publisher Ellora's Cave. Whether you prefer e-books or paperbacks, be sure to visit EC on the web at www.ellorascave.com for an erotic reading experience that will leave you breathless.

www.ellorascave.com